P9-CLB-045

Praise for the Black Sheep Knitting Mystery series

"The fast-paced plot will keep even nonknitters turning the pages."

—*Publishers Weekly*

"Congenial characters and a mystery that keeps you guessing."

—*Kirkus Reviews*

"Maggie and her group are as efficient with their investigation as they are with their knitting needles."

—*Library Journal*

"Small-town crafty ambience. . . . This enjoyable tale is similar in style to the work of both Sally Goldenbaum and Cricket McRae."

—*Booklist*

"An engaging story full of tight-knit friendships and a needling mystery."

—*Fresh Fiction*

"A slew of interesting characters."

—*Single Titles*

"Enthusiastic, engrossing, and exciting."

—*The Mystery Gazette*

"An intriguing mystery with a few surprising twists and turns."

—*Romance Reviews Today*

"Delightful. Enchanting. Humorous. Impressive. Witty. Those are just a few adjectives to describe Anne Canadeo's effervescent cozy."

—*Book Cave*

**Also in the Black Sheep Knitting Mystery Series
by Anne Canadeo**

Meet the Black Sheep Knitters

Maggie Messina, owner of the Black Sheep Knitting Shop, is a retired high school art teacher who runs her little slice of knitters' paradise with the kind of vibrant energy that leaves her friends dazzled! From novice to pro, knitters come to Maggie as much for her up-to-the-minute offerings like organic wool as for her encouragement and friendship. And Maggie's got a deft touch when it comes to unraveling mysteries, too.

Lucy Binger left Boston when her marriage ended, and found herself shifting gears to run her graphic design business from the coastal cottage she inherited. After big-city living, she now finds contentment on a front porch in tiny Plum Harbor, knitting with her closest friends.

Dana Haeger is a psychologist with a busy local practice. A stylishly polished professional with a quick wit, she slips out to Maggie's shop whenever her schedule allows—after all, knitting is the best form of therapy!

Suzanne Cavanaugh is a typical working supermom—a realtor with a million demands on her time, from coaching soccer to showing houses to attending the PTA. But she carves out a little "me" time with the Black Sheep Knitters.

Phoebe Meyers, a college student complete with magenta highlights and nose stud, lives in the apartment above Maggie's shop. She's Maggie's indispensable helper (when she's not in class)—and part of the new generation of young knitters.

The Postman Always Purls Twice

A Black Sheep Knitting Mystery

Anne Canadeo

GALLERY BOOKS

New York London Toronto Sydney New Delhi

To Susan Davis Pereira, with love and gratitude for your friendship.
How lucky to have found each other in Mrs. Hammer's class.

Gallery Books
A Division of Simon & Schuster, Inc.
1230 Avenue of the Americas
New York, NY 10020

This book is a work of fiction. Any references to historical events, real people, or real places are used fictitiously. Other names, characters, places, and events are products of the author's imagination, and any resemblance to actual events or places or persons, living or dead, is entirely coincidental.

Copyright © 2015 by Anne Canadeo

All rights reserved, including the right to reproduce this book or portions thereof in any form whatsoever. For information address Gallery Books Subsidiary Rights Department, 1230 Avenue of the Americas, New York, NY 10020.

First Gallery Books trade paperback edition April 2015

GALLERY BOOKS and colophon are registered trademarks of Simon & Schuster, Inc.

For information about special discounts for bulk purchases, please contact Simon & Schuster Special Sales at 1-866-506-1949 or business@simonandschuster.com.

The Simon & Schuster Speakers Bureau can bring authors to your live event. For more information or to book an event contact the Simon & Schuster Speakers Bureau at 1-866-248-3049 or visit our website at www.simonspeakers.com.

Cover illustration by Mary Ann Lasher

Manufactured in the United States of America

1 3 5 7 9 10 8 6 6 4 2

Library of Congress Cataloging-in-Publication Data

Canadeo, Anne
The postman always purls twice / Anne Canadeo. -- First Gallery Books trade paperback edition.
pages. cm. (A black sheep knitting mystery)
I. Title.
PS3553.A489115P67 2015
813'.54--dc23
2014033459

ISBN 978-1-4767-6749-9
ISBN 978-1-4767-6751-2 (ebook)

All the world's a stage,
And all the men and women merely players;
They have their exits and their entrances,
And one man in his time plays many parts,
—*As You Like It,* ACT 2, SCENE 7, WILLIAM SHAKESPEARE

All the hate and revenge has left me, but is it all out of you?
—*The Postman Always Rings Twice,* JAMES M. CAIN

Chapter One

"It's a mystery to me. The movie people haven't told me much." Maggie shrugged as she set down a platter of sushi on the long oak table at the back of her shop. Lucy and Dana, the first to arrive, sat in their usual places, sipping wine and gently coaxing yarn and needles from their knitting bags.

"The cast and crew arrive in town tomorrow," Maggie continued, "and they'll be invading this place on Saturday, at the crack of dawn. The shop's busiest day of the week. What can you do? The show must go on."

"Where else are they filming? Is the shop the only spot in town?" Lucy was almost done with her latest creation, Maggie noticed; an airy, oatmeal-colored, dropped-stitched scarf, perfect for the warmer weather. But now she seemed more interested in hearing about the movie than moving in for the kill on her project.

"Suzanne said they also rented a big house on the beach where they'll shoot other scenes. I think they'll be in town about a week. I know I should feel honored, but somehow I already regret agreeing to this."

Maggie was quietly proud of the Black Sheep Knitting Shop. She had found the perfect spot for her business years ago, the first floor of a beautifully renovated Victorian building that had once been a private home.

But she wasn't surprised at all that the entire town of Plum Harbor had caught the eye of movie location scouts. A classic New England village on the Cape Ann coast, it was as picturesque a spot as any movie set, its tree-lined lanes filled with historic houses, and a row of well-kept shops along Main Street, which led down to a harbor and green.

But now that reality was setting in, Maggie had serious doubts about whether she'd made the right choice.

"Come on, Mag. You're our Hollywood connection. How will we talk our way into being extras if you come off like a big grump?" Phoebe, Maggie's assistant, walked out from the storeroom, balancing a serving tray laden with other dinner necessities: a stack of flat sushi plates, little bowls for soy sauce, and a pile of chopsticks and napkins.

Maggie enjoyed cooking dinner for a knitting night, but didn't have the spare time today. Sushi was a crowd-pleasing choice, and the chopsticks and knitting needles seemed somehow related.

"I think Suzanne is our official Hollywood connection, and I'm not ready to give up my day job yet." Maggie began handing out the napkins and chopsticks to her hungry-looking guests.

"I'll skip the audition, too," Dana added with a smile. "But I'd love to watch them film a scene or two, and see how the actors and director work. That would be interesting."

Lucy suddenly looked up from her knitting. "I wouldn't

mind going behind the scenes with the actors. Especially Heath O'Hara."

Lucy was a fan? Maggie had no idea. "Sounds serious. Does Matt know he has such famous competition?"

"He drifts into a happy daze every time I mention Trina Hardwick is in the cast, so I'd say we're even."

"She doesn't seem his type at all. She's such a 'bad girl,'" Maggie replied.

"All the more attractive as a fantasy," Dana noted. "Like most celebrity crushes."

"Very true. But that's just common sense," Maggie mumbled around a bite of spicy tuna. "No offense."

Dana shrugged, rarely offended by the group's gentle teasing about her profession. When advice from a calm, thoughtful voice was needed, Maggie knew Dana, their resident psychologist, was the first they turned to.

"I can't believe that in like . . . less than two days, all those movie stars are going to be in this shop. Maybe even sitting in *these* chairs." Phoebe gazed down at her own chair in awe. "It's totally freaking me out."

"Hang in there, Phoebe. They're not here yet." Such a vivid imagination; Maggie admired that.

"Sorry if you don't think that's really cool, Mag. But it totally is."

"And good publicity for the shop," Lucy reminded her.

"Yes, yes . . . That's how Suzanne talked me into this. I'm hardly the most starstruck person you'll ever meet."

"That we'd all agree upon, for sure," Dana assured her.

"I hope Suzanne is coming. I saved her some sushi." Maggie glanced at her watch. "She must know a little more. I'm not sure if I should straighten up the place, or if they want that lived-in look. Will they be using the merchandise as props? Not that I mind, if they're careful with everything. I'd just like to know."

"Don't stress. I'm sure you can email someone who will answer your questions. The shop looks neat as a pin, as always," Lucy assured her.

"We try our best." Maggie glanced at Phoebe, who was suddenly staring at her food as if she expected the bits of fish to leap off her dish.

Keeping the shop in order was one of Phoebe's main duties; making sure all the project books, needles, and other knitting necessaries were in their proper place and each skein of yarn in a cubby on the big wall, or tucked in a basket, carefully organized by color and fiber type. Phoebe kept up with this task most of the time. But she could so easily get distracted.

"Who else is in the movie besides Heath O'Hara and Trina?" Phoebe asked.

"Jennifer Todd is the big star," Dana replied. "I saw her once on Broadway, in *Hamlet*. She was amazing as Ophelia. She won all kinds of awards."

"Jennifer Todd is a better actress than Trina any day. Trina is mainly famous for being famous. And for her bad behavior," Lucy added.

Maggie had to agree. After some early success in teen movies, Trina ran right off the rails—if one believed half the news about her in gossip magazines—trashing hotel rooms, causing scenes in exclusive restaurants. Arrests for shoplifting and driving under the influence. And all her dirty laundry, mug shots, and shocking outfits captured for the world to see on the covers of supermarket tabloids.

Jennifer Todd's image would be found a few rungs higher

on the magazine rack, gracing the cover of *Ladies' Home Journal* or *Vogue*. Maybe sharing a favorite recipe or beauty tip in her interviews.

"Let's face it, the media doesn't want stories about how happy and settled a movie star's life is. Scandal sells more magazines," Lucy observed.

"The film's director, Nick Pullman, has had one or two of those," Dana recalled. "I remember years ago, he was involved in the death of a very young actress. I think she drowned in the pool at his mansion. A real tragedy. She was very young, not even twenty."

"That's awful. I've never heard that." Lucy put her knitting down. "When was this? I don't remember."

"Oh . . . about fifteen years ago. He got off without any big legal problems. I don't even think the girl's family sued him. But it was pretty messy, tarnished his reputation for a while."

"Interesting." Maggie looked over her sushi, selecting a next bite. "But some celebrities have a way of smoothing over rough patches that would derail mere mortals."

"They do," Lucy agreed. "Maybe he paid the girl's family to keep it out of the courts."

"And not discuss it openly," Dana added. "Reporters refer to the incident from time to time, but he's pretty much shaken it off and moved on."

"Few people are untouched by tragedies. Even if their lives seem golden from a distance," Maggie noted.

"How true, and Trina's had some tragedies in her life, too. Her father and older sister were killed in a car crash when she was only a teenager." Dana had set her plate aside and was already back to work, counting the pale yellow stitches along one needle, just about the color of her straight, chin-length hair. "It's no wonder she has so many issues now."

"Trina is a walking cry for help," Phoebe agreed. "But I heard she's been in rehab. This is her first big movie clean and sober."

"Well . . . good luck to her," Maggie said sincerely. "It's awful to see someone that young, with such great opportunities, throwing everything away."

Dana nodded. "I think Hollywood actors lead a hard life. So much pressure and temptation."

"Jennifer Todd seems to be completely the opposite. So down to earth, the type of person you could talk to. Or even be friends with. I think she even knits." Lucy sounded as if Jennifer was already their friend, Maggie noticed.

"Absolutely," Dana agreed. "Except for her chauffeur, housekeeper, chef, personal assistant, fitness trainer . . ."

"Okay, not *exactly* like us. But you know what I mean. She's a real girl-next-door type. Though she's probably about forty?" Lucy guessed.

"I just read she's thirty-seven, and she is—or was—the girl next door. Didn't you know that she grew up around here?" Maggie was surprised her friends didn't seem aware of that connection.

"I heard that somewhere, too." Dana looked up from her knitting. "Is she from Plum Harbor?"

"Newburyport," Maggie recalled. The village a few miles north was the last town on the Cape Ann coast and practically a metropolis compared to sleepy Plum Harbor.

Lucy seemed cheered by the news. "Maybe they'll hold a Welcome Home, Jennifer parade."

"I wouldn't be surprised. 'Any excuse for a parade' is the motto around here," Maggie said.

"So . . . that means she graduated high school almost twenty years ago," Phoebe calculated aloud. "Was she ever one of your students, Mag?"

Maggie shook her head. "I was at Plum Harbor High. Newburyport has its own secondary school."

It seemed like another lifetime, her days as a high school art teacher. She had been teaching more than twenty years when her husband, Bill, had unexpectedly died. Maggie was paralyzed with grief at first, but eventually decided to pursue her "someday dream" and turn her love of knitting into a full-time career.

A wise choice, she often reflected now, five years after she'd opened the doors of the Black Sheep Knitting Shop. She'd been devoted to teaching, but she loved owning her own business, too.

"I'm sure there are plenty of people around here who did know her well. Or will claim they did," Maggie added.

"I wonder how many Jennifer Todd will actually remember. Or if she keeps in touch with any friends she grew up with," Dana mused. "I always think it's a sign of good character when people do."

"Yes . . . but her life must be so demanding compared to ours, I think we can cut her some slack," Lucy replied.

"I hope you're all talking about me," Suzanne sang out from the front of the shop. "Letting me off the hook for being so late and not even sending a text?"

"Don't worry . . . we still love you," Phoebe called back sweetly.

"Maggie saved you some sushi. That says it all." Dana pushed a clean place setting over to an empty spot at the table.

Maggie rose and headed for the storeroom, which doubled as a kitchen. "Sit down and relax. I'll get it for you."

"Thanks. You're a pal." Suzanne dropped her big leather tote and landed in the seat with a sigh.

"Were you stuck with a client?" Lucy asked.

Suzanne worked in real-estate sales for a busy agency in town, Prestige Properties, somehow managing to fit her career around caring for her three children and her husband. Amazingly, she seemed to thrive on her demanding, fragmented schedule.

"I wish. Clients are fun. Most of the time. I was stuck figuring out some mix-up with the extra insurance on the house the movie crew is renting. It's still not straightened out."

"We were just talking about that," Maggie called from the next room. "Do you know how long they'll need the shop? Will they do all their scenes in one day, or do they need to come back? There's really so much they haven't told me yet."

Maggie knew she sounded anxious, but she couldn't help it. She emerged with Suzanne's dinner and set it down near her place.

"What service, thanks so much. All my favorites, too . . . yum." Suzanne surveyed her dinner, chopsticks poised to attack.

"Enjoy." Maggie took her seat, eager to hear more details.

So were the rest of their friends, who all sat quietly now knitting and waiting for Suzanne's report.

"I've had a few emails with the location manager today. As far as I can see, the schedule seems to change from day to day."

Maggie shrugged. "I can go with the flow. As long as I have some idea which way I'm flowing."

"Here's the scoop. The cast and crew are flying into Boston

and New York over the next few days. I think Jennifer Todd and Nick Pullman are staying at the Copley Plaza for a night. Everyone is due in Plum Harbor on Friday night and your shop is the first stop on their schedule. They say now they only plan on shooting here for one day."

Maggie liked that news. "That's a relief."

"But of course, that can change. If they don't get all their scenes done," Suzanne reminded her. "I think the town will be insane. I'm picturing a big caravan of trucks for equipment, and fancy trailers for the movie stars rolling in. I also heard they've booked most of the Lord Charles Inn."

"That makes sense. It's the only really nice place around here." Lucy frowned down at her knitting, counting stitches on the needle. She didn't look happy, but hadn't called out for rescue yet. Maggie gave her a moment to sort it out herself, knowing that built knitting confidence.

"What's the name of the movie again?" Dana asked.

"*Love Knots.* I heard it's a thriller, but there's a romance in there, too. I'm not really sure of the plot." Suzanne dipped another bite of sushi into some soy sauce.

"Maybe there's a website. Let's take a look." Lucy reached for Maggie's laptop, which sat on the table near her place. She slid it over and began typing.

Lucy was a graphic designer who worked at home, and her computer was her best friend . . . next to her two dogs and her boyfriend, Matt. She did tend to search online for the answer to every question her life posed. Which was not always the best approach, Maggie sometimes reflected.

"Let's see . . . no official website yet, but there's loads of publicity. 'Partners Off Screen and On: Jennifer Todd and Nick Pullman Team Up for *Love Knots.* How will this

Hollywood couple handle the knotty mix of producing, directing, acting . . . and marriage?'" She looked up from the computer. "I didn't even know they were married."

"They're the iconic LA power couple." Suzanne sounded positively offended by Lucy's ignorance. "Where've you been? Living on a desert island?"

Lucy laughed. "Sorry . . . I fell behind with my celeb marriage scorecard. I'm still stuck on Brad and Angelina."

"What else does it say? Anything we should know?" Maggie asked.

"Let's see . . . 'This romantic thriller is the couple's first collaboration in over ten years, though Nick Pullman has made three feature-length films with Todd's costar, Heath O'Hara. Trina Hardwick also gets top billing in a supporting role.'"

"I guess that means she doesn't get the guy?" Suzanne speculated.

"Or she gets killed off." Maggie shrugged. "They do say it's a thriller. Someone must get murdered. Or close to it. Don't you think?"

Lucy scanned the rest of the article. "Doesn't say much about the plot. A lot of effusive adjectives, though. 'The windswept shores and winding lanes of a coastal New England village provide the moody backdrop for this dark drama, centered around the owner of a knitting shop, played by Todd, who is tempted by the crosscurrents of a passionate love triangle. Love, jealousy, and betrayal prove a dangerous mix . . .'" Lucy looked up. "Wow, that sounds good."

"But not a temptation I've had to resist lately," Maggie said, laughing. "In my experience as a *real* knitting shop owner."

"Never mind dull, old, real life. That sounds pretty juicy. I can't wait to see it," Suzanne countered.

"I bet Trina Hardwick plays the 'dangerous crosscurrents,'" Lucy added.

"She was born for that role," Phoebe agreed.

Lucy laughed. "Here's what they say about her: 'As Hardwick prepares for her first role in a major motion picture in over three years, the young star will be tested to prove she remains a box office draw and a bankable commodity.'"

Dana shook her head, her gaze fixed on her knitting. "Goodness. That's awful. They talk about the poor actors as if they're cattle. No wonder they all have self-esteem issues and turn to drugs and alcohol."

"I was thinking race horses," Suzanne offered. "But we're on the same track . . . no pun intended. Filmmaking is a big-money business, and a flaky movie star is a high risk for investors."

"Looks like the biggest investors in this film are the power couple . . . along with Heath O'Hara." Lucy still studied the computer screen. "They've formed their own production company, Three Penny Productions."

Lucy looked up at her friends. "Matt and I can do yard work together or even grill. But I'm not sure how long the relationship would last if we tried to make a movie."

"Kevin and I can't even do yard work . . . and he knows better than to come into the kitchen before the food is on the table," Suzanne replied. "Enough of this business stuff. What about Heath?" She drew out the name on a breathy note. "Besides being the sexiest, yummiest man alive, I mean." Her friends laughed, but she remained unfazed. "You all know what I'm talking about. Lucy . . . don't even try to hide that little smile."

Lucy did not reply as she typed a bit more, though Maggie

noticed a flush of color in her cheeks. "Here's the official Heath O'Hara website. Feast your eyes, Suzanne."

She turned the computer around for Suzanne to see, but the rest of the group looked over just as eagerly, Maggie noticed.

Suzanne was not embarrassed to let out a loud, long sigh, worthy of any love-struck fourteen-year-old. "The man is just so gorgeous. Who cares if he says a word?"

"Luckily . . . because he's not a very good actor," Dana practically whispered. "Rather one note, I'd say."

Suzanne glared at her, then replied in her tough-love-Mom tone. "Dana . . . I want you to go to your room and think about that."

Dana laughed. "Beauty is in the eye of the beholder. No argument, my friend."

"Look, his hobbies are listed. Maybe he's not just a pretty face," Lucy offered. "Let's see if you two have anything in common, Suzanne." Lucy clicked the link and read aloud: "'Heath devotes his spare time to many passions—rescuing wild horses, helicopter skiing, fund-raising for humanitarian efforts around the globe, and vegetarian cooking.' Oh, and he knits! Look, here's a picture."

Lucy laughed as she turned the computer around again. "Do you think any of that's true?"

"Of course it's true," Suzanne insisted. "A lot of men knit. Especially actors. They have a lot of time on their hands, waiting around on the movie sets."

Maggie shook her head. "Suzanne, you're such a loyal fan."

Dana was trying not to smile, but couldn't help grinning a little. "I suppose it could be true. The story includes a knitting shop. Maybe he was chosen for his role because he already knows how?"

Suzanne didn't look happy about that comment, either. "How about he got the role because he's the hottest actor in the world? They can always find some extra person to knit and then just splice in the hands or something."

"So . . . now you *don't* think he knits? I'm confused," Maggie teased. "Do you think he's really a vegetarian, or does helicopter skiing?"

Suzanne lifted her chin, a bit self-conscious now that she'd defended her idol so fiercely. "You know what I mean."

Maggie laughed. "I'm sorry . . . I couldn't help teasing you. But it is hard to sort out all the hype from reality. If there is any. I guess we'll find out what all these celebrities are really like on Saturday. And draw our own conclusions."

"Yes, we will," Suzanne agreed. "We'll find out a lot of things."

"I bet the entire town is here, looking for autographs," Lucy predicted. "Or just plain looking."

"And the local news outlets. The newspaper and TV stations," Dana added. "This is a big story for Plum Harbor."

"It's so exciting. I can't even knit, thinking about it." Suzanne practically shivered.

Maggie laughed, though she could hardly think of a life event that had been so distracting she couldn't knit. If anything, knitting calmed her mind in stressful times. Or provided a way to express her joy and celebrate a happy moment.

She picked up her needles and turned to them now for the first reason. "I'm excited, too. But for different reasons."

It was hard to imagine half the town stampeding her territory . . . along with an entire movie crew. But she had signed on the dotted line and had no choice now but to go through with it.

⌒

When Saturday morning rolled around, Maggie trudged out to her car in the frosty air, carrying a travel mug full of coffee, her purse, and her knitting bag—equipped the same as she would be heading to her shop for a full day of teaching classes and helping customers.

Except that this morning it was barely 6 a.m., a few hours earlier than she normally left. If all had gone according to schedule, her shop would already be filled with actors and movie equipment, and who knew what else. And very soon, she would be standing on the sidewalk, trying to catch a glimpse of someone famous. Or just trying to see what was going on within.

That will get old pretty quickly, she reflected, starting up her little SUV. But she did want to be part of the hubbub for a little while. She was no autograph hound, but was as curious as the next person.

She wondered if they would let her into the shop because she owned the place. Funny how she had forgotten to ask that important question. Though her other questions had been answered in the agreement she'd signed with the production company, giving them permission to use the space. She just hadn't read it closely enough the first time, Suzanne pointed out.

As she rounded the turn on Main Street, she would have thought a town holiday was in full swing—the annual tree lighting or Founder's Day parade. Blocks away from her shop and not a parking space to be found.

She was feeling rather hopeless, wondering if she had to park down at the harbor, when she spotted a car pulling out. She quickly steered into the space and grabbed her belongings.

Once on the sidewalk, she found herself in a stream of walkers, headed in the same direction, most chatting eagerly, some practically running. All hoping to spot movie stars, as if they were creatures in the wild. Many had field glasses and cameras slung around their neck. Some even carried knapsacks and lawn chairs, prepared for a long wait. Such devotion. She was amazed.

The line of cars on Main Street quickly gave way to a row of very large, box-shaped trucks and white RV-type trailers. Many busy and official-looking people were climbing in and out of the trucks that held mysterious equipment and large black cases and boxes.

But quite a few of the movie people were just milling about, looking over silver clipboards and chatting with each other. Or speaking into the headsets that were wound around their heads. They paid little mind to the onlookers. They were used to doing their jobs with an audience, Maggie realized.

A deep crowd had already assembled around the front of the shop, spilling out onto the street. Wooden barriers—set up by either the movie people or the village police?—stood around the perimeter of the property, keeping the fans at a reasonable distance. The white picket fence that enclosed the property helped, too.

She always welcomed the first sight of her shop. A wide porch wrapped around the front and long windows that were trimmed with wooden shutters. Stark looking at this time of year, but it would soon be covered with flowers, the window boxes filled, hanging pots trailing petunias, along with the garden blooming in front.

Phoebe, who attended a local college part time in addition

to working for Maggie, lived in an apartment upstairs. A convenient arrangement. Though not today, with all the noise so early, Maggie realized. Her young friend could sleep until noon on days she was not due at school or downstairs to work. Sometimes, even when she was.

As Maggie approached, she felt a small pang in her heart, as if seeing a friend in some distress, but not knowing how to help her.

Don't worry, you'll be all right, Maggie told the shop silently. I know it seems like an invasion of ruffians, but it will all be over soon. Then you'll have fun telling the story. Isn't that what her friends had promised her? More or less?

Maggie was thankful for the wooden barriers, keeping some of the barbarians at the gate. It had been a long winter and tender green shoots were just starting to sprout in the flower beds that rimmed the walk and the edges of the fence and porch. She did fear for their survival.

She was glancing around, wondering if anyone was there yet, when she felt a firm grasp on her shoulder.

"Maggie . . . we've been waiting for you."

Suzanne stood right behind her, dressed for her role of Real Estate Lady to the Stars in brand-new black skinny jeans, a slim leather jacket, and a fine peach-colored scarf she knit herself in Maggie's ribbon yarn class. The color set off her dark brown hair and big brown eyes perfectly. Huge designer sunglasses that hid half her face were the finishing touch. Even though the sun had barely risen past the horizon.

"I almost didn't recognize you . . . Are you hiding from the paparazzi, too?"

Suzanne ignored the question and grabbed her arm. "You

just missed Jennifer Todd. She came out of her trailer and walked into the shop."

"She did? When was that?"

"A few minutes ago. She's so beautiful in person," Suzanne added. "And she was so nice. She stopped to sign autographs for everyone who asked, though you could tell the poor woman was hardly awake."

"I'm hardly awake, either. Maybe I should go home and go back to bed."

"Don't be silly. The other actors didn't pass yet." By that, she meant Heath O'Hara, of course. "And they should let you inside, even for a minute or two. You do own the building," Suzanne reminded her

"I wondered about that. Who do I ask?"

"The location manager, I guess. Give me a minute, I'll look around for him."

They'd worked their way through the throng, to where Dana and Lucy stood against the picket fence on the left side of the property. The spot afforded them a clear view of the porch and lawn, and of everyone walking up the brick path and into the shop.

"Primo perch. What time did you get here?" Maggie asked.

"Phoebe came out around four a.m. With a lawn chair and sleeping bag," Lucy reported.

"That's crazy. The poor thing. She must be freezing. I hope she doesn't catch a cold." It was early April but still very chilly at night. "Where is she?"

Lucy smiled and pressed a finger to her lips, then glanced over her shoulder.

Maggie saw her poor assistant curled in a beach chair just behind them, a hood pulled over her head, the rest of her stuffed into a sleeping bag like a caterpillar in a thick cocoon, a few hand-knit afghans tossed over that.

"She said not to wake her until the other stars show up," Dana whispered.

"At least she looks warm enough." Maggie rubbed her gloved hands together. She wasn't sure how much longer she wanted to wait. Even to see the famous Heath O'Hara. She was not bitten by the Hollywood bug like the rest of her friends—and most of the town—seemed to be. Some scrambled eggs and toast with a hot cup of coffee at the Schooner Diner down the street seemed like a better idea. She wondered if anyone else felt the same. But all her friends looked mesmerized by the star watch.

The door opened at the front of the shop. Everyone turned to see who would emerge. Maggie felt jostled by the crowd, all the bodies shifting and pushing to get a better view, like the Wave in the stands at Fenway Park.

"Who is it? Can you see?" Suzanne stood behind them, jumping up on tiptoe. Lucy, the tallest, was closest to the fence.

"Just another guy in a baseball cap and a headset," she reported. "Must be part of the crew."

Suzanne peered over Lucy's shoulder, then flung herself forward, waving her hand.

"Lyle . . . yoo-hoo! Over here . . . Suzanne Cavanaugh, from Prestige Properties!" She turned back to her friends. "That's Lyle Boyd, the location manager. Maybe he can get us inside."

The young man stared at Suzanne with a puzzled expression, then seemed to recognize her. He hopped down the porch steps and loped across the lawn, a silver clipboard tucked under one arm.

"Hey, Suzanne, I was just about to text. Do you know how we can get in touch with"—he paused and checked his clipboard—"Maggie Messina?"

"No problem. She's right here," Suzanne said smoothly. "Maggie, Lyle Boyd. The location manager for Three Penny Productions."

Maggie nodded in greeting. "How can I help you?"

"Could you possibly come on the set a few minutes? Ms. Todd has some questions."

It was odd to hear her own shop called "the set." But today that's what it was.

"I'd be happy to." She smiled and shrugged, as if she was asked to advise movie productions every day. "Can my friends come, too? They'll be quiet as mice."

Lyle glanced at the row of hopeful faces. "I guess it would be all right. It's so insane in there right now. Nobody will even notice. Just come around to the gate and I'll meet you at the security guard."

As he walked away, Suzanne gripped Maggie's arm. "That was brilliant!"

"Good work," Lucy commended.

Dana agreed. She had already turned to jostle Phoebe. "Wake up, Sleeping Beauty. We just got permission to go on the set."

Phoebe stood up and stumbled a bit, as if starting off in a sack race. "Whoa . . . wait for me."

Dana caught her just before she tumbled. "You go ahead; we'll catch up."

"Don't take too long," Maggie warned before being dragged along by Suzanne.

Maggie had noticed a few of the local police, but hadn't

realized that security guards were also stationed in the crowd. Which made perfect sense. There were probably a lot of overly enthusiastic—even emotionally unstable—fans who hung around movie stars on location. You couldn't be too careful these days.

They made their way slowly along the sidewalk and finally reached the gate in the middle of the fence.

A big bald man with a tiny goatee stood just inside the fence. Dressed all in black, he looked like a former pro wrestler or football player. He smiled and a few front teeth capped in sparkling gold seemed to support that guess. He blocked the entire opening of the gate quite effectively with his broad body as he peered down at Maggie, much like a genie that had popped out of a bottle.

"Open sesame?" she was tempted to say. But of course, she held her tongue.

Luckily, Lyle Boyd appeared. "It's okay, Victor. They're visiting Jen."

Victor took out a clipboard and asked for everyone's name.

"Two more of my friends are coming, Dana and Phoebe. They were held up in the crowd," Maggie explained.

"You go ahead. I'll wait for them," the location manager replied. "Ask around for Alicia Littel, Jennifer's assistant."

Maggie nodded and headed up to the shop. She felt self-conscious walking up the brick path. The entire town seemed to be standing there, watching. A few onlookers called out to her.

"Way to go, Maggie!"

"Get Heath's autograph for me!" a teenager girl called out. "Please? I'll make it worth your while . . ."

"Hey, Maggie . . . are you going to be in the movie?"

someone else shouted. She must have known the person, but couldn't pick a face out of the crowd.

Maggie shook her head, eyes cast down as she steadily walked forward. Lucy walked alongside her and Suzanne followed, waving and smiling, as if she was a famous star, too.

"Suzanne . . . you're such a ham." Lucy was laughing when they reached the porch.

Suzanne shrugged as she rearranged her scarf and pulled a tube of lipstick from her pocket. "We all have a cross to bear." Her makeup freshened, she pulled open the shop door with firm resolve. "Okay, let's do this."

Maggie felt strangely apprehensive entering her own familiar territory. She stepped inside and paused. A swarm of activity hummed all around her, the worker bees dressed much the same, men and women wearing a sort of uniform—T-shirts, jeans, and walkie-talkie headsets. Some accessorizing with baseball hats and hoodies.

Moviemaking equipment was everywhere. Maggie could only guess the use of the objects—huge lights on metal stands, cameras, microphones hanging from poles, and rolling tripods. Some of it was already set up and some was still being assembled, or pushed over the wooden floors on noisy, rattling wheels.

She hardly recognized her shop, reorganized and refurnished with all the equipment, most of the area rugs and some of the furniture pushed into the alcove near the front door, where she kept an antique loveseat and sitting chairs, a cozy knitting nook no more.

"Oh my," was all she could say, then stopped in her tracks near the front door as a huge round light in black metal casing rolled by.

Luckily, Suzanne remained sharp. As usual. She nabbed the first person who passed by—a young woman busily unrolling green cable across the floor, pausing every few feet to secure the trail in place with duct tape. Her black T-shirt displayed the movie title on the back and the chopped-off sleeves revealed impressive tattoos.

"Excuse me . . . do you know where we can find Alicia Littel?"

"She was at the table in the back a minute ago," the girl replied without pausing in her task.

"Thanks." Suzanne turned to Maggie and Lucy. "That must be her, the blonde with the glasses, sitting next to Jennifer Todd."

Maggie could hardly get a good view with the bustling crew and all the equipment in the way. But yes . . . there was Jennifer Todd, sitting at the table next to a younger woman.

Jennifer was a beauty on screen, but even more stunning in person, with smooth, honey-colored hair pulled back in a ponytail at her nape and a radiant, peaches-and-cream complexion. She wore little or no makeup and just ordinary workout clothes—black yoga pants and a magenta wrap around her top that showed off a toned, superslim figure. Maybe her outfit was the best money could buy, but it was still just athletic wear, the only hint of her fame and fortune a huge, square diamond that sparkled on her left hand, visible from all the way across the room.

Jennifer and her assistant sat shoulder to shoulder, looking over a large binder that sat opened flat on the table between them.

Maggie had expected Alicia to be older for some reason, but she looked quite young, with a round, friendly-looking face, pink cheeks, and pin-straight blond hair cut to her chin in a hip, choppy style. Long bangs brushed the top of large, tortoiseshell-framed glasses. Maggie felt encouraged, noticing her quick, dimpled smile; she looked efficient but pleasant to deal with.

"Do you want us to come with you? Or do you want to go over by yourself?" Suzanne asked.

Maggie didn't answer, suddenly tongue-tied. Funny, since she never considered herself awed by famous people.

"Why don't you go with her, Suzanne? I'll wait here for Dana and Phoebe," Lucy suggested.

"Good idea. We don't want to stampede them. Ready?" Suzanne turned to Maggie again.

Maggie fluffed her curly hair with her fingertips. "I didn't expect to consult with movie stars today. I would have dressed up a bit."

Suzanne grinned. "You never know what's going to happen when you wake up in the morning, do you?"

"Thank you, Forrest Gump." As Suzanne laughed off her testy reply, Maggie squared her shoulders and took a breath. "Lead on. I'm ready to consult to the queen of England."

"Is she in this film, too?" Lucy asked. "That would really draw some publicity."

Maggie smiled but was too nervous to laugh. Her gaze was fixed on the familiar worktable where the world-famous actress Jennifer Todd sat with her assistant.

As Maggie drew closer, she saw Jennifer pick up the binder and Maggie realized it was a script.

"I'm going to grab a water. Do you want one, Jen? Or maybe some tea? I can run back to the trailer for your teapot," Maggie heard Alicia tell the movie star.

"I'm fine, thanks. But can you text Heath again? Nick will throw a fit if he finds out we didn't run through the changes yet," Jennifer added in a quieter tone.

"No problem." Alicia took out her phone and tapped a message.

Maggie had noticed a large folding table nearby laden with food—a coffee percolator, boxes of donuts, muffins, and bagels, bottled water, and a tray of sandwiches covered with plastic wrap. Alicia was obviously headed in that direction.

Maggie watched the assistant finally depart and saw her chance to approach the star.

Well, here's my cue. Enter stage left . . . Or something like that.

Just as Maggie headed for her target, a horrific sight filled her gaze. She heard people gasp and even scream as a long metal pole, poised on a metal stand and topped with a square grid of flood lights, suddenly fell toward the table.

Maggie felt as if she was watching a slow-motion film as the heavy fixture swayed and then headed for the floor. She heard more screams as all the lights flickered and blacked out completely for a moment. The metallic monster crashed on the table in a spray of broken glass and sizzling, exploding lightbulbs, then finally settled, an acrid, burning smell filling the air.

Maggie had already raised her arms to shield her face out of sheer reflex, though she and Suzanne stood several yards away.

When she looked again, almost everyone in the shop was running toward the accident. She could hardly see a thing.

She turned and stared at Suzanne. For once, Suzanne was speechless.

"Jennifer Todd . . ." Maggie whispered. "Is she under there?"

The actress would be smashed like an insect, all that metal and cables . . . and broken glass.

Maggie winced and squeezed her eyes closed, imagining the fate, too horrified to look back and find out what had happened.

Chapter Two

"Jennifer! Are you all right? Answer me . . . please!"

As Maggie and Suzanne moved toward the back of the shop along with the rest of the crowd, all they could hear was Alicia, crying and screaming.

Some of the crew members, along with Alicia, rushed to the spot where Jennifer had been sitting, but the star could no longer be seen.

While they shouted at each other, there was no reply from the actress for the longest moment. Maggie glanced at Suzanne, who stood with her hand over her mouth, pale and shocked.

Finally, they heard a weak but familiar voice. "I'm all right. I'm okay . . ."

"Step back, please! Give her some space!" one of the crew members shouted as he and Alicia dove under the table and helped Jennifer to her feet. She stood on shaky legs while Alicia frantically brushed bits of broken glass from Jennifer's clothing and hair, heedless of her own hands touching the jagged bits.

Jennifer had either fallen, or perhaps purposely dropped to the floor to protect herself. Alicia and the young man helped her walk to a canvas folding chair a few yards away from the table. It said "Todd" on the back in white block letters, Maggie noticed.

"Call first aid! Somebody, please!" Alicia hovered over Jennifer and continued to gently pick bits of debris off Jennifer's clothes and hair. The poor girl looked very shaken herself, weeping as her own hands trembled.

Jennifer gently patted Alicia's arm, quite ironic, all things considered. "Please, don't cry. It's all right. I'm fine."

Alicia gasped for a breath. "I saw it falling . . . I couldn't reach you, Jen. You could have been crushed."

Maggie sympathized with Alicia's reaction. She felt shaken to the core herself. The sight had been heart stopping.

"Yes, dear. But I wasn't hurt at all. At least I don't seem to be. Any scratches on my face? That's the main thing," she said quickly.

Alicia checked, then shook her head. "No, thank goodness."

"We're okay, then. But look at your hand. You've got a big cut."

Alicia held out her right hand to check. Maggie saw a slash on the side oozing blood.

"It's nothing. Doesn't even hurt. I'll just cover it." Alicia took a hand towel that was draped on the chair and quickly wrapped it around the wound. She glanced around. "Where's Nora Lynch? I thought she was already on the set?"

Before anyone could answer, a young woman wearing a dark blue windbreaker with a red cross symbol on the back ran up to Jennifer, obviously a medical technician of some kind.

"Nora . . .please check Jennifer first," Maggie heard Alicia say as she stepped aside so that Jen could be examined.

Finally, the med tech turned to Alicia and examined her hand. "This is nasty," Nora said, checking the cut. "I don't think you need stitches, but I'll put on a few butterflies."

She took out a box of first-aid supplies, cleaned the wound, and applied the bandage, while Jennifer looked on, holding two ice packs, one in each hand, apparently not feeling any aches or pains yet.

Maggie turned to Suzanne. "Thank goodness no one was seriously hurt. Jennifer jumped under the table just in time. I don't even want to think about what we could have just witnessed."

Suzanne quietly agreed. "It's a miracle. Let's not even think about it."

Before the friends could say more, Suzanne stumbled to one side and glanced over her shoulder. Someone had pushed her, and rather rudely, as they stomped by.

Maggie caught sight of a tall man with broad shoulders and long, thick, silver-gray hair combed back straight from his forehead.

"Is she hurt? Did anyone call an ambulance?" the silver-haired man shouted. "Out of the way! Idiots," he grumbled.

Just as quickly, he was gone, rushing toward the accident like a heat-seeking missile. Several more people followed in his wake, all talking into their headsets as they trotted after their leader.

"Nick . . . for goodness' sake, calm down. You'll have another heart attack," Jennifer greeted him.

"That must be Nick Pullman." Maggie could tell from Suzanne's tone she was quite impressed.

"He probably calls everyone an idiot. Or worse. I won't take it personally," Maggie whispered back.

"Under the circumstances, I'll let it slide this time, too," Suzanne agreed.

They watched Nick hover over Jennifer alongside Alicia. He conferred with Nora Lynch a moment, then spoke to his wife again. Although Maggie couldn't hear what he said, it was obvious that he was trying to be certain she wasn't hurt.

He held her face in his hands and examined it with narrowed eyes and slow scrutiny. A gesture of cherishing adoration? Maggie wondered. Or was he checking his property for damage, as if she was an expensive car that had just been in a fender bender?

What a cynical thought, Maggie scolded herself. Of course he's worried about her safety. Anyone would be, and he's her husband.

The medical technician was dismissed and Jennifer was left with the ice packs.

Maggie heard Jennifer laugh. "I guess you won't be satisfied until I stick these on something. How about on you, Nick? You're our fearless leader. You can use some epaulets."

Jennifer rose and draped an oblong blue ice pack on each of her husband's shoulders. Then laughed.

"Very funny." He stared down at her, unsmiling. "Are you sure you didn't hit your head?"

Jennifer mocked an apologetic expression. "A little joke, honey. To lighten the mood? It was an accident. I'd rather get to work and forget all about it."

"We have to change the schedule now," Nick replied sharply. "And find out who hooked up that equipment," he barked at an assistant nearby. "I'm going to fire their ass."

He glanced at his watch. "Damn it . . . look at the time."
He glanced around at the crew, most of whom were staring at
him, awaiting instruction. "Close this set and clear this mess
away."

Several crew members had already started cleaning up,
and a few followed Nick like confused goslings as he stomped
off, his flock of assistant directors, Maggie guessed. She'd
heard there would be a lot of them.

"My oak table. I love that piece. I hope it's not scratched.
I bought it at a tag sale the same day I made the decision to
open the shop," she told Suzanne.

"It's going to have a few dings, no doubt. But you can have
it refinished. It probably saved Jennifer Todd's life. I'd say that
gives the piece added value, scratches and all."

Before Maggie could respond, one of Nick's underlings
walked up to them, waving his hands. "Closing the set. The set
is closed to everyone but cast and crew." He looked straight at
Maggie and Suzanne as he swept by.

"Guess we're being kicked out," Maggie said quietly to her
friend.

"Looks that way." Suzanne seemed reluctant, but moved
along with the group headed for the door. Most wore press
passes slung around their necks.

A more persistent reporter had broken from the pack and
clung to Nick Pullman, asking questions about the fallen fixture.
He shook his head and walked on, without giving her a comment.

Interesting, she thought. She turned to Suzanne, but her
friend had disappeared.

Drat . . . where did she go? She wouldn't have left without
me . . . would she?

Maggie's gaze swept the shop, suddenly finding Suzanne

right next to Jennifer Todd's chair. Chatting with Alicia and the actress like an old friend. In her inimitable Suzanne way.

Maggie stared at her. Suzanne smiled and waved her over.

She's one in a million, that girl. That's all I can say. Maggie would have laughed out loud, but didn't want to draw attention to herself.

"Jennifer, Alicia . . . this is Maggie Messina, owner of this beautiful shop and our fearless knitting leader." Suzanne introduced her with a flourish.

Jennifer extended her hand, looking sincerely interested to meet her. "Maggie . . . thank you so much for coming. We had a little accident with some equipment . . ."

"We saw what happened. How awful for you. What a scare."

"Just a big mess." Jennifer rolled her eyes briefly, as if the incident was nothing at all.

"Does equipment fall down like that a lot on movie sets?" Suzanne asked.

"Not usually, thank goodness." Jennifer rose from her seat. "I've only seen that happen once before. On a very low-budget film . . . which this is most definitely *not*," she added quietly, then laughed.

"I'm glad you stuck around. I have loads of questions to ask you. But it's a madhouse here now." Jennifer glanced at the crew of gaffers, who had already started rigging new lights. "Can you come back to my trailer? We'll have some privacy there."

Maggie met Suzanne's bright gaze. She looked about to burst with pleasure, the edges of her smile spreading to her earrings.

"We'd love to. Lead the way," Maggie answered for both of them.

A short time later, they had followed the star outside and another large security guard met them on the porch. Maggie saw Lucy, Dana, and Phoebe standing at the gate. They all waved when she looked their way.

"Oh dear . . . I forgot all about them," Suzanne gasped, and covered her mouth with her hand.

"I did, too," Maggie admitted. Understandably, in all the excitement. Lucy must have been asked to leave when the set was closed, and Dana and Phoebe probably never even made it inside. "Is something wrong?" Jennifer stopped and turned. She wore a white down coat draped over her shoulders and tugged the edges toward her chin.

Maggie was about to say, "Nothing." But Suzanne answered first. "Our friends . . . the rest of our knitting group. They're *dying* to meet you. Could we just stop and say hello?"

Jennifer smiled. "You have a real knitting group? I'd love to hear all about that. Ask them to join us. It will be fun."

Maggie was shocked at the star's generosity. "It's not too much of an intrusion? I'm sure you don't have much time . . ."

Suzanne jabbed her with an elbow. "Thank you so much! I know they'll be thrilled."

"It's fine. And will help me enormously. Even though I knit a lot on the set, I buy most of my materials online and I've never been part of a group. Or spent much time in knitting shops," she admitted. "It will add so much to the role if I have more of a feeling for this character's life—her routines and relationships."

"I can definitely help with that," Maggie promised. All the while thinking how boring her life will seem compared to Jennifer Todd's.

Quiet and predictable. But that's the way I like it. I doubt I would enjoy being a movie star, even if it was a possibility, she reminded herself.

Right, Maggie, a little voice—a lot like Phoebe's—chided her. Tell me another one . . .

Everyone called the vehicle a trailer, but it was really a super-luxury RV, quite daunting from the outside and even wider and more spacious inside than Maggie had expected. She felt as if she had entered a small, expensively furnished condo. Or maybe the cabin of a multimillion-dollar yacht.

Alicia, who was working on the refreshments in a galley kitchen, smiled as Maggie and her friends entered and looked around, unabashedly in awe.

"I'm just fixing some tea and snacks," Alicia called out. "Does anyone want anything special?"

"Don't go to any trouble for us," Maggie assured her.

The actress had led them to a sitting area with a dark blue cushioned-back couch wrapped around the space in a U shape.

A blond-wood coffee table, with a raised rim—so cups and glasses wouldn't slide away if the trailer was moving?—was secured to the floor. Matching cabinets, flat-screen TV, and bookcases had been built in around and above the couch.

"This is my own custom-fit trailer. I have someone drive it to locations for me, whenever possible. There's already so much stress when we're on location. It makes life easier to be in your own space."

"It's beautiful," Lucy said, gazing around.

"Like a home away from home," Dana added.

"As much as it can be," Jennifer replied.

Maggie noticed many personal touches—a photo of Jennifer and Nick on their wedding day and another with the couple posed at the Great Wall of China. There was also a framed poster from one of her early film successes and a large vase of fresh flowers near the window. Lily of the valley.

"Lovely flowers," Maggie remarked. "I have some in my garden. They don't bloom around here until May, though."

Jennifer smiled. "I love gardening. When I have the time. I can't get lily of the valley to grow very well where I live, but friends know it's my favorite. Regina Thurston, our executive producer, sent that bunch. To wish me good luck on the film," she explained. "Take a seat, everyone, I think there's enough room," the star said graciously. "Alicia, can you bring some of those kale chips and the green drinks . . . oh, and the strawberries?"

Maggie was more inclined to pairing her tea with a blueberry scone, or even plain butter cookies. But of course, white flour, sugar, and butter were pure poison to a movie star. Jennifer Todd was so slim—practically skeletal. She probably lived on nothing more than kale chips and filtered water.

"Please help yourself." Alicia set down a tray with several small teacups, made of dark green pottery, alongside a cast-iron teakettle with a coppery sheen. Maggie had seen such kettles in specialty tea shops and knew they cost a small fortune.

There was also a dish of what looked like green potato chips and a more approachable-looking bowl of ripe strawberries, along with several bottles of a healthy-looking green drink.

"Nick and I have these smoothies flown in almost every day from a terrific little vegan restaurant in Laguna Beach. I practically live on them. Try one," Jennifer encouraged them. She picked up a bottle and twisted off the cap, then poured it into a tall glass.

Maggie and her friends all took cups of tea. Phoebe was

the only one tempted by the green drink. She sniffed it curiously before tasting, like a little cat.

"So . . . where shall we start? Maybe I should tell you a little about the character I play. Her name is Renee Woods. She's a young widow without children who has thrown herself into running her knitting shop the last few years, since her husband died. A bit reserved. Maybe even shy."

"That's weird. She sounds a lot like Maggie," Phoebe blurted out, then looked embarrassed. "Sorry, Mag. I don't think you're shy," she assured her.

"Thanks for that. It does sound like me . . . a little," Maggie admitted. "I opened my shop right after I lost my husband. Though I'm not all that young. I do have a daughter; she's in college. I used to be a high school art teacher, but I decided it was time for a change," she added.

"An art teacher? How interesting. That's a wonderful detail." Jennifer seemed delighted by the disclosure. As if Maggie had made up some fascinating embellishment in a work of fiction. Except that it was her real life story, she reflected.

"Alicia? Can you get this down for me?" Jennifer turned to her assistant, who sat in a chair beside the star.

"I'm all set." Alicia already had an iPad, opened and booted up on her lap. The large bandage on her left hand didn't slow her down a beat as she began tapping out notes. "This is interesting," she agreed, smiling at Maggie.

Jennifer looked back at Maggie. "Please go on with your story . . . So I'm a former art teacher. Do I miss teaching? Working with students and all that?"

Maggie was getting confused with all these points of view—Jennifer, her character, Renee . . . and her own life. She felt as if she was suddenly walking in a hall of mirrors.

"I do think about my art room years once in a while. And I stay in touch with many of my special students. It's mostly fond memories. But I don't miss it. I'm using my teaching skills every day with the classes I lead at the shop. It seems almost synchronistic, the way this new career path evolved for me. Equally as rewarding as working at the high school. Maybe even more."

"That's wonderful. I love that perspective. Life just . . . evolving for you. I'm going to use that, if you don't mind."

"I don't mind at all." Maggie had thought that Jennifer would be asking about practical matters—how to use the yarn winder for instance, or ring up a sale. Not her own life story.

But she had no experience with actors and how they worked. It appeared that they created the characters they had to play much the same way that writers created a character on a page. It was fascinating, she thought.

"I love that word, 'synchronicity.' I love that wise perspective." Jennifer nodded.

"Maggie's very wise," Lucy remarked, making Maggie blush.

"With a lot of insight," Dana added.

"Quite a character in her own right," Suzanne quipped.

"Yes, I can see that." Jennifer smiled. She had dazzling blue eyes and amazingly white teeth.

Maggie wondered if they were the original set. It didn't seem possible; they had to be caps or some sort of cosmetic enhancement. Otherwise, the actress was a natural beauty. No obvious nips and tucks, or frozen, tight spots that hinted at too many Botox shots.

"So . . . did you always knit, or was that taken up recently?"

"I learned from my grandmother, when I was a teenager.

But I didn't spend much time on it until I was pregnant with my daughter, Julie. I came across a simple pattern for baby booties in a magazine, waiting for a doctor's appointment. I decided to make them by the time she was born. I ended up with booties, a jacket, a hat, and a matching blanket," she rattled off, making everyone laugh.

"I never heard that story before," Dana remarked.

"Me, either," Lucy noted.

Maggie shrugged. "Maybe I just made it up."

"If you did, you're a better actress than I am." Jennifer's quick comeback made everyone smile. "So you took to knitting quickly. Sounds like you were a natural."

"Not quite. Those early attempts were far from perfect. The toes on the booties curled, like little elf shoes. I don't think the baby noticed," she added with a laugh. "I'd had a miscarriage before I became pregnant with Julie. Knitting calmed me down and distracted me. A very therapeutic hobby for pregnant women. Especially if they're put on bed rest."

"I never thought of that. What an authentic story. And what a lovely image—an expectant mother, creating something so protective and comforting for her baby." Jennifer seemed enchanted. "Alicia, make sure you get this down. Every word."

"I've got it. Great stuff," Alicia added, looking up for a moment to smile at Maggie again. She typed on steadily, like a court reporter taking down intense testimony.

"I can see Renee knitting a little jacket or some booties. It's perfect. We have to tell Theo to write that in to one of the later scenes." Jennifer turned to her assistant again, then back to the knitting friends. "In the plot, Renee has been longing for a baby, but she and her late husband couldn't conceive. Then

Tyler Hanson comes along. Well, I don't want to ruin it for you."

"Tyler Hanson . . . that's the character Heath O'Hara plays?" Suzanne sat up at attention, eager for tidbits about her idol.

Jennifer nodded. "Heath brings so much to the role. He's such a gifted actor."

Maggie smiled, though she couldn't see how a handsome hunk would have any problem playing the role of . . . well, a handsome hunk who sweeps a shy, widowed knitting shop owner off her feet. Which seemed to be the bare bones of the story, from what she could glean from Jennifer's description.

"So, do they end up together, Renee and Tyler?" Suzanne asked eagerly. "I love a good romance."

Jennifer smiled. "Oh, it's a good romance. But for one thing, Heath is married to Trina's character, Sabrina . . . and he dies rather tragically, very bravely in fact." She looked suddenly sad, as if these characters were real people. "But at least Renee has the baby," she added. Her eyes suddenly widened and she covered her mouth with her hand. "Oh my gosh . . . I spoiled it for you now, didn't I? I'm so sorry . . . I didn't mean to."

"That's all right. We'll definitely see it anyway," Lucy assured her.

"I'll see it a few times," Suzanne promised.

Jennifer looked relieved, but before she replied, a black iPhone on the table buzzed, signaling a call or text coming through. Alicia quickly picked it up. "It's Nick's assistant. They want you in makeup in five."

Jennifer sighed and picked up her teacup. "Tell them I'll be right there. This is important, too."

She looked over at Maggie and her friends again. "It's been amazing talking to you, Maggie. It's already been a huge help. And I didn't even get to ask you any of my technical questions about running the shop. Or what you all do in your knitting group. Can we talk some more later?"

"Absolutely," Maggie said graciously.

"Would you like to come to a knitting group meeting? You'll get some great material touches for your character," Suzanne solemnly promised the movie star.

Maggie sat back, stunned by Suzanne's nerve. She could see her other friends felt the same. Who would ever imagine inviting Jennifer Todd to one of their humble meetings? The thought would have never crossed Maggie's mind.

Maggie sometimes wondered why Suzanne wasn't selling million-dollar properties every day with her just-do-it—or say-it—philosophy.

Of course Jennifer wouldn't come, though Maggie expected a polite excuse.

"I'd love to. When is it?"

"When can you come? That's when we'll have the next one," Suzanne promised, moving in quickly to seal the deal.

"Let's see . . . Alicia, do you have the schedule handy?" Jennifer turned to her assistant, who had quickly brought up another screen on the tablet.

"Monday night looks possible." Alicia nodded and glanced at Jennifer.

"Yes, that looks good. I can come for a little while on Monday night, around seven. Does that work out for you?"

Maggie wasn't sure what to say. She couldn't recall whose turn it was to hold the meeting. They usually rotated between their homes and the knitting shop. But Jennifer probably wanted to visit the shop. She probably had questions about her character's job as the proprietor and all that.

"We can meet at seven in the shop, provided the movie crew isn't there," Maggie added with a hopeful smile.

"We're filming at the beach house most of next week. Didn't you get a schedule from Lyle?" Alicia asked.

"No . . . I didn't. Is that who I should ask for the particulars?"

"He must have emailed it. Maybe he had the wrong address. What's your email address, Maggie? I'll send you one right now." Alicia looked down at her iPad, fingers poised.

Maggie told her, grateful for the young woman's efficiency. "Thank you so much."

"So we'll meet on Monday night and help Jennifer prepare for her role?" Maggie looked around at her friends, who nodded eagerly, though she suspected Monday night was not ideal for all of them. But she was also sure they would cancel any previous commitments to hang out and knit with Jennifer Todd.

Maggie rose from her seat. "This has been lovely. Thank you both."

Her friends stood up, too, and also thanked their hostess and Alicia.

"It was great meeting you. I'm really looking forward to Monday night," Jennifer replied.

Dana took a last sip of tea before setting down the cup on the tray. "This tea had such an unusual flavor. What kind is it?"

Jennifer seemed pleased by the question. "A special blend of green tea. It's very difficult to find. I purchase it through a contact in Australia. It's just chock-full of wonderful vitamins and antioxidants that come from bamboo," she enthused.

The brew did have a distinct fragrance and a smooth taste, Maggie had noticed, one that didn't seem at all familiar. "Is it made from bamboo leaves?"

"Not the bamboo exactly. It's the panda poo. It's used to fertilize the tea plants," Alicia explained. "Pandas eat only wild bamboo and hardly digest their food, so their excrement is filled with amazing nutrients."

"I feel so vitalized after a cup or two . . . and strangely calm at the same time," Jennifer added.

Phoebe nodded. As if this all made perfect sense. "Pandas are very calm animals. Playful, too."

Suzanne looked like she was going to playfully barf some back up. "Amazing," she said, putting down her teacup.

"I can't offer anything that exotic. But we always share a nice dinner and some wine with our knitting. And we look forward to seeing both of you," Maggie added, extending the invitation to Alicia.

A few moments later, Maggie and her friends regrouped on the sidewalk, a short distance from the shop. Fans still waited five deep around the fence, but the TV news vans were gone.

Maggie was about to suggest that they all head to the Schooner. It was half past eleven, and having woken up at five, she was definitely ready for lunch.

But before she had time to speak, Suzanne gripped her arm with one hand and pointed with the other. "Look at the limo! I wonder who's in there?"

Lucy stepped around Maggie for a better view. "Looks like we're going to find out. It's pulling up at the shop."

Maggie and her friends scurried down the sidewalk, chasing the sleek luxury car that cruised along like a great white shark.

When it finally parked, two large, brawny men wearing tight charcoal-gray suits, black shirts, and black ties climbed out. They gazed in all directions as they walked around the car and out to the sidewalk. One of them held his hands out and asked the group of onlookers to step back, while the other two flanked the passenger-side door of the vehicle.

After a few moments, the back door on the passenger side opened again. A long, elegant leg—clad in a fishnet stocking and a tight black boot—emerged.

Then a swish of a golden fur, trimmed with fluffy white stuff.

Before the rest of the body appeared, Maggie had already guessed the identity of the mystery arrival.

"Trina Hardwick. She knows how to make an entrance," Lucy murmured.

"You'd think it was the red carpet at the Academy Awards," Suzanne noted.

"Maybe stars need to practice in out-of-town markets. The way they get the kinks out of Broadway shows?" Dana asked.

Trina Hardwick, in all her glory, stepped out of the car and raised a slim arm above her head, waving to fans who greeted her with cheers and wolf whistles.

She turned a few times, tossing a mane of thick, reddish-gold hair, as one hand pushed back her fur coat and rested on a lean hip, showing off her Barbie doll figure to full advantage. Long, slim legs, a tiny waist, and a full, bouncing bosom. She leaned against the limo in a sultry pose. Or maybe her boots were so high she needed the fender for balance. Either way, she twisted from side to side with a dazzling smile while fans and a few strangling reporters ran up to take photos.

"She is beautiful," Lucy noted.

"If you like the obvious type," Suzanne sneered.

"As in . . . obviously gorgeous bombshell?" Phoebe countered.

"I'd text a picture to Matt, but I don't want to give him any encouragement," Lucy confessed. "That's too much competition for me."

"Maybe . . . but do you think that's all . . . real?" Phoebe raised a pierced eyebrow.

"The glossy mane is full of hair extensions. As for the rest, *these* are real . . . and I have the hips to prove it." Suzanne looked down at her own chest. "Those things? I doubt it. Though I'm sure they're the best set money can buy."

"Suzanne . . . you just can't assume that," Dana scolded her.

"Phoebe asked a valid question and I'm answering with fact-based knowledge. First of all, no arm fat. And when she twists and turns, they're still pointing straight ahead. No natural bounce and jiggle. Dead giveaway," Suzanne added knowingly. "I bet if she laid down flat, it would look like two Tupperware bowls stuck under her dress."

"Suzanne . . ." Dana turned to her, shaking her head. "That's not fair. And possibly not even true. About breast implants or Trina's body," she added in a reasonable tone.

"Think what you like. I know reality from illusion, ladies. And I can tell synthetic enhancements, let us say, from Mother Nature's natural blessings," she added, tugging her sweater down.

"Thanks for keeping it real, Suzanne. We can always count on you for that." Lucy laughed and patted her pal's shoulder.

Trina had finished posing and slowly sauntered down the sidewalk, then down the brick path toward the shop, still waving and smiling, flanked by her bodyguards. Who looked like a doo-wop trio from the sixties in their matching outfits, Maggie thought.

"Speaking of keeping it real, how about some real food? Lunch at the Schooner?" Maggie suggested as the redheaded bombshell disappeared into the knitting shop.

"The panda poo tea and kale chips weren't enough for you?" Lucy teased.

Before she could answer, Dana interrupted, reading off her cell phone. "Before we dis that nutritious snack, I just Googled the tea. It's one of the most expensive blends in the world, next to tea leaves covered in gold leaf," she added with a little laugh. "While the health benefits are hotly debated, each tiny cup of panda poo brew cost about fifty dollars to prepare."

"So Jennifer Todd isn't exactly a hometown girl with simple, unspoiled Lipton tastes?" Lucy surmised.

Suzanne shrugged. "If I was raking in zillions of dollars a day making movies, maybe I'd go all the way for the gold leaf stuff. It doesn't mean she's not a nice person. I bet she comes to our meeting Monday."

"Do you really think she will? Or is she just too polite to refuse?" Lucy asked. "She did seem interested in asking you more questions, Maggie."

"I suppose it depends on her schedule and how tired she is after a day of working on the movie. What's the worst thing that could happen? We'll all get together and do some knitting."

"Good point," Lucy agreed.

The rest of her friends did, too. And none wanted to miss a chance to hang out and knit with Jennifer Todd.

Chapter Three

On Monday night, five minutes before nine, everyone but Suzanne seemed to accept that they'd been stood up. But Maggie could have guessed that.

"Movie stars are always late. It's part of their mystique," Suzanne reminded her friends.

"Two hours is a lot of mystique." Lucy yawned and covered her mouth with her hand.

"Stop that, Lucy. It's not that late," Suzanne snapped. "You'll make us all sleepy."

"At least we're being productive," Dana pointed out.

"Yes . . . but it's distracting, waiting for her. I'm not getting much done," Phoebe admitted.

"Neither am I . . . though this pattern is so simple I could make it in my sleep." Maggie shrugged and set her work aside. She had started the group on a ribbed summer tank. It was hardly warm enough out yet to wear it, of course, but no one seemed to mind that. They all liked the flattering style and squared-off neckline, and thought it would look fine with most any summer outfit, and even under a blazer. She'd also pulled some patterns for Jennifer's baby booties and a hat.

"I'll make coffee and bring out Suzanne's cupcakes." Maggie rose, knowing dessert would cheer her friends.

"What kind?" Phoebe asked with keen interest.

"Chocolate, gluten free. I wasn't sure if Jennifer was on a GF diet, but it seems likely," Suzanne added. Maggie knew Suzanne was the last one to worry about healthy ingredients. She obviously wanted to please their guest of honor. Now she felt doubly bad for Suzanne, about Jennifer failing to keep her promise.

"If you have chocolate, who needs gluten?" Phoebe's tone was persuasively logical.

"Very true," Suzanne agreed. "What are you working on, Phoebe? That looks too big to be a bootie . . . unless it's for a giant baby? Hey, I thought you broke up with Josh, at least a month ago."

They all knew Phoebe had dumped her slacker musician boyfriend, Josh, with no regrets. Though his memory and the name of his band, the Big Fat Whining Babies, still supplied a few laughs.

"Good one. I'm filling an order. I got a lot of hits this week on Crafty-Cricket.com."

"Really? That's fantastic. Another female entrepreneur in our midst," Suzanne said.

"I'm so impressed," Lucy added.

"Good for you, Phoebe," Dana said. "Good things happen when you follow your bliss."

"Thanks, guys. I'm wondering why I didn't think of this sooner. I was definitely giving a former boyfriend—who shall not be named—way too much of my precious time, energy, and brain power."

"How true. You're unleashed, Phoebe. Go for it, girl," Suzanne advised.

Phoebe's knitting passion had always been socks. But instead of making them for herself, or an unappreciative boyfriend, Phoebe was busily filling orders.

Encouraged by her knitting pals, Phoebe had begun to sell her footwear originals online at Crafty-Cricket, a site that gave fledgling designers and artists a way to market their handmade products without setting up and servicing their own website.

Her knitting friends were very proud of her. She was making extra money for college tuition and gaining a lot of confidence, too, Maggie thought.

"She's turning into the Betsey Johnson of socks, right before our eyes. Pretty soon you'll quit your day job," Suzanne predicted.

"Oh . . . I hope not." Maggie had returned with the cupcakes and a pot of decaf. As she set the dessert on the table, she and her assistant shared a warm smile.

"Don't worry, Mag. I'm not running out on you yet," Phoebe promised. "I'd miss the knitting group . . . and the food around here."

Suzanne leaned over and helped herself to a cupcake. "A consolation prize for being stood up," she added glumly.

"Now you agree?" Lucy asked.

Suzanne just shrugged. But before she could reply, the bell on the front door sounded and they all turned to see who was coming in. Suzanne's cheeks were stuffed like a squirrel, her eyes bugging out as she caught sight of Jennifer Todd, followed by Alicia Littel.

"Hello, everyone. Sorry we're late. We were shooting at the

beach today and it went way overtime. Hope you're not done with your meeting?"

"Not at all! We're just getting started," Suzanne managed.

"Come right in. We're just having some coffee and dessert. Gluten free," Maggie added. "I was showing everyone this summer tank top pattern. I also pulled a quick baby bootie pattern for you, Jennifer. The needles and materials are all set out for both," Maggie said graciously.

A short time later, Maggie was showing Jennifer how to start the summer sweater. And how to act like a knitting teacher.

Alicia took a seat beside Phoebe, content to watch. The bandage on her hand made it hard to hold the needles. "I'm pretty uncoordinated anyway. Even with two hands in working condition," she apologized with a laugh. "It does look like fun, though. Maybe Jen can teach me sometime."

"Don't be silly, Alicia. You'd be very good at it. You're very creative," Jennifer encouraged her. "I'll teach you," she promised. "We'll be a mini knitting group on the set."

Alicia seemed to like that idea, but still didn't want to try now. She was interested in Phoebe's socks and took a moment to look at the wares on Crafty-Cricket, too.

"Wow, these are great. I'm going to order some," Alicia promised. Phoebe looked pleased.

Was a celebrity endorsement in the offing for Phoebe? Maggie wondered. She imagined the quote: "I love my Socks by Phoebe. I have a fresh pair flown in daily!" Signed, Jennifer Todd.

Maggie was suddenly snapped from her daydream by a question from the movie star, who was quite an experienced knitter.

"Do you walk around and help people? Or only if they ask?" Jennifer asked.

"I do walk around if it's a class. But I only help my friends if they send up a flare," Maggie explained. "This is basically what we do. Sit and knit. Learn a new stitch or two. Have some dinner and chat," she added.

"We have been known to dish the dirt about mutual acquaintances, too," Lucy admitted.

"That sounds fun. Did we miss any good gossip?" Jennifer asked.

"The movie crew coming to town is definitely the hot story this week," Dana replied.

"Especially since you grew up right in Newburyport," Maggie added. "Has it been hard to come back and film a movie here? It must look very different to you."

"When I read the script, all I could picture was this part of New England. I suggested the location to Nick and our producer, Regina Thurston. They loved the idea. But I don't have much family here anymore. My parents got tired of the cold winters. They live near me now, in San Diego."

In a beautiful home Jennifer had built for them, Maggie had read somewhere.

"There are a few friends I've kept in touch with over the years," Jennifer added. "I hope to visit some of them while we're here."

"I bet everyone says that they knew you," Suzanne said.

"Not everyone. But there are a few that do and I have no recollection," Jennifer admitted with a small laugh. "Maybe I'm just getting old and my memory is going."

"There are a lot of people I went to high school with I'd like to forget," Suzanne said.

"Have you ever thought of being an actress, Suzanne?" Alicia asked. "Your energy totally projects. Doesn't it, Jen?"

"Oh yes. She's a natural." Jennifer agreed.

Suzanne looked surprised, then lit up with pleasure. "Thanks for the compliment. But I think my talents are best used around here for now. In the real-estate biz. I should get an Academy Award for the way I handle some of my clients."

"If not acting, maybe just stand-up comedy," Lucy observed. Maggie thought she was joking, but Suzanne took the comment seriously. Hamming it up for the visitors?

"That has crossed my mind. Maybe after the kids go off to college. I know they'd kill me now for embarrassing them," Suzanne mused. "But how do you get to be a personal assistant for someone like Jennifer?" Suzanne asked Alicia. "I bet there was some tough competition for that job."

Alicia smiled and glanced at her boss. It was obvious the two had a close bond. Jennifer was a little young to be Alicia's mother, but seemed to be a mother figure in some way to the younger woman. Alicia clearly adored her.

"Let's see . . . it's hard to remember how it all came about. I think I started off just walking Jen's dogs and watering the plants, and maybe cooking sometimes for her and Nick. That sort of thing."

"I can hardly remember, either," Jennifer admitted. "But she was clearly a gem. When my last assistant left for a job writing sitcoms, Alicia was the obvious choice. For one thing, she already knew our entire schedule. And all our little quirks."

"It was my dream job. Quirks and all," Alicia confessed. "But I never thought Jen would actually hire me."

"Where did you grow up, Alicia? In California?" Dana asked.

"My dad was career military. We lived all over. I came back to the West Coast for college because I like the weather so much. I studied education, but I couldn't find a teaching job. I volunteer with kids when I can, though. It's very rewarding."

"Good for you." Maggie smiled at her. "There are so many ways to share our knowledge and help others. A person doesn't need a teaching certificate to do that."

"But I bet your experience as a classroom teacher is helpful, here in the knitting shop," Jennifer said, turning the conversation back to Maggie.

"It does help most of the time. But maybe some of the time, I'm *too* instructive." Maggie shrugged. "I don't know, ask my friends."

All of her friends smiled and rolled their eyes.

"I think 'bossy' is the word we're looking for," Lucy said quietly.

"Lucy . . . you really shouldn't use the word 'bossy' that way," Suzanne cut in. "It's like saying it's all right if a man is assertive and acts with authority. But the same behavior is unattractive or unbecoming for a woman."

Phoebe's head popped up from her sock in progress. "You tell her, Suzanne."

"Excuse me. Let's just say she likes things done her own way, at times. Wouldn't you both agree with that?" Lucy asked.

Suzanne and Phoebe glanced at each other, then nodded.

"I do, too," Dana added.

Maggie laughed. "Guilty as charged, I guess. What can you do?"

Jennifer sat up straighter in her seat. "Wow, that was fun. So this is what a knitting group is like. I didn't know what I was missing."

Jennifer had more questions and Maggie answered as thoroughly as she could, though it was hard to describe her day and routines exactly. Maggie gave her a quick tour of the shop, showing her how to arrange the stock and displays, ring up a sale, or search for buttons in the big cabinet behind the table.

"I was wondering what you kept in there. I can use that in a scene, sorting through all those buttons. They're so pretty, too," Jennifer added.

"We need a lot of choices on hand. Sometimes you find the perfect match for a sweater right away. Other times, it's endless," Maggie explained.

"Just like relationships," Jennifer replied.

"Exactly," Maggie agreed, appreciating the analogy.

Despite their enjoyable conversation, her life did sound deadly dull, Maggie realized. The most challenging moment, matching buttons to a project?

But it was the simple truth.

Meanwhile, Jennifer Todd seemed to find everything Maggie said utterly fascinating. Was she just trying to flatter her? But for what reason? It wasn't as if Maggie was a mover and shaker in the film industry. Jennifer was charming, with amazing social skills. That was for sure.

Jennifer turned from the button cabinet to the knitting group. "I've had so much fun at your meeting. I'd love to do something for all of you."

Suzanne's face lit up. Maggie guessed she was thinking an introduction to Heath O'Hara would be the perfect way for Jennifer to show her gratitude. Lunch maybe?

"Would you like to visit the set this week? I thought Thursday night would be a good time. We're shooting a big scene here, with my character and Trina Hardwick's. From about seven until who knows when. I know that you didn't get to see anything Saturday, except a bunch of lights fall down," she recalled.

"All of us?" Phoebe asked eagerly.

Maggie wondered about that, too. She hoped her friends were included. She didn't want to come without them.

"Of course." Alicia quickly took out her iPhone. "I'll put everyone's name on the security list. Just send me the proper spellings, Maggie."

"I will do that ASAP," Maggie promised.

"I'm so totally there," Suzanne enthused. "Thank you, thank you, thank you."

"Great. I'm glad it works out for you. I have an early call tomorrow. We'd better get going," Jennifer said finally. "I have to look fresh for those close-ups. Even the best makeup artist can only work so much magic."

Jennifer Todd hardly needed any magic wand from a makeup artist. Though Maggie was sure that it was hard for an actress to get older, her looks constantly scrutinized, as if they'd been stamped with an expiration date. Men could get craggy and mature looking. Or be cast against an actress half their age. But it was an entirely different ball game for women. A harsh reality of the profession.

The actress gathered up her knitting, looking pleased at her progress. Maggie gave her a Black Sheep Knitting Shop tote to carry it. She'd just had them made up for the shop—a black recycled shopping bag with the shop logo printed on one side in white. On the other side, one of her favorite mottos read: So much yarn, so little time.

"That's adorable. I can really use this, too. I left my knitting bag on the plane. The airline still hasn't returned it," Jennifer explained as she held out the tote, admiring it.

Another celebrity endorsement? Could be, Maggie realized, though she certainly hadn't given Jen the bag for that reason.

"You've given me so much good material. I'm going to talk to Theo, the scriptwriter, tomorrow and see if he can work some of these details into the shop scenes. Maybe we should have a knitting group in the background," she mused aloud.

"If you need any experienced extras, let us know," Suzanne jumped in. Maggie could see her other friends silently react, shocked once again at Suzanne's boldness.

"You're at the top of the list," Jennifer promised.

Did they really have a chance to be extras in the movie, or was Jennifer just being nice? They'd been joking about that the other night, Maggie recalled. Wouldn't it be amazing if it happened?

"I guess you should text Victor and tell him we're ready," Jennifer told her assistant.

"I just did," Alicia replied.

Jen glanced at Maggie again. "We tried to sneak over on our own, but security insisted on driving us. Poor Victor hadn't even eaten dinner yet, so I told him not to wait. He's just up at the inn. He'll be here in a minute."

Before Maggie could reply, a sharp knock sounded on the door. Maggie was surprised. "That was fast. He's very efficient, isn't he?"

Maggie opened the door, ready to face the bearded giant. But the threshold was empty.

She glanced back at Alicia and Jennifer, who stood just behind her, about to leave. Maggie wondered if the security guard had returned to his car. But only the familiar cars of the knitting group stood parked within view.

Alicia stepped out on the porch behind Maggie and glanced down the street in both directions. "I don't see the car, Jen. Don't come out yet," she warned her boss.

"Oh brother . . . I'm not in witness protection." Jennifer sounded cranky about having to be so cautious. It must be odd, Maggie realized, to worry about moving freely around the community where you were raised. She could understand Jennifer's irritation.

"Goodness, what's this?" Maggie suddenly noticed a bunch of flowers on the top step and picked them up—a huge wicker basket, full of long-stemmed yellow roses, the handle of the basket decorated with a dark blue satin ribbon and a big bow. She held it out for Alicia to see.

A large card set right in the middle of the bouquet read, "For Jennifer, My True Love" in large, cursive script.

"It looks like a gift for Jennifer. Special delivery?"

Alicia did not look pleased. In fact, she looked very alarmed. "You'd better put that down, Maggie. Please. We can't be too careful."

Alicia looked worried and Maggie quickly did as she was told. Though she wondered what menace might lurk in the beautiful bouquet, besides a few thorns on the rose stems.

"Jen has some really obsessive fans. You wouldn't believe some of the things they do to get close to her," Alicia confided in a hushed tone.

"Can I come out now?" Jen asked in a playful, singsong tone. "Is the coast clear?"

She stood in the doorway, a silhouette backlit from the lights within the shop. Maggie saw that her friends had gathered in the front room as well, and were standing just behind the movie star. Saying good night, perhaps.

As Jennifer began to walk out to the porch, a voice called out from the empty street: "Jennifer! I love you! We were made for each other . . . We need to be together now . . . You came back . . . to be with me . . . finally."

"Get back in the shop! Quickly!" Alicia spun and pushed Jen back inside, then slammed the door closed behind her.

Maggie was left alone on the porch. She knocked on the door with one hand behind her back, afraid to take her eyes off the street. She swallowed hard, staring out at the empty scene.

Not a shadow stirred. She had no idea where the voice had come from. From across the street somewhere? It had seemed so at first. But she wasn't sure.

Suddenly, it sounded closer. Much closer.

"Jen . . . please. Don't run away . . . Don't be like that. It makes me so . . . upset."

The voice didn't sound upset. More like angry. And louder . . . and closer. Though Maggie still couldn't see anyone as she huddled against the door, peering into the darkness.

"Let me in! You've locked me out here!" she called to her friends, trying hard not to sound panicked.

Finally, the door flew open. Maggie practically fell into the shop, but Phoebe caught her, her own face pale with concern. Suzanne yanked Maggie's arm and pulled her aside while Dana slammed the door again and twisted the locks.

"Maggie . . . get in here! What are you doing?"

"What do you mean? I got locked out," Maggie insisted.

But before anyone replied or even tried to explain, Lucy ran out of the storeroom. "I locked the side door. Just to be safe." Alicia stood huddled next to Jennifer, as if ready to block a bullet.

"Did you see anyone?" Alicia asked Maggie.

Maggie shook her head, feeling silly now. It was just a

lovelorn fan. Obviously. "I didn't see a thing. I wonder how your admirer knew you were here, Jennifer."

"I do have some overly enthusiastic fans. It comes with the territory," Jennifer said calmly.

"They stalk her. They're obsessed. They crawl out of the woodwork. They leave these scary notes on her fan page." Alicia shivered with a chill.

"I think we should call the police. At least report the incident. They can take the flowers away and examine them," Maggie added.

She doubted the roses were rigged to cause the star harm. But what did she know about passionate, besotted fans?

"Oh no . . . don't do that. Nick will have a fit." She sounded more worried about her husband's reaction than about the stalker, Maggie noticed. "I slipped away from the inn tonight without telling him. He thinks I turned in early."

Maggie wondered where Nick Pullman was. Not in the hotel room he shared with his wife? Or did that mean they were staying in separate rooms?

"He hates negative publicity," Alicia added. "We'll tell Victor," she added, mentioning the security guard again. "He knows what to do."

Maggie nodded. It did make sense. The movie people had their own experienced security staff who would know how to deal with crazy fans.

Another knock sounded. Alicia ran to the shop's front window. "It's Victor. Rick is with him. I see the car there, too." Alicia sounded relieved. "I'll just call and explain what happened. They might want to check the street before you come out."

The star nodded. She did seem a little apprehensive about going outside now.

"Good idea," Suzanne said. "You can't be too careful these days."

"No . . . you can't," Jennifer agreed quietly.

There was an awkward silence while the women waited for the security guards to call back. But a few moments later, Alicia's phone buzzed and she glanced over at Jennifer.

"He says it's fine. They're waiting on the porch."

A look of relief flashed across Jennifer's lovely features, quickly replaced by one of her trademark brilliant smiles.

"So sorry for the surprise ending to your meeting. And all this drama." She rolled her eyes, as if they'd all shared a big joke.

"No apology necessary. We're glad there's no harm done. Thanks again for the invitation to visit the set," Maggie added.

"Yes, hope to see you there." Jennifer bid them all good night again, departing with her authentic Black Sheep Knitting Shop tote tucked under her arm.

Alicia quickly said good night as the two women were met at the doorway by a pair of serious-looking security guards. Maggie remembered both of the men; they'd been guarding the gate to her property on Saturday. They escorted the actress and her assistant to a long black limo that waited on the street, right in front of the shop.

Maggie closed the door and locked it. The rest of the group watched from the window as the limo drove away.

"That was so weird." Phoebe shivered. "It really freaked me out."

"I know what you mean," Maggie agreed. "I hope they took the roses. I don't want to carry them out to the trash and be worried they might explode or something."

"Explode? Why would Jennifer's adoring fan want to blow her to smithereens?" Lucy asked.

"Unrequited love?" Dana asked mildly.

Maggie laughed. "Haven't we all been on the unrequited side at one time or another?"

"This is different. This isn't 'She's just not into you' stuff," Suzanne pointed out. "This is nutcase, super fantasy land, if-I-can't-have-you-nobody-can caliber. I'd be worried stiff if I were Jennifer Todd."

"I hope it's not that serious. But they should report this to the local police, even if they do it quietly. You don't know what people are capable of these days," Dana said with concern. "Not that I think that flower arrangement will explode, either."

"Of course not. That's silly." Suzanne glanced out the window again. "But does anyone else smell . . . smoke?"

Maggie and her friends stared at each other, frozen with fear as Suzanne craned her neck to get a better view out the window.

"You're kidding . . . right?" Lucy asked quietly.

Suzanne turned slowly, her serious expression cracking into a grin. "Sorry, gang. Just goofing on you."

"Suzanne! You scared us half to death," Lucy scolded her.

"That wasn't funny." Phoebe still looked worried.

"No . . . it wasn't. I'm sorry," she added more sincerely. "I get it from the kids. I can't resist teasing you guys. You're all so gullible." She shook her head with remorse, though Maggie detected a small smile.

"Are the flowers still out there? Can you at least tell us that?" Maggie asked.

"No, they're gone. Victor must have taken them away."

"Really? I didn't see them carrying anything. Maybe I didn't notice," Lucy said.

"Maybe the stalker saw his gift had been rejected and came back for it." Phoebe looked around at her friends, her theory clearly making her nervous all over again.

"Oh dear. I hope not." Maggie felt goose flesh rise on her arms. "I wish Jennifer had let me call the police."

"You can still call. It is your shop and you have a right to be concerned about your property," Suzanne reminded her.

"Not to mention poor Phoebe, alone upstairs tonight," Lucy added. "Are you going to be all right?"

Phoebe did look a little nervous, Maggie thought. She shrugged her thin shoulders. "Oh . . . I'll be fine. All the doors are locked and there's the alarm. And I have Van Gogh," she added, mentioning her cat.

"Right, that very scary watch cat. He'll protect you." Dana smiled. Van Gogh ran under the nearest piece of furniture at the sight of a stranger. Though he clearly adored Phoebe.

"Why don't you come home with me?" Maggie suggested. "I'll be worried about you. I won't sleep a wink."

"Me, either," Suzanne and Lucy said in unison.

"It's unanimous," Dana added.

Phoebe sighed. "All right. If it makes you all feel better. I'll just grab some stuff . . . and my cat," she mumbled.

"I heard that. It's all right," Maggie added with a sigh. The truth was, even though Maggie had initially balked about having the cat in the shop, she was getting used to him. Even as a houseguest.

A few moments later, Maggie had checked all the doors and windows, set the alarm, and followed her friends out to the porch. She locked the door and double-checked the knob.

A few yellow petals remained in the spot where the big basket of roses had stood, the only evidence that it had been there at all.

Maggie glanced at them a moment and checked the door again.

"Come along now. Time to go." Lucy tugged her arm. "No one is going to bother the shop. Jennifer Todd is gone. That's the only person this weird delivery guy is interested in."

"He was obviously following her. Maybe he followed her back to the inn," Suzanne said logically.

"Yes . . . that's probably true." Maggie accompanied her friends down the path to the street. "But thank you for waiting until I closed up."

"Don't be silly. Safety in numbers," Lucy said quickly.

"Especially true for sheep, come to think of it," Maggie quipped. "Though you're hardly a timid bunch."

"Are you kidding? We're pretty darn *baaah-aad* ass, if you ask me," Suzanne insisted.

Phoebe rolled her eyes. "Oh please. Can we go now?"

"After that, we really ought to," Maggie agreed. It was definitely time to head home, but good to end the strange evening with a laugh.

Chapter Four

"**C**ome on, Lucy . . . just say yes. You know you *want* to."
Suzanne's tone was tempting. So was her invitation. Lucy still wavered.

"I do . . . but I have a project due Friday. I don't think I should skip work tomorrow."

"Oh, come on. It won't take the whole day. Just an hour or two. You can catch up at night. Just drink some coffee, like you always do."

That was true. She should have been back at her desk already, but got sidetracked after dinner, watching a baseball game with Matt. The spring season had just started and they were both suffering from Red Sox withdrawal.

With her cell phone balanced between her ear and her shoulder, Lucy carried a bowl of popcorn from the kitchen to the sofa. Tink and Wally swirled around her legs, two panting, furry crocodiles, lured by the scent of their favorite snack. The dogs watched vigilantly for a stray kernel to drop in their direction.

She handed the bowl down to Matt, who responded with

a pleased smile. Then jumped, nearly spilling the entire pile. "You moron! Throw to *first*! How hard is that?"

"Hey . . . did I get you guys at a bad time?" Suzanne sounded concerned.

"Matt's just yelling at the TV. Red Sox are playing the Yankees. You know how that is." Lucy was amused. She and Matt rarely argued. In fact, she couldn't remember the last time.

"Wait a second, if you have time to watch grown men run around a field chasing a little ball, I don't understand why you can't find the time to support a friend in a courageous adventure. And maybe even get to see Heath O'Hara running on the beach . . . with his shirt off," she added for good measure.

Lucy had returned to the kitchen to make her coffee.

She had to laugh. "I thought we were going to meet all the movie stars Thursday night."

"Jennifer never said Heath was in that scene. She only mentioned Trina. He might not even be there Thursday." Suzanne had obviously given the question careful consideration.

"He might not be there tomorrow, either." Lucy couldn't resist playing devil's advocate.

"I'm willing to take my chances. I thought you'd be excited about the idea. I'm not going to force you." Suzanne suddenly sounded distracted, as if she didn't care one way or the other.

Another technique her pal had learned in some sales seminar, Lucy suspected. But she allowed herself to fall for it anyway.

"Okay, you got me. What time did you say again?"

"I'll pick you up at ten. You'll have plenty of time to work in the afternoon. Since you don't have a herd of children invading the house, asking for snacks, help with homework, and need-ing to be driven to the ends of the Earth and back," she added dryly.

Lucy ignored this obvious bid for sympathy. Suzanne groused at times, but totally adored her Mom routine, often moaning that her brood was growing up too quickly.

"What's your excuse for going over there again?"

"The addendum from the insurance company finally came and I have to drop it off for Lyle. A totally valid reason," she insisted.

Lucy guessed that this document could be emailed to the location manager in seconds. But she didn't bother with further debate. Suzanne was right. Why put up such a fuss about meeting Heath O'Hara? She might not get another chance.

"Guess I need to get up early. To wash my hair and work on a good outfit."

"That's the spirit, Lu. I knew you'd see reason if I worked on you long enough." Suzanne sounded cheered by Lucy's change in attitude.

Lucy had returned to the TV room, where she found Matt slumped back on the sofa, looking forlorn. The Yankees were ahead three runs. Most of the popcorn had spilled and the dogs were happily grazing.

"See you tomorrow. And don't chicken out on me. I'll *never* forgive you," Suzanne warned in a solemn tone.

Lucy knew her friend was only kidding. Under her brassy, sassy persona, Suzanne was loving mush. Though her temper might flare, she was always the first to forgive and forget.

"Don't worry, I won't chicken out. See you at ten." Lucy flopped onto the other end of the sofa and put her phone aside.

"Who are you not chickening out on?" Matt smiled at her curiously.

Lucy shrugged. She was embarrassed to admit that she was joining Suzanne on this star-stalking scheme. They were almost as bad as the nutcase who'd left the roses for Jennifer Todd.

"Oh . . . nothing." She quickly sensed he was not satisfied with that answer. "Hey, how did the Sox fall behind like that? That's not good."

"Error in the outfield. We'll catch up . . . and you're trying to change the subject. This must be good."

That was the trouble with Matt. He could always see right through her. Lucy gave up and decided to divulge the silly plan.

"Suzanne has to drop off some papers at the movie set, and she asked me to come with her."

"Sounds like fun." Matt looked back at the TV. "I thought you were all going on the set Thursday night."

"We are. But Heath O'Hara might not be there then. Suzanne is very concerned about that. She hopes she can catch a glimpse of him tomorrow."

Running on the beach, with his shirt off, was her friend's exact fantasy. But Lucy didn't bother to admit those details.

"How about you? Are you hoping to *catch a glimpse* of him, too?" Matt grinned, echoing her nonchalant tone.

"Honey . . . why would I look twice at Heath O'Hara, when I have you?" Lucy took a sip of coffee, hiding behind the rim of her mug.

Matt laughed and then, to her surprise, slid across the cushions and loomed over her. "Good. That was the A answer."

"I didn't know it was a test."

He took the cup from her hands and put it aside. "It was. But I still might have to tag along tomorrow. I'm not sure I should let you near that handsome, millionaire heartthrob all alone. You might sweep him off his feet."

Lucy laughed out loud. Matt had both his arms around her so that she was captured. Lovingly captured. She lifted her hands and touched his face. "That's sweet. But the only way I could sweep Heath O'Hara off his feet is with a broom."

Matt smiled and kissed her nose. "Not true. I fell for you at first sight . . . Or maybe you did have a broom with you? I can't remember now."

Lucy had a feeling he recalled their first meeting better than that; the fateful day she'd brought her dog to Matt's veterinary practice. She remembered. Every last detail.

He gazed into her eyes, then pulled her closer as their lips met in a deep, warm kiss. While Lucy wiggled around to stretch out next to him, Matt leaned over and shut the light . . . and then clicked off the TV.

"Wow, you're missing the game for me?" Lucy teased him, kissing his ear. "That is passion."

"Absolutely. I just want to remind you that I know I'm a lucky guy. Luckier than Heath O'Hara any day of the week."

Lucy was more than satisfied with that explanation. She thought she was pretty lucky, too.

She didn't have another thought about movie stars, either, and vaguely wondered now why she'd even agreed to join Suzanne.

Suzanne's SUV pulled into the driveway promptly. Lucy was ready and waiting, wearing good jeans, a long, smoky-blue cardigan, and a scarf she'd made from very fine yarn in hues of blue, gray, and purple.

"Hey, you look great. Nice work on the hair," Suzanne complimented her as she backed out of the driveway and onto the road in one smooth move. "You hardly ever wear it down like that."

"It's a pain to dry it. But this is a special occasion."

"Absolutely. I tried to get a wash-and-blow with my hairdresser this morning, but the salon wasn't open yet."

Lucy laughed at Suzanne's concern. "Don't be silly, you look great. I love that outfit."

Suzanne had dressed in a gray wool suit with a tailored silk blouse underneath, a vibrant shade of pink with small cream-colored polka dots. Large gold earrings and a chunk bracelet said successful realtor, Lucy thought.

"Thanks. It's my 'closing outfit.' Is the blouse too much?"

The blouse was definitely bright. But if anyone could pull it off, it had to be Suzanne. "It suits you."

"Dumb, right? We might not even see Heath O'Hara. Even if we do, what would I do? What would I say?"

Lucy wasn't sure if Suzanne was asking for suggestions, or just thinking out loud. "I'm sure you'll think of something. Ask for an autograph?"

"Good plan. Promise you'll give me a poke if I just stand there and babble . . . or maybe drool on myself, struck dumb." Suzanne's anxious scenario made Lucy laugh.

They'd quickly driven through the Marshes, a comfortable family neighborhood near the beach where Lucy and Matt lived. Suzanne knew all the back roads and drove a maze of streets to finally emerge on the Beach Road, which swung past the Plum Harbor Country Club and an affluent waterfront neighborhood, where stately old houses and large estates stood hidden behind tall trees, brick walls, and wrought iron gates. Lucy had only been inside one of these homes since moving to the area, the Lassiter estate, where she and her friends had attended both a wedding and a funeral within a week. She wondered if Suzanne was also remembering those strange events. She glanced at her driver, who seemed totally swept up in today's adventure.

"Where are we going?" Lucy asked, gazing around. "Downton Abbey?"

"We'll definitely be in the neighborhood. But the house they rented for the movie is very modern. Looks like an off-kilter layer cake, with loads of windows and balconies. I have a feeling Trina Hardwick's character gets pushed off one. So Heath's character can be free to marry Jennifer's," Suzanne speculated.

"Are you sure you aren't just wishing that would happen, so he'll be free to be with you?" Lucy teased her.

"Do you think so, Dr. Freud?" Suzanne replied. "You should have been a shrink, Lucy. Except, from what Dana says, it's not as easy at it looks."

"Nothing is. Not even being a famous movie star. I wouldn't want to live like Jennifer Todd, flanked by bodyguards every time I walked down the street."

"How about having some creep whining at you from the shadows? *Jennifer . . . please . . . I love you!*" Suzanne imitated the fan who had called out Monday night at Maggie's shop, making Lucy laugh.

"Suzanne, stop . . ." Lucy warned between laughs. "It's not funny. And that wasn't even what he said, was it?"

"That's what he meant. But you're right, it was more like,

'Jennifer, you came back . . . We can be together now . . . Even though I'm crazy as a loon.'"

Lucy still couldn't help laughing at Suzanne's silly voice. "Suzanne, it's sad. That guy is in pain. He was really troubled."

Suzanne nodded, looking serious again. "Very true. I shouldn't make fun. It's just that entire situation was like a scene from a low-budget slasher flick. You know that kind of movie that's supposed to scare you to death, but it's so badly done you end up laughing?"

Lucy scared easily. She'd never seen a slasher movie, low budget or otherwise. She could barely watch a trailer for a scary movie without ducking under her seat.

"It was a bit absurd," she acknowledged. "But I'm just realizing now, when you think about what the fan said, it sounds like he knew Jennifer at some point. Maybe they dated in high school?"

"Good point. At that stage of the game, you can really inflict some psychic damage. Even if you don't intend to. Sometimes I still think about this kid who broke up with me over the PA. It was in between 'The Star-Spangled-Banner' and the daily announcements."

"Over the school loudspeaker? You're kidding, right?"

"I wish. Talk about high school humiliation." Suzanne shook her head, then raised her chin a notch. "That guy would be eating his heart out if we met again . . . if I hadn't run him over with my mom's minivan."

"You didn't. You're just pulling my leg again."

Suzanne stared straight ahead at the road and shrugged. "No, I didn't. But I really wanted to," she added, finally cracking a smile.

Before Lucy could reply, she swung the big vehicle around a sharp turn Lucy hadn't even noticed. They drove down on a narrow, private road, lined with tall grass and dunes. Lucy could tell they were heading toward the water, though she couldn't see the beach yet.

"It's about a mile or so more this way," Suzanne told her. "Right on the water. Some famous architect designed it. Completely sustainable. Awesome curb appeal. The owners are traveling through Asia on business. They were thrilled to rent the place. They might want to put it on the market soon, and I'd get an exclusive listing. They can't wait to see it in a movie."

Lucy was about to reply when she suddenly heard an approaching siren. Suzanne glanced in the rearview mirror, then quickly pulled to the shoulder of the road, nearly driving into the beach grass.

"Police car. I wasn't speeding, was I?"

The two women stared at each other a moment. But the blue-and-white cruiser sped by. Suzanne breathed a sigh of relief.

"You never know. These police officers have to meet their quota of tickets every month and they'll pull you over for the slightest thing sometimes."

She pulled back onto the road and soon turned onto a new road that ran parallel with the water. Lucy's jaw practically dropped, taking in the huge, fantastic properties.

"Wow . . . I don't think I've driven down here lately," she said.

"There's been a lot of new construction. I'd love to sell one of these beach plums. Or even co-broke. That would be a year of college tuition. We just have to come up with . . . eleven more?"

Suzanne laughed while Lucy silently did the math. With her daughter in high school and twin boys in middle school, Suzanne and her husband had a lot of tuition to cover. The sum was daunting. To say the least.

"I'm hoping the couple who owns this house will decide to sell soon, or even rent. I think they're relocating their business to New York."

"That would be good for you," Lucy agreed.

"Yes it would . . . .but not if the house burns down!" Suzanne's optimistic musings suddenly took on a dire note. Her daydreamy smile melted into an expression of horror.

Lucy followed her gaze down the road, to the sight of two fire trucks and an ambulance blocking their path. Along with the police cruiser that had just sped by.

"Is that the house you rented to the movie company?"

Suzanne nodded bleakly. "Unless *another* house is on fire and they just had to park there?"

Unlikely, Lucy thought. Fire trucks generally tried to get as close as possible to the flames, didn't they?

But Lucy tried not to panic. When she turned to reassure her friend, Suzanne was driving with her face puckered up and her eyes squinched.

"Suzanne . . . you can't drive with your eyes shut, please!"

"I know . . . but I don't want to see." She opened her eyes and stared straight ahead. "It *is* the house, Lucy. Look. There's another fire truck sticking out of the driveway." She pointed in that direction. "It's a big piece of property. You can't see the house from the road. But that's the entrance of their private drive."

"Maybe it's not that bad. It could be a little kitchen fire. A piece of burned toast could set off a smoke alarm connected to the fire department."

"That's true," Suzanne agreed in a dull tone.

"You know how eager the volunteer firemen are around here. They send ten trucks out for the least little thing."

Suzanne nodded, then slowed down as they drew closer.

A police officer stood in the middle of the road, flagging down cars.

Lucy suddenly smelled smoke. Suzanne sniffed the air, too.

"That smells like a lot more than toast," Suzanne said bleakly.

It did, Lucy had to admit. An acrid scent, like burned rubber. Or something electrical. Not pleasant at all.

"I hope no one was hurt," Lucy said, trying to remind Suzanne of what was really important right now. "The ambulance is still here. That's a good sign."

"You're so right. Of course I don't want to find the house burned to a shell . . . since I did persuade that couple to rent it to the movie people . . . but as long as nobody's hurt. That's the main thing. If I'm washed up as a realtor, well . . . so what. I can just leave town, change my name, and start a new life somewhere else."

"Let's find out what happened before you go into deep cover."

Just beyond the police car, a long fire truck that was not in use, as well as an ambulance, blocked the view of the entire scene, but Lucy got the idea. A large number of the film crew members milled around in the street, along with some curious neighbors.

The police officer walked up to the SUV and Suzanne rolled down her window. "This road is closed right now, ma'am. Do you live down here?"

"No . . . but I was coming to this house, Officer. I have to get on the property and see what happened."

"Are you the owner?" He stared at her curiously.

"I'm a real-estate agent and I represent the owners. They're away right now. I rented the house to a movie company and I have to see if there's any damage. Was the fire very bad?"

Suzanne had started off in a reasonable, professional tone which quickly deteriorated, finally bordering on hysteria. But her concern seemed to sway the officer, who considered her question . . . and how much he might tell.

"No damage to the house. The fire was out here . . . in one of the movie trailers." He waved his hand in the direction of the fire truck. Lucy still couldn't see past it, but did notice a thin plume of smoke rising some distance down the road.

"A trailer? Was anyone hurt?" Suzanne asked quickly.

The officer shook his head. "No injuries."

"Can I just come out a second and speak to the location manager, Lyle Boyd? I need to get some information to tell the property owners, even though the house wasn't affected," she said quickly.

Was that really true? Suzanne's explanation sounded good, but somehow Lucy doubted it. Suzanne probably just wanted to check out the situation firsthand . . . and make sure Heath O'Hara was safe and sound.

"Can I see some ID?" he asked. Suzanne quickly handed over her license, then turned to Lucy. "Give me your license, Lucy. The police officer has to see it."

"But . . ."

"We work together. She's in training," Suzanne fibbed to the officer. He didn't seem to care. Lucy actually did feel like she was in training when she went off with Suzanne on one of her adventures. Training for what, she wasn't quite sure.

He quickly checked her ID and handed it back.

"You can park over there." He pointed to a space across the road, next to a stand of beach grass.

"Thank you, Officer," Suzanne said sincerely. She closed her window and swung the big vehicle around. "I'm so relieved that no one was hurt. But I really want to see what happened . . . don't you?"

"I guess so," Lucy replied, hardly sharing her friend's enthusiasm. "Or we could wait for the local news. I'm sure they'll have the story . . . Look, there's a TV truck."

A white van that said "News Five—Alive!" on the side drove off, headed for town. There probably was not much left to see, if they were leaving.

"They have to report this tonight on TV. But we have a higher authority to answer to." Suzanne checked the time. "Let's dig up the dirt and go back to Maggie's shop for lunch."

"I have to get back to my office. I think you have to file this story on your own."

"Okay, I'll handle it. But we're here now—let's get the details. I promised you an adventure, didn't I? Isn't this more fun than designing a brochure for a nursing home?"

"It's 'assisted living at its finest.' But you have a point," Lucy conceded.

Lucy and Suzanne climbed out of the SUV and walked back toward the police officer. He was talking to the driver of another car and waved the two women forward.

Suzanne glanced at Lucy and poked her with an elbow as she started to speed-walk. "Pick up the pace, before he changes his mind."

Lucy followed her lead, though Suzanne was a speedy rabbit when she put her mind to it. Even in her black heels.

The road was wet with a stream of water that grew wider and wider as they approached the fire truck, and Lucy was mindful to avoid the puddles. They soon reached a truck, where firemen were putting away their equipment and a few had already climbed on board.

On the other side of the fire-fighting equipment, they saw some members of the movie crew standing about, watching the last of the firefighters at work. There were more of the boxy movie equipment trucks on both sides of this portion of the road and a row of fancy trailers used by the film stars.

The house was barely visible from the road, just a few jutting pieces. It did look like a pile of boxes set one on the other, at off-kilter angles, plenty of balconies and decks, as Suzanne had mentioned. The landscaping along the road and private drive hinted at the luxury beyond, with a wide trellis of green vines and tiered layers of plantings. Spring flowers flourished, banks of tulips and daffodils, already in bloom.

Lucy turned back to the trailers. The fire had obviously been in the last trailer in the line. The back of the vehicle was charred and a thin plume of smoke rose from a hole in the roof, from the open door, and from the rear windows, which had been broken. Sudsy white foam puddled nearby.

Suzanne sighed. "What a mess. Thank goodness no one was hurt." She pressed her hand to her chest. "I wonder whose trailer that is?"

Before Lucy could answer, Suzanne was on the move again. "There's Lyle. Let's ask him." Lucy quickly followed as Suzanne trekked off to catch the location manager.

"Lyle . . . what happened? Whose trailer is that?" Suzanne asked breathlessly.

"Heath's. But he's all right," he added quickly. Though not fast enough to prevent Suzanne's gasp of terror.

"Oh no! Are you sure? Where is he now?" She quickly looked around, as if searching for one of her own children.

"He fine," Lyle answered quickly. "The trailer was empty but somebody smelled the smoke and called the fire department. They got here pretty quickly, before it could spread."

"Wow . . . close call." Suzanne laughed off her crazy reaction. "So the house is all right?" she asked again. Of course she was nervous about that and wanted to make sure.

"The house is fine. You can't even smell the smoke up there. Well, we didn't when it started. It wasn't much. Just annoying for everyone now. I guess if Heath was in there asleep it could have been a problem," Lyle mused. "Now it's just another production delay. What are you guys doing here anyway? Did you get cleared to come on the set again?"

Trying to meet Heath O'Hara, Lucy knew was the truth of the matter. She stood silently and waited for Suzanne's answer.

"I was in the neighborhood and thought I'd drop off your copies of the addendum to the rental agreement. But now I forgot all about that. The envelope is in the car . . . I'll run back and get it."

Lyle shrugged. "That's all right. You can just scan it and send me an email."

"Right . . . will do." Suzanne nodded.

"So . . . thanks for coming by. I'll watch for your email." He smiled, obviously trying to get rid of them.

"Right . . . See you, Lyle," Suzanne said brightly, starting to walk away. Lucy sensed that her friend felt defeated underneath her cheery smile. Was she going to give up this easily?

Lyle watched them; making sure they went straight back to their car? Suzanne was about to say something as they walked away when they heard voices coming from a trailer that was parked on the other side of the road.

The door of the trailer opened and one of the security

guards came down the steps, looked around, and waited. Lucy and Suzanne waited, too, watching without saying a word.

Trina Hardwick soon appeared in the doorway, clutching a papery-thin blanket around her shoulders, the kind given out in emergency scenes. Her long, thick hair fell across her face in a seductive tangle, her mascara smeared in dark circles around her eyes. Below the blanket, her legs were bare. Lucy thought she saw the edge of a short pink robe, but it was hard to tell. It didn't seem she was wearing much beside the blanket and a smug expression.

Trina hopped down the steps, followed by a security guard, then scampered across the street and disappeared into another trailer.

Lucy turned to comment on the sight, but Suzanne gripped her arm, pressing her free hand to her chest. "Look who *else* is in there," she whispered.

Heath O'Hara opened the door a crack and poked his head out. Then the rest of him emerged. He wore an outfit similar to Trina's, the same sort of blanket draped around his shoulders. Shirtless underneath, he also wore a pair of jeans that were curiously miles too big and gripped the waistband with one hand as he walked down the steps, barefoot.

"Matching outfits," Lucy murmured. "That's cute."

"Those jeans look like loaners," Suzanne added. "I bet they belong to Nick Pullman."

"Or maybe Victor?" Lucy added, noticing the security guard who followed Heath from the trailer and led him across the street, to the same trailer Trina had entered.

Lucy turned to Suzanne. "We did see Heath O'Hara without a shirt on. I wouldn't call the trip a total loss."

"Not by a long shot," Suzanne agreed. "Though I hate to

think he and Trina have something going on. That's what it looks like."

"Maybe they were rehearsing a scene?"

Suzanne gave Lucy a look. "You are naive. But I mean it in a good way. It's sort of cute."

"All I'm saying is, you can't assume. And what's the difference to us anyway?"

"Agreed." Suzanne nodded as they headed back to her SUV. "And all I'm saying is, if it looks like a duck, and it walks like a duck—who waddles by with practically no clothes on. *Twice*—it's probably two ducks who were in bed together. But not in Heath's trailer."

She smiled and shrugged. Lucy just laughed. It was hard to argue with Suzanne's circuitous logic.

A few minutes later, as Suzanne cruised through Lucy's neighborhood, Lucy felt the tug of her deadline pulling her back to her office. But the workday was too far gone to be recouped, she reasoned. "I'll just drink a lot of coffee and work tonight," she told Suzanne.

"That a girl. There's a reason you have your own business, Lucy," Suzanne reminded her as they sped off toward the village.

"There is. Though I'm fairly certain it has nothing to do with goofing off in order to chase movie stars."

Suzanne laughed. "Sounds like a perfect reason to me."

A short time later, they were at the Black Sheep Knitting Shop, eating take-out salads as they sat side by side in the small knitting nook to the left of the entrance.

Maggie had just finished teaching a class, Spring Fling: Felted Flowers. Most of her students left quickly, though Lucy noticed that two lingered at the back table, looking over pattern books. Maggie left them to bustle up front with her knitting and a cup of tea. She dropped with a sigh into the wing chair. "The coast is clear. I have a few minutes before the next class. Are we waiting for Dana?"

"She's with a patient. We'll have to fill her in later," Lucy said.

"She'll see it on the news tonight. But we have the inside story. Inside Trina Hardwick's trailer, you might say. Where there's smoke, there's fire."

Maggie cocked her head. "That all sounds very titillating, but I haven't the foggiest idea what you're talking about. Can you tone down the celebrity gossip slang a bit?"

Lucy laughed. "We went to the house where the movie company is filming. Suzanne wanted to drop off some papers for Lyle Boyd. When we got there, there were fire trucks and an ambulance. There'd been a fire in one of the trailers."

"In Heath's trailer," Suzanne continued. "And we were so worried about him when we heard—"

"I wasn't worried," Lucy scoffed.

Suzanne gave her a look. "Yes you were, but that's besides the point . . ."

"The point being, he wasn't in his trailer?" Maggie guessed.

"Exactly. A TV news crew came to cover the fire. But right after the van left, we saw Heath and Trina sneak out of some other trailer. Wrapped up in blankets and not much else. They'd obviously been caught. Together . . . well, up to something."

Maggie's brows jumped up a notch as she took a sip of tea. She set her mug aside and took up her needles. "I guess that's no great surprise."

"Maybe not. But it would be a juicy item for the media,"

Suzanne replied. "Too bad I didn't have my phone handy. That photo would be worth serious money."

"I'm so glad you didn't," Lucy said with a sigh. "Don't you think people deserve some privacy, even if they are movie stars? And everyone's always making assumptions about their behavior. It's awful the way photographers climb trees and hide behind bushes to snap candid pictures with all kinds of telescopic lenses. As if these poor actors were animals out in the wild."

Her two friends stared at her. "My goodness. You feel very strongly about that, don't you?" Maggie asked.

Lucy shrugged. "I just think it's very low to make money from embarrassing people publicly." She glanced at Suzanne, hoping she wasn't offended. But it was true.

"When you put it that way, I have to agree. I wouldn't have tried to sell the picture. Or blackmail them," Suzanne promised, digging into her salad. "Though someone with less scruples might have done both. At least I got to see Heath, in all his glory. My life is complete. And no one was hurt—that's the main thing."

"Yes, it is," Maggie agreed. "But this movie isn't going very smoothly, is it? First that light tower practically smashes Jennifer Todd, then a fire breaks out."

"And let's not forget that weird flower delivery," Lucy reminded them.

"You mean 1-800-Lovelorn-Stalker?" Suzanne asked. "How could we?"

"Do you think every movie crew has these problems?" Maggie asked. "I suppose there are always going to be mix-ups and setbacks. Equipment breaking down and accidents. Even stalkers."

"I think movie people are used to a few speed bumps. But it's starting to seem like this production is jinxed. Hate to sound superstitious," Suzanne added. "The bottom line is they keep losing time and that costs money. If someone wants to throw a monkey wrench into the works, this is a good way to undermine the picture."

"It is now," Lucy agreed. "I guess they need to stay in town longer than planned. Or work around the clock to make up for lost time." Late nights with lots of coffee. She knew that drill.

"Where was Jennifer? Did you see her this morning?" Maggie asked.

Lucy and Suzanne shook their heads. "No, we didn't." But before Lucy could say more, the bell on the shop door sounded. Lucy expected to see Phoebe, returning from her morning classes, or maybe even Dana, dashing down the street between appointments.

But it was Alicia Littel. She took a few steps into the shop and smiled shyly.

"Alicia . . . hello," Maggie greeted her warmly. "What a nice surprise."

"Hi, everyone. Am I interrupting something?" she asked politely.

Maggie shook her head. "Not at all. We're just . . . chatting." Of course she didn't want to admit they were gossiping about the movie crew. "How can I help you? Ready to start your knitting lessons?"

"Not quite . . . but I'm getting there." She held up her hand and showed them a smaller bandage that crossed her palm. "Jen has been knitting like wild, though, and asked me to pick up more yarn. I'm not sure what kind. She gave me a label," the assistant explained, pulling a slip of paper from her jacket pocket.

Maggie rose and slipped on her glasses to read it.

"We were at the beach house this morning and saw the fire trucks leaving," Suzanne told Alicia. "Thank goodness no one was hurt."

"Oh yes, the fire," Alicia said. "Jen wasn't needed on the set this morning, so we stayed at the inn. But we heard about the whole thing. Heath probably did something stupid, like dumped cigarette butts in a trash basket."

"Heath smokes? I thought he was a vegetarian and meditates and all that." Suzanne sounded shocked.

"Whoops . . ." Alicia covered a smile with her hand. "I wasn't supposed to say that."

"We won't tell, will we, Suzanne?" Lucy glanced at her friend. Suzanne shook her head, looking disappointed at this disclosure.

They hadn't spent much time with the movie people, but there did seem to be an awful lot of secrets among them, Lucy reflected.

"I'm just relieved Trina didn't come running out of Nick's trailer half naked." Alicia rolled her eyes. "Trina is such a slut. She didn't get any therapy for *that* while she was away."

The knitting friends glanced at one another. Strong words coming from the otherwise demure girl.

Was that what had happened, Lucy wondered—Trina and Heath ran out of Trina's trailer when the fire started? Alicia seemed to be saying that was what she and Jennifer had heard. And from what she and Suzanne had seen, it seemed possible.

But why did Alicia allude to Trina and Nick being involved, too? Was it just some groundless fear because Alicia saw the young actress as a threat to Jennifer? Or was there something more to that comment?

Lucy wasn't bold enough to ask. But Suzanne was.

"Do Nick and Trina have something going on, too?" she practically whispered. "I thought Jen and Nick were rock solid."

"They are," Alicia insisted. "But this is Trina's big break since she screwed up and she's not on screen much. Everyone knows she'd do anything to see more Trina Hardwick in the movie. Nick is . . . well . . . he's getting older and it doesn't take much to flatter him." She sighed and shrugged. "I just feel sorry for Jen. Women are always throwing themselves at him."

Alicia was fiercely loyal to Jennifer, that was for sure. And many people took an instant dislike to Trina, from her reputation alone. Especially other women, Lucy had noticed.

Maggie found the yarn Alicia needed in one of the baskets near the register. Lucy was glad that she had not needed to go back to the storeroom and miss all this juicy gossip.

"Here you go. How many skeins does she need?"

"Just one will do," Alicia replied.

Maggie thought she'd given Jennifer enough to finish the pattern, but if she had a tight stitch, she would need more. Maybe she was making the project as a gift, in a larger size than her own. She might have wanted extra just in case.

Maggie put the skein in a plastic bag, knowing Jen already had a tote. Alicia began to open her purse but Maggie waved at her. "Don't worry. It's on the house."

"Oh, Maggie, you don't have to do that. Jen wants me to pay you," Alicia said.

"Tell her it's a thank-you . . . for inviting us on the set again," Maggie reassured her.

"If you insist. That's very generous."

"It's my pleasure. I don't have many customers who are

movie stars. In fact . . . I'd say Jennifer is my first and only. And we're all excited to visit Thursday night. Tell Jennifer I look forward to seeing her progress on the knitting project."

"I will," Alicia promised. "She's been sort of bored today. She was supposed to give a speech to the students at her old high school in Newburyport, but she had to cancel at the last minute."

"Is she feeling all right?" Maggie asked with concern.

Alicia shrugged. "She's all right. It was just that . . . something came up."

She caught herself from saying more. Lucy exchanged glances with her friends, but didn't speak. Their silence seemed to draw Alicia out.

"That crazy fan again," Alicia admitted quietly. "He left more flowers in the middle of the night, right outside her hotel room, and a really weird note. It scared her. She was afraid to go out today. Even with security."

Maggie looked alarmed by the report. "That is frightening. I think it's very wise of her to be careful until this person is caught. What do the police say?"

Alicia shrugged, her gaze downcast. "I don't know . . . she didn't tell me. I did hear her talking to Nick about it. He's handling everything."

Lucy wondered what that meant. She'd already heard how much the temperamental director disliked bad publicity.

"As long as someone gets to the bottom of it. It's probably best for her to be on the cautious side," Maggie said.

"I think it is, too. I worry about her. She takes too many chances. She'll stand right in the open, signing autographs all day. She never wants to hurt anyone's feelings," Alicia told the women.

Suzanne smiled. "That's why she's America's Sweetheart."

"I guess so. One of the reasons," Alicia agreed, finally smiling again. "Thanks again for the yarn, Maggie."

"It was nothing. I hope you and Jennifer just kick back and have a relaxing day. That will be the perfect distraction," Maggie advised.

Alicia waved as she stepped out the door. "Thanks . . . we will."

Maggie took up her knitting and waited a moment after the door closed behind Jennifer's assistant. "That was enlightening. There's a lot going on behind the scenes of *Love Knots*, isn't there?"

"Oh yeah," Suzanne agreed. "It sounds as if Jennifer has to keep her eye on Nick. Could you imagine? He's only married to one of the most beautiful women in the world. Men are never satisfied, are they?"

"Some men," Maggie agreed. "But we don't even know that for sure. It sounds as if Alicia has just observed Trina flirting. Which might not mean a thing."

"Alicia is very protective of Jennifer. Devoted to her," Lucy added.

"And more worried about the stalking fan than Trina Hardwick. With good reason," Maggie added. "I must confess, I don't have a clear sense of where the police are in all of this. I'm not even sure it's been reported."

"I'm not, either. Alicia didn't seem to know for sure," Lucy observed. "Would they take that kind of chance with Jennifer's safety? Even considering bad publicity?"

"Hard to say. But maybe I should tell Charles," Maggie said, meaning Charles Mossbacher, a detective for the county police department who Maggie had recently begun dating,

"Not really report it, but just put him on the alert? But we did promise Jennifer and I don't want to go back on my word."

"I think the information can only get to the media if someone makes an official report and it goes on the police blotter," Lucy said. "That's how reporters pick up these things. Or they have inside information, like Dana's husband."

"Or they listen to one of those police-band radios twenty-four/seven," Suzanne added. "I had a boyfriend once who did that."

"Was he a reporter?" Lucy had finished her salad and snapped the plastic lid shut.

"Nope. Just a little nutty. He didn't last too long." Suzanne rose and gathered her trash, then grabbed her big handbag and checked her phone. "Got to run. Sales meeting this afternoon. I have to make big smiley faces about Marcy Devereaux being crowned salesperson of the month again." Suzanne made a big fake smile and stuck out her tongue at her office rival.

"Don't worry, Suzanne. Every dog has their day," Lucy said sympathetically. "You'll land some big deal soon and win another travel mug. I have a feeling."

"If the listing doesn't burn down or explode in the meantime," Suzanne replied. "I will say this has been a worthwhile morning, even without earning a red cent. Don't tell me you didn't have fun, Lucy. I won't believe you."

Lucy grinned. "It was definitely more exciting than designing a brochure for assisted-living condos."

"Wow-ee . . . More fun than watching paint dry, too, I guess," Suzanne mumbled under her breath.

Lucy just laughed. Maggie shook her head. "You did miss your calling as an actress, Suzanne. It's very clear to me now."

Suzanne stood at the door and waved good-bye in a slow,

theatrical manner. Lucy could tell she had enjoyed the comment. "What can I say, Maggie? All the world's a stage. And we are all actors of one kind or another. Farewell, *mes amis!*" she added, blowing kisses from both hands.

Two more customers had wandered in and turned to peer at Suzanne curiously, then whispered to each other. Maggie scooted over to give them some attention. "Oh dear, I hope she hasn't scared them off."

Lucy doubted that. The ladies seemed too interested in a new yarn display—organic fibers and light, bright spring colors. Lucy would have checked it out, too, but it was well past time for her to head home.

She didn't live far from the village and set out at a brisk pace. Matt had late hours at the animal hospital tonight and wouldn't be home until ten. She still had a good stretch of time to work and catch up with her deadline.

It had definitely been fun to skip work for a few hours. More than Lucy had admitted to her partner in crime . . . for fear of encouraging her. The plain truth was, you never knew what's going to happen when you rode shotgun with Suzanne.

Chapter Five

"Just got the email with instructions for tonight. Alicia put our names on a list with security. There are a lot of other dos and don'ts for visitors on the set. Alicia is very efficient, isn't she?"

Maggie had printed the email and showed it to Phoebe. Her assistant looked up briefly from the newspaper she was reading but didn't reply. Perhaps she thought Maggie was intimating that her own assistant was not as efficient? Maggie didn't mean it that way at all . . . though the two were completely different. Still, given the choice, she'd choose Phoebe's creativity over Alicia's crisp efficiency any day.

On Thursday morning, Maggie and Phoebe had opened the shop at the usual hour, but would have to close early, definitely by three.

That was when the movie company would arrive to set up again. They planned to start shooting at five, though there was no telling when they would be done, Alicia had mentioned in her note. She'd also hinted it might take hours to film a single scene before Nick Pullman was happy with it.

Maggie knew she wouldn't last that long. She just wanted to watch the actors for a little while and get a sense of how it was done.

From all that she'd heard so far, watching the process of filming a movie certainly threatened to ruin the magic. Like seeing how sausage was made. A saying of her mother's that seemed to apply fairly well.

Phoebe should have started setting up for a class, Knitting 101, but she was still sipping her coffee and paging through the latest edition of *The Plum Harbor Times*.

"Alicia told me that they've added a knitting group to the scene we're going to see, sitting in the background," Maggie told her. "That will be fun. To see actors who are supposed to be . . . well, us. Don't you think?"

Phoebe frowned, still staring down at the paper. Maggie could tell she was in a pout about something.

"*We* should have been extras in the scene, playing *ourselves*. We gave Jennifer the idea." She glanced over at Maggie and back at the newspaper again. "I was reading about it online. There's some dumb rule, even if she did ask them to hire us. The movie company has to hire a certain number of union actors first, like thirty or something, before they can hire amateurs. So unless they were doing a big crowd scene, we didn't have a chance."

"Too bad. Maybe next time." Personally, she was relieved. Maggie had always been more of an observer than a performer. Expressing herself through mediums like yarn or paint, that was her way of performing.

But of course, so much of life required a little acting. Being a shopkeeper and a teacher, for example. William Shakespeare had been right: all the world was a stage, and men and women merely players, with their exits and entrances, and one man playing many roles in his lifetime.

"Did you print out the instructions and the picture for the class?" Maggie asked.

"It's all in the folder, next to the register . . . and the needles and yarn are in the storeroom." Phoebe finally looked up. "Look at this, a big article about the movie."

Phoebe turned the paper so she could see. The article took up two pages side by side, with several photos. Still shots from the movie that would probably be used in promotion—Jennifer and Heath, embracing on the beach, and one of Jennifer and Trina in the shop.

"Another? I thought the paper did an article last week, when the crew came to town."

"This one has a different slant. It's more about Jennifer growing up in Newburyport. There are photos from her yearbook. She was in the chorus and Drama Club . . . and the Science Club."

"The last is a surprise, but the first two seem logical," Maggie replied.

"Look at that hairdo . . . I barely recognized her."

"It's a challenge," Maggie agreed, taking in the big-hair style of the era and the shoulder pads in Jennifer's dress that made her look like an NFL player in drag. "Why is it that when we look back at old styles, we always think that we looked hideous, but at that time, we thought we looked so good?" she murmured.

"I'm still wearing the same styles since high school. I guess I'm not old enough to figure that one out."

That was true, Maggie thought. Though she did wonder what Phoebe would think twenty years from now, seeing her streaked hair and piercings. Or maybe she would still dress that way. She was very much her own person.

Phoebe picked up her coffee again. "I guess it's fun for her fans to see the old photos. And read about her memories growing up here."

"And generate some positive publicity. After the fire," Maggie noted.

It seemed the movie crew had been in the news every day since they'd come to town. Reporters who had been on the set Saturday had witnessed the light fixture fall and added that to their fluff story about the village being used as a location for the big feature film.

Then there was the fire, just a few days later.

Not to mention the stalker who had cornered Jennifer at the shop Monday night and crept up as close as the star's hotel room door the night after. That situation had not made the news, effectively contained by the powers that reigned. But it would be equally newsworthy, if it had been discovered, Maggie thought.

Phoebe glanced over the article once more. "They interviewed Heath O'Hara and Trina Hardwick. And Nick Pullman, too. They asked him what it's like to direct his wife in a love scene."

"That's a good one. What did he say?" Maggie asked curiously.

"'We're all professionals and close friends. We actually have a good laugh afterward.'" Phoebe looked up at Maggie. "Do you think that's true? He doesn't feel the least twinge of jealousy watching his wife kiss a hunk like Heath?"

Maggie wondered about that herself, considering Nick's hot temper. "Who knows? If he does, it's unlikely he'd ever admit it to a reporter."

"True." Phoebe closed the newspaper and stretched. "Time to get cracking on our summer tanks and cropped tops. It's heating up out there." She picked up the paper and fanned herself.

She's mocking me, Maggie realized, though she couldn't take offense. She actually had to smile. She was glad to see Phoebe in better spirits. Moving past the disappointment about her thwarted acting ambitions already.

"Yes, it is. I hear the mercury will hit the midfifties today. We should serve the class umbrella drinks. But we'll have to make do with tea and coffee. Let's get ready. It's a short day. It's going to fly by," Maggie predicted.

And so it did. The trucks were already lining up on Main Street as Maggie closed out the register at three. A few of the movie crew people came into the shop, with their ubiquitous clipboards and headsets.

Maggie gently chased out the last of her customers and headed home. She and her friends had agreed to meet back at the shop at seven. Alicia had warned in her email that waiting in between takes was sometimes tedious and they ought to bring something to do as a diversion. Like their knitting.

An ironic twist, considering they would usually be sitting together on any other Thursday night for their knitting group meeting. This time, they'd be watching a movie being filmed . . . . with a knitting group in it. Like looking in a mirror, inside a mirror, inside a mirror.

Maggie didn't dwell on the confusing notion very long. She really didn't have time.

When Maggie returned to the shop at seven, equipment

trucks and actors' trailers were parked in a row along Main Street again. The yellow sawhorses and film crew security guards were stationed around the shop, as they had been on Saturday. A group of fans hung around on the sidewalk, but far fewer than she'd seen on Saturday morning. Maybe the good citizens of Plum Harbor had already grown immune to the lure of celebrities in their midst. Or since it was a weeknight, most were at home, cleaning up dinner dishes, helping kids with homework, and getting to bed at a decent hour.

She met her friends across the street from the shop. No one had dressed up for the event, except Suzanne—of course. She looked stylish in a long black skirt, black boots, and a big cream-colored cowl-neck sweater. Not to mention freshly blown-out hair and a new manicure.

"You look ready for the red carpet, Suzanne," Lucy noted.

Suzanne shrugged. "I couldn't resist dressing a bit for Heath. I don't want to look all raggedy when I ask for his autograph."

Just then, Phoebe appeared in the drive next to the shop. She'd come down from her apartment from the outside entrance, though she easily could have gone down to the set from the stairs inside the building. She trotted across the street to meet them.

"I'd rather go in with you guys than go down from my apartment. I don't want to be standing there alone . . . with all those movie stars and officious crew people."

"And your name is on a list with a security guard at the gate," she told them. "So it's probably better that you didn't just appear," said Maggie. "Security is tight, from what Alicia told me in the email."

Maggie took the message out of her knitting bag, in case

there was some question with the guard. Perhaps they'd tightened up entrance to the set since Jennifer's flower delivery incidents and the falling light fixture. Or maybe it was always like this. She had no way to judge.

The security guard looked over the email and checked the list for each name, then looked inside knitting bags and purses with a flashlight. No body pat-down or metal scanner like at the airport. Maggie was relieved at that.

He finally let them pass and they entered the shop.

It was buzzing with activity, but not quite as frantic as Saturday.

A section toward the back of the shop was set off for the scene, circled by the big lights on tripod stands. Overhead hung a microphone hanging from a long pole. Front and center, a big camera on a rolling mechanism with a seat was positioned next to a canvas chair that said "Pullman" on the back.

She saw Jennifer standing nearby, talking with her husband, Nick, and Trina. Both the actresses were in full makeup and outfitted in character. Jennifer wore a beige turtleneck and a nubby brown cardigan with patch pockets that all but camouflaged her perfect figure. The big sweater definitely looked handmade, found in a thrift shop by some costume designer, Maggie suspected, along with a brown wool skirt.

Is that what Hollywood thinks knitting store owners look like—dowdy, timid librarians? Is that what *I* look like? she thought with horror. The cliché of a librarian, actually. All the librarians Maggie knew dressed very fashionably.

Maggie stared down at herself, relieved to see a stylish— even sexy—dark red cardigan with a draped neckline and hem, designer jeans, and black suede boots.

Never underestimate the power of a cliché.

Trina wore a much more glamorous outfit than Jennifer's, a tailored satin blouse, with several buttons undone, slim black pants, and stiletto heels. Huge hoop earrings could have doubled as bracelets, and her cocktail ring would have come in handy for self-defense. Layers of mascara and a slash of vibrant red lipstick were bold accents to Trina's heavy stage makeup.

"I guess Trina is playing a 'Real Housewife of Plum Harbor' role," Suzanne whispered.

"If her film career stalls out, she'd definitely have a chance in reality TV," Lucy murmured back.

Just then, Jennifer strolled over to greet them, along with a young man Maggie could not recall seeing before. He wasn't dressed in the movie crew uniform, no headset or black T-shirt. He wore a light blue sweater with jeans, had thick, reddish brown hair, and large glasses that gave him a serious, intellectual air. He carried a movie script, Maggie noticed, and so did Jennifer.

"You made it. That's great . . . Did Alicia tell you? I told Theo about the knitting group, and he worked it into the scene."

"Yes, she mentioned that," Maggie replied.

"Too bad he couldn't come to the shop to observe before he did the revision, but we had to call the extras and do the costumes on the fly." Jennifer paused and turned to her companion. "Theo, this is Maggie Messina, the owner of this beautiful shop. These ladies are her friends and knitting group. Theo is Nick's son. He's done a lot of work on this script. Really brought it along. He's very, very talented," Jennifer added effusively.

Though the way her glance darted to the side as she

delivered the compliment made Maggie wonder if she really believed it.

"Nice to meet you." Theo nodded politely without quite making eye contact. He seemed shy. Or maybe just anxious, Maggie thought. Certainly eager to be on his way. Quickly dismissing them as fans and "looky-loos"? Maybe he had important work to do before they started filming. Everyone on the set seemed a bit keyed up, she noticed.

"I'd better get to work. Alicia will show you where to sit." Jennifer turned to her assistant, who had appeared like a loyal pet and stayed with the knitting group once the star left to join her husband and Trina on the set.

"I saved a good spot back here." Alicia led them to a circle of plastic folding chairs about midway through the shop, off to one side and a few yards back from the set.

"Hang out as long as you like. There's plenty to eat and drink. Please help yourself." She pointed to a table near the front door, laden with catering trays—sandwiches, cookies, bottled drinks, coffee, tea, and other snacks. "They're doing a last check of the sound and lighting for Jen and Trina. In a few minutes, the lights will dim and you'll hear 'Quiet on the set.' An assistant director will check the sound and another one will make sure the camera is rolling. Then they'll announce the scene and the take number. Be superquiet until you hear someone say, 'Cut.' Nick can flip out if he thinks the actors are being distracted," she added in a whisper.

Maggie's friends listened to the instructions with solemn expressions. Even Suzanne paid complete attention.

"Can we knit? When they're not filming anything?" Maggie didn't want to upset Nick Pullman with the sound of clicking needles. Maybe the people who were supposed to be knitting on the set were using silent knitting needles. Was there such a thing?

Alicia smiled. "Please do. You'll have plenty of time for that. There's a lot of downtime between takes. I'll be back later to say hello again. And maybe finally get my knitting lesson?" she added hopefully. Maggie noticed the large bandage on her hand was gone, though she did see a nasty-looking scab, stained with iodine marking the spot.

"Anytime. We'll be right here," Maggie promised.

Maggie watched Alicia scamper back toward the set. Jen was already standing on her mark, turning her face this way and that while someone with a light meter waved it around her head. Alicia stood just outside the circle of light, watching.

Alicia was a dear girl and worked so hard. It would be impossible to describe her duties. Most seemed to be anticipating Jennifer Todd's every need. Part secretary, part mind reader, part . . . extra brain.

Maggie wondered if Alicia had career plans beyond this job. Right now, she was paying her dues, as they say. Jen had mentioned that her last assistant had gone on to write for TV. Alicia would certainly have the necessary connections to do something in film or television. Maggie guessed most young people took a job like that to network, and others were simply lured by the glamorous atmosphere. It wasn't clear where Alicia fit on that question.

"Are we all clear on proper movie set etiquette?" Maggie asked the group.

"Perfectly," Dana answered for the group. She already had her knitting out and was lining up her needles. Suzanne had brought along her knitting bag but paid it little mind, her gaze darting in all directions, watching the activity on the set, but most likely on the lookout for her idol, Heath O'Hara. Who had not showed up yet. Maggie wondered if he would be acting in any scenes being filmed tonight. Maybe he wouldn't show up at all.

That would be a great disappointment for Suzanne, and Lucy. Though she wasn't quite as vocal about her star crush.

Lucy and Phoebe got up together. "We thought this was a good time to grab some snacks," Phoebe said as they strolled toward the food table. "We'll bring something back for you."

"I hope they don't bring back too much. It all looks fattening," Maggie said to the others as she set out her knitting.

"I bet there are lots of healthy choices up there," Dana replied. "Like the green drinks Jennifer has flown in from California? I see a few of those."

"That's true. But I have a feeling the stars hoard the really pricey stuff in their trailers. Like fine wine," Maggie said.

"You're probably right," Dana whispered, softly laughing.

Nick was on the set, alone with Jennifer. Maggie noticed Trina at the catering table, selecting a bottle of sparkling water from a large tub of cold drinks. As Nick spoke quietly, Jennifer nodded with a thoughtful expression. She had a pile of button cards spread on the table and was showing Nick how she'd use them as a prop.

Nice touch, Maggie thought. She felt gratified she'd contributed this small detail.

Nick turned to Trina next, who now stood near the camera. Nick seemed to be reminding her where she needed to enter the scene and to stand. He held her by the shoulders and led her to her place.

She asked him a question. He laughed and swept back his thick silver hair. He was a very handsome man, Maggie realized. When he smiled. He had a lionlike look to his features, straight white teeth, and a tall, strong build. He looked about ten or more years older than Jennifer, and ten more than that compared to Trina.

He stood with one hand on his hip, chatting with the younger actress. Then leaned forward and whispered something, their faces very close.

Not just their faces. Maggie noticed his hand touch her hip, giving her a pat.

Trina didn't seem a bit surprised by this encouraging, even intimate, touch, as if Nick were a coach sending a star player into the big game.

Maggie wondered how Jennifer felt watching them. She was fiddling with a bundle of large safety pins Maggie used to hold stray buttons together or mark a spot in a project. Maggie noticed that Jennifer did glance at Nick and Trina, and accidently stuck herself with a pin. She put her fingertip to her lips a moment and frowned. Because of the tiny pinprick or the sight of her husband flirting, Maggie could not be sure.

But Jennifer seemed very grounded. She probably took this behavior in stride, as if it was part of her husband's job as a director, a way of bonding with a leading lady. Trina was a fragile flower and needed reassurance, Maggie guessed. Not like Jennifer, who seemed more confident.

Nick soon returned to a spot by the camera. He spoke to the cinematographer, who was operating the camera, then stepped back, just beyond the bright stage lights. One of his many assistants was talking to the extras who played the knitting group, and soon walked off the set as well.

A few moments later, the assistant director—or perhaps the assistant to the assistant? Maggie was not clear at all on the pecking order—called out, "Quiet on the set."

Lucy and Phoebe raced back to their seats just as the lights were dimmed. Phoebe muffled the rattling sound from a bag of chips next to her sweater. Maggie gave her a sharp look. She didn't want to get kicked out just as things were getting started.

Luckily, her friends were not the only ones grabbing a last-minute snack. She saw an assistant run over to Nick Pullman and hand him something. It looked like a cold drink. He twisted the top off the bottle and took a big gulp.

Dana and Lucy put their knitting down and everyone faced the set just as the digital clapboard appeared.

"Scene fifty-seven, take one," a young woman standing beside the camera announced. She held up the clapboard a moment, then quickly stepped aside.

"Sound . . . Camera rolling," another voice said quietly. There was silence for a moment. Then someone said, "Action."

Nick Pullman stood next to the camera, gazing intently at the set. Jennifer seemed engrossed in her button-sorting task, oblivious to all the lights, equipment, and onlookers. Maggie had never realized how many people and distractions were around the actors while they were being filmed. They needed amazing powers of concentration to transport themselves to some distant, imagined reality, didn't they?

Something about Jennifer's expression and posture was suddenly transformed. As if another personality had floated into her body. Before she'd spoken a single word of dialogue, she projected the essence of a totally different person. She really was a very talented actress.

Trina walked toward Jennifer. Her steps were sinuous and sultry, her heels clicking on the wooden floor. She stood in front of Jennifer, casting a shadow across the table. She didn't seem any different from the Trina who had exited the limo Saturday in all her glory. But maybe that was enough.

Jennifer slowly looked up. Her eyes widened. "Ms. Fuller . . . I didn't see you come in."

Trina didn't reply. Then she slammed a Louis Vuitton knitting tote on the table. Maggie had only seen such accessories in magazines and at knitting shows. She certainly didn't sell them in her store.

"I came for my lesson," Trina announced in her gravelly tone. "Or maybe to teach you one?"

Jennifer stood up straighter. "It's not what you think . . ."

Trina laughed. "How stupid do you think I am? Do you think you're the first?" She leaned closer and whispered harshly. "I'm not worried. Tyler is playing with you. He's done this before."

The button cards slipped from Jennifer's fingers. Her mouth grew tight and she blinked.

"Cut!" Nick jumped forward. "*Super!* Both of you. Great work." He smiled and nodded in approval. "But I guess in the next take, I'd like you try it a little more . . ."

Maggie couldn't hear the rest of his critique. She sat back and looked at her friends.

"What do you think? They don't let the actors say very much, do they?"

"No, but this is fun." Phoebe tore open a bag of pretzels and munched a handful.

"It is fun," Dana agreed. As soon as the lights went back on, her needles had jumped into action. "But it's amazing they can make an entire movie at this rate. Maybe they need to warm up a little before he lets them go full throttle?"

Maggie hoped so, though there was no time to reply. The lights dimmed again and the girl with the board appeared.

As the actors began speaking their lines, Maggie noticed that Suzanne's gaze had wandered in the opposite direction of the set. Then her eyes widened and her face got pale. Maggie could tell she was about to either scream or shout as she rose from her chair.

Maggie leaned over, about to stuff a ball of yarn into Suzanne's mouth. Luckily, Nick shouted, "Cut!" Maggie dropped back down with a huge sigh.

"What on earth is the matter?"

Suzanne didn't answer, just pointed, her eyes bugging out of her head. Maggie followed the gesture, along with the rest of her friends.

Heath O'Hara stood right beside them, his arms crossed over his well-developed physique, biceps bunching up attractively under a tight white T-shirt.

He'd snuck up on them, coming from somewhere at the front of the shop. He leaned over Phoebe's shoulder and Lucy nearly swooned. "Hey, ladies. How's the view? Sight lines good? You found a cozy corner, didn't you?"

Suzanne blinked, and her face turned beet red. Maggie was afraid she would faint.

"We're very comfortable, thank you," Maggie replied with a tight smile.

He looked amused by her reply. Or maybe by the fact that she wasn't wowed off her chair? As the rest of her friends seemed to be, including Dana. Despite her cool attitude when they'd talked about movie stars—Heath in particular—she stared up at him now with her knitting hanging from her hands. Her mouth hanging open a bit, too.

His looks were dazzling; Maggie had to grant him that. But a bit of a peacock, she thought.

"So, you're the *real* knitting group. Jen told me about you," he added.

Jennifer Todd had been talking about them? To Heath O'Hara? Maggie wished she could have been a fly on the wall for that conversation.

"We're the real thing, all right," Lucy replied.

"But we don't belong to the Screen Actor's Guild, of course, so we couldn't be in the movie," Phoebe explained glumly. "That's supposed to be us up there." She pointed to the extras on the set.

"You're not missing much. They'll be shooting the same five lines of dialogue until tomorrow," he predicted.

"So we've heard," Maggie replied. "I don't think we'd last that long."

Suzanne stared as if he'd floated down from a cloud. She finally snapped out of her daze. "Could I please have your autograph, Heath?"

"I'd be happy to." He walked over to her chair as she frantically searched for a scrap of paper in her knitting bag. She finally came up with one and handed it to him, along with a fine-point marker.

"Could I have one for my daughter? Her names is Natalie . . . N-A-T-A-L-I-E."

The movie star quickly complied and handed the paper back. Suzanne practically pressed it to her chest, then slipped it back into the knitting bag.

"Oh drat . . . I don't have any more paper." She looked around, panicked. "Wait, I saw someone do this at a rock concert." She stood up and whipped off her sweater. Maggie squeezed her eyes shut, not daring to see what was next.

To her great relief, Suzanne wore a T-shirt under the

sweater. She handed him the marker and twisted around so that her back faced him. "Could you sign my T-shirt? It's Suzanne . . . with a Z, double N."

Heath chuckled as he scrawled a bold signature, amused at her resourcefulness. "No problem, Suzanne with a Z, double N."

"Thank you so much." Suzanne sighed, craning her neck to get a view of the autograph on her back. Close to impossible without a mirror. Suzanne would complain of a crick in her neck tomorrow. Maggie felt sure of that.

"Could you sign this for me, please? It's Lucy. The usual spelling." Lucy shyly held out a knitting pattern, the blank side of the page showing.

The movie star directed his dazzling smile Lucy's way as he signed his name again. "My sister is named Lucy. It's one of my favorite names."

Maggie smiled, though she wondered about that claim, even though Lucy seemed to believe him. Maggie might check later on the Internet, not that it made any difference.

Heath O'Hara glanced at Maggie and Dana, but neither of them jumped forward with pen and paper. He slipped his hands into the front pockets of his tight jeans. "I hear that one of you owns this shop?"

"I do," Maggie replied.

"The set designer loved it. She didn't do a thing to the displays or the way the furniture is arranged. That's saying something," he added quietly.

"Thank you, that's nice of you to tell me." Was he this friendly to all his fans? Or just bored and thinking he would give them a little thrill?

Dana had picked up her knitting and started working

again, though she wasn't totally recovered from this close brush with stardom. "We read on your website that you like to knit, too, Heath."

She didn't add, "Is that true?" But Maggie sensed she was probing a bit.

"I do. It's a good way to kill time and a lot cheaper than playing poker with the gaffers and grips." Maggie knew what gaffers and grips were: electricians and other set technicians.

Maggie looked up at him. "Are you working on any knitting projects right now?"

"I just started a vest, to use in the movie as a prop. My character is supposed to learn how to knit, too," he explained. "It's not coming along that well."

"Maybe I can help you. I'd be happy to take a look," Maggie offered, then wasn't sure why. To call his bluff and find out if he really did knit? Silly, but she was curious.

"Maggie is like a brilliant surgeon for knitting projects," Phoebe promised. "If she can't fix it, there's not much hope."

Heath grinned, his smile as white as his shirt. "Great, I have the stuff right here." He walked over to the director's chair that said "O'Hara" on the back and slid it over to their group. He opened a leather pack that was slung over the arm of the chair and carefully removed his project.

So he *did* knit. Maggie thought for sure he was only saying that to up the fantasy of his carefully crafted image.

"Any hope?" He held up the work, which did look a mess.

"Give it here. I'll see what I can do." Maggie held out a hand and slipped on her reading glasses.

Phoebe sat back and gripped the arms of her chair, staring up at the ceiling. "Am I the only one who cannot believe that

Heath O'Hara is actually knitting with us? Would somebody pinch me . . . please?"

Phoebe stared around at her friends, her eyes wide with shock. Heath laughed lightly. Maggie could tell he thought her reaction was very cute. Maggie did, too.

"I'm not going to pinch you. But I will take a picture." Suzanne pulled out her phone and jumped up from her chair. "Is that okay?" she asked Heath.

"Absolutely. You can post it on my Facebook page," he added.

"I'm going to post it on my mine first, don't worry . . ."

"I'll take the photo, you sit in my chair," Dana suggested.

Heath's seat was right next to Dana's and she was the least in awe. Along with Maggie. Though she did find him a likable fellow.

Lucy had gone very quiet and looked a little mesmerized.

"All right, bunch up together and smile," Dana instructed. Suzanne had found an even better excuse to move closer to Heath, Maggie noticed. If she was any closer, she'd be wearing his clothing. But he didn't seem to mind. He smiled even wider and put his arm around her shoulder. Suzanne's smile was so wide it looked painful. Maggie thought she might faint.

Dana snapped a picture and a second for good measure. Then handed the phone back to Suzanne, who took it in her two hands as if was the Holy Grail. She quickly found the photo, tapped out a message, and posted it on her Facebook page.

"What did you write, Suzanne?" Lucy asked.

"'Yes, that is Heath O'Hara. You are not dreaming. Neither am I!'"

"Funny," he said with a grin.

"Thank you, Heath." Suzanne's tone was so sincere, as

if he'd just said she was the most beautiful woman he'd ever seen.

"I've tagged all of you . . . except Maggie, of course, who hasn't joined the twenty-first century."

"I have a page for the shop," she reminded Suzanne. "Put it there. I'd like a copy to hang in the shop, too," she added, glancing at the movie star. "Maybe you could sign that for me?"

"I'd be happy to. Don't forget to put it on my fan page, Suzanne," Heath added.

Suzanne gazed at him. "Will do."

Maggie nearly laughed out loud at her adoring tone. She concentrated on repairing Heath's knitting instead. She had picked up quite a few slipped stitches. She showed Heath the tinks and how she'd fixed them.

"One loop at a time. Unless you want to decrease your stitches. You're not ready for that part of the pattern yet," she explained.

He took the knitting and needles back carefully. "Thanks . . . wow, this looks much better."

"No problem, happy to help," Maggie replied. Just then, someone called, "Quiet on the set," again. Maggie turned her chair so she could see the set. So did Phoebe. The rest of her friends already sat facing the set, with Heath sitting cozily between Suzanne and Lucy.

I am glad I have a picture of this, Maggie thought. Even I might not believe it happened by tomorrow, she decided.

She'd thought Heath O'Hara was a bit full of himself when he'd first sauntered over, but his swaggering charm did grow on a person. Some people—men especially—could be total egotists but in a very beguiling way, she'd often found. The lights were dimmed again, except for the big floods shining on the actors. Maggie put her knitting aside and so did her friends.

"Camera rolling," someone called.

Nick Pullman had been coaching the actresses but sat in his chair now. He took a wad of tissues and patted his brow, then slipped off his linen blazer. An assistant stood by to take it away and handed him a bottle of cold water, which he drank thirstily, then pressed it to his forehead for a moment.

The digital clapboard appeared. "Scene fifty-seven. Take three."

Maggie wasn't sure if she wanted to stay after this one. Though she expected that her friends, especially Suzanne, would not budge an inch until Heath O'Hara left their midst.

Trina had just delivered her line, "I'm here for my lesson . . . Or maybe to teach you one," when Maggie heard a horrendous sound, like someone choking.

She saw Nick Pullman stand up, gasping for breath. Then grabbed at his chest, with a horrible grimace. Eyes bulging, he staggered forward.

They were all in the dark, except for the actors on the set. Everyone was shouting. "It's Nick . . . he's sick . . . get some help . . . dial 911 . . ."

Maggie and her friends jumped from their seats, their purses, knitting bags, and knitting clattering to the floor.

"Oh my God! What's wrong?" Jennifer ran toward her husband. "Put the lights on! Call an ambulance!"

Nick grabbed Jennifer's arm. His mouth hung open but he couldn't speak. He fell to the floor, gripping his chest again. Trina stood beside him now, too, along with a circle of crew members.

"Help him, someone . . . he can't breathe!" Trina screamed.

The lights flashed on as the cast and crew ran to help. Jennifer knelt by her husband's side. Nora Lynch, the nurse practitioner, had pushed her way through the crowd and knelt down next to the fallen director, too.

"Is he choking on something?" Dana asked quietly.

"I think he can't breathe. Maybe it's a heart attack," Maggie whispered back. She recalled that Jennifer had told her husband to calm down when the light fixture fell on Saturday. *Do you want another heart attack?* she'd asked him.

Maggie saw the nurse administer mouth-to-mouth resuscitation. Heath was down on the floor, too, and began chest compression. Maggie saw him counting under his breath, forcing himself to focus.

"Nick . . . please. Open your eyes, man. Come on. Don't do this . . . Do you hear me? Open your eyes . . ." Heath was half begging, half crying as he pumped his friend's chest with his hands.

Jennifer knelt next to her husband, looking shocked and frightened. She pressed her hand to Heath's shoulder to steady him, her gaze fixed on Nick's pale face.

"An ambulance is coming! They're on their way," someone in the crowd shouted.

Nick stared up at the ceiling, his brown eyes unnaturally wide. Then he closed them with a groan.

Maggie feared Nick was gone. Nora and Heath kept working in a steady rhythm. Heath was crying openly but didn't miss a beat.

The shop door burst open and several police officers entered. They ran back to the fallen director. One of Nick's assistants began to explain the situation to one of the officers: "He was watching the take and started choking and couldn't breathe . . ."

Another officer knelt by Heath and took over the CPR from the actor. Heath rose on trembling legs, his handsome face grim and ashen. He stepped over to Jennifer and put his arm around her shoulder. It was hard to tell who was comforting who. He hooked the other arm around Trina, who buried her face in Heath's chest.

Jennifer turned away a few moments later to answer questions from a police officer. "Yes . . . he had a heart attack last February and had a bypass operation."

Maggie heard a siren approach, and seconds later EMS technicians ran into the shop with a stretcher and cases of equipment. Nora let them take over and they quickly assessed the situation. Nick was breathing again on his own and they covered his mouth with an oxygen mask. The director was quickly strapped to a stretcher and rolled toward the door.

"Stand back, everyone," police officers instructed the onlookers.

Suzanne gripped Maggie's hand and squeezed her eyes shut.

Maggie could hardly watch. But she couldn't help it, she had to see what was happening. Dana, Lucy, and Phoebe were huddled together on the other side of the crowd, watching intently, too.

Heath, Trina, and Jennifer followed the stretcher, along with several security guards. Everyone moved to the front of the shop to watch the stretcher being rolled out and lifted into the ambulance. The crowd of onlookers on the sidewalk and street had grown; quite a few had cell phones out and were snapping pictures. She expected that news of Nick Pullman's health crisis would be on the Internet instantly. Maybe it was already.

Jennifer spoke quickly to Alicia as they walked together

toward the ambulance. Maggie couldn't help overhearing their conversation. "—and you'd better call Dr. Wang in LA. The ER doctors will want to speak to him . . . And call Regina right away. I'll check in with her later, when I know more."

Maggie guessed that was Regina Thurston, the film's executive producer

Alicia patted Jennifer's arm. "Don't worry, I'll take care of everything. I'll come to the hospital in a little while," she promised.

Jennifer smiled briefly in thanks and Alicia gave her a quick hug. Then the star was helped into the back of the ambulance, the doors slammed, and it drove off, siren blaring. Heath and Trina climbed into the backseat of a big black car, escorted out by the massive, silent giants who guarded them.

"Where do you think they'll take him?" Lucy asked.

"Harbor Medical Center, in Newburyport. It's the closest hospital," Dana replied.

"I hope he makes it," Lucy said quietly. "At one point, I thought he was gone."

"So did I," Maggie admitted. "Thank goodness the ambulance got here so quickly—"

Her words were interrupted by shouts from the crew. "Okay, back inside. Let's break it down and pack this stuff up," one of Nick's assistants shouted, herding the crew back into the shop.

The movie crew looked dazed, drained of their crackling energy. They moved like zombies, murmuring to one another. Maggie and her friends stood on the sidewalk, watching.

"It's so frightening." Lucy sounded shaken. "He was hard at work one minute. On the floor the next, fighting for his life."

"It was a shocking sight," Maggie agreed.

The drama off camera had been far more intense than the drama on the set. But based on an undeniable, unavoidable truth: life was fragile. Any moment could be our last.

We all took it for granted, didn't we? Cocooned in our routines, our plans, our projects and expectations. Who could live a normal life, conscious every moment of our mortality?

Our entrances . . . and exits.

Maggie reached out and took hold of Lucy's hand on one side and Phoebe's on the other. "He's fairly young and in good shape. And he has everything to live for. He could be back on his feet in no time. Let's hope for the best."

"Yes . . . let's send him waves of positive thoughts," Phoebe suggested.

"And Jennifer, too," Lucy said. "She must be terrified."

Maggie nodded. Of course, they didn't know the actress very well, but she'd been so kind to them and did seem like a friend in a way. Maggie's heart went out to her, too.

She hoped Nick Pullman would recover, and not make Jennifer a young widow, like the character she played in their film.

Chapter Six

ight before heading for bed, Maggie turned on the late news. As she'd expected, there was a report about Nick Pullman. A brief, blurry video—most likely sent in by an on-looker using a camera phone—showed the stretcher bearing Nick being loaded into an ambulance and Jennifer climbing in behind it.

". . . A spokesperson for Harbor Medical Center in New-buryport reported Pullman in critical condition after a medical emergency earlier this evening. Doctors suspect the director suffered cardiac arrest, though an official diagnosis has not been released. Pullman, along with his wife, actress Jennifer Todd, were filming on location in the village of Plum Harbor when he collapsed on the set."

The female reporter turned to face the camera at a differ-ent angle. "We'll be right back with Accurate Ed's weekend forecast, Red Sox highlights, and more . . ."

Maggie switched off the set. If it had been a heart attack, wouldn't doctors know by now? Maggie remembered only too well when she'd had a health scare, years ago. Heart monitors, EKG, blood work, and all sorts of tests told the story fairly quickly. Harbor Medical Center was not at the level of Mass General, in Boston, but it was a good hospital with the latest equipment. They should be able to discern if the man had suffered a cardiac "episode," as the doctors like to call it.

She wondered if the doctors had confirmed it, but Nick Pullman—and/or his public relations people—didn't want the news released. More bad publicity? But news like that couldn't be held back for long.

What was ailing him, if not his heart? Perhaps something surprisingly minor that would clear up quickly. He might be back at work tomorrow, or the day after. She certainly hoped so.

But her high hopes for Nick's speedy recovery were soon deflated by a phone call that woke her from a sound sleep. She glanced at the clock. Half past two. Maggie fumbled with the receiver, feeling her pulse race. She hated calls in the middle of the night. They rarely brought good news.

"Maggie? It's Charles. Sorry to wake you."

Maggie pushed herself up in the bed. "That's all right . . . Is something wrong?"

"Not exactly . . . I'm at work."

Maggie had started dating Charles Mossbacher a few weeks ago. A detective with the Essex County Police Department, he sometimes pulled the night shift, but had never called her after eleven.

"A case just landed on my desk. It has to do with the movie crew."

"They were filming at my shop tonight," Maggie said. "Nick Pullman had a heart attack . . . or something. He was rushed to the hospital."

"Yes, I know. Pullman was poisoned. I've been assigned to the team that's investigating."

"Poisoned? That's awful! Is he going to survive?"

"He's still in ICU, but at least they know what's wrong and he's getting the correct treatment. The thing is, the shop is now a crime scene. I've got two uniforms there already, just to make sure no one comes back and tampers with evidence."

Does the villain always return to the scene of the crime? Maggie wasn't sure about that. But her heart fell to hear that her shop would be picked over, inch by inch.

"Oh dear . . . do you really have to? An entire movie crew moved in and out of the shop today. It was like a herd of buffalo. Then they packed and cleaned everything up. I doubt if you'll find a single clue."

Charles laughed quietly at her protest. Not at all in a mean way, but with sympathy for her situation. "I'm sorry. I know what you're saying. The scene has been seriously compromised, no question. But the tiniest bit of physical evidence can turn a case. Personally, I have high hopes for the trash. Did they take that away with them, or leave it there?"

"Let's see . . . On Saturday they bagged it up and left it on the side of the building, by the other pails. I'm not sure what they did tonight. I went home right after the ambulance left."

"You were there?" She could hear the surprise in his voice and pictured his brown eyes growing wide.

"Jennifer Todd invited the knitting group to the set since we didn't get a chance to see any filming Saturday. She was just being friendly. I helped her a little with her role. She plays a woman who owns a knitting shop and she wanted to know how I got started in the business, that sort of thing."

Charles was quiet a moment. "I see . . . I knew from the report that the movie crew was at your shop and that's where Pullman experienced the effects of the poisoning. But I didn't know that you and your friends were witnesses."

Again, he might have added.

Maggie wasn't sure how this always seemed to happen, but her "traveling sisterhood" of knitters always seemed to find themselves in the middle of a police investigation. In fact, that was how she and Charles had met.

When Phoebe's friend Charlotte Blackburn had been involved in a murder investigation, Charles was assigned to investigate the case. Which turned out to be tangled with a local knitting graffiti group, the Knit Kats.

The investigation touched upon her shop and friends, and she found herself in many conversations with Charles. Official conversations, and not all of them pleasant. But his intelligence, humor, and kindness did shine through, even during some very tense moments.

Maggie never expected to be attracted to a police officer. But something had clicked with Charles right from the start. He'd obviously felt the same, making excuses to visit the shop when a phone call would have done fine.

So far, her initial impressions still rang true. The more she knew of him, the more she liked and respected him. And enjoyed his company.

"What sort of poison was it? You didn't say." Not that she knew much about poison. But she was curious.

"Now that I know you're a witness, I'm not sure I can say. You have to be officially interviewed . . . and ruled out," he reminded her.

"Oh, Charles . . ." Maggie sighed and laughed. Sometimes

he was a stickler for rules. But she could be, too. "All right. Be like that. I'll see it on the news soon anyway."

"That's true. Okay, I'll tell you, but don't tell anyone it was me. This is a high-profile case. A guy like Pullman doesn't usually put a toe in Essex County. No less get poisoned here. The chief assigned an entire team, and I should probably recuse myself, considering our relationship."

They had a relationship? Hmm . . . She liked that idea and was glad to hear he thought so.

"It's all right. I don't want to make any trouble for you," she said quickly.

She heard him sigh. "No big deal. Toxicology report found an excess of digitalis in his bloodstream, which was particularly toxic since he already has a heart condition."

"How awful," Maggie replied quietly. "Isn't digitalis a heart medication? An overdose could be dangerous, right?"

"Exactly. It *should* have been fatal. Except that Pullman is a lucky guy. From what we can see so far, the composition of the drug is chemically unusual . . . not in the typical form you might find in a pharmacy. So we know he didn't do it himself, by accident."

That was the next question Maggie had—maybe Nick had just mixed up his medication.

"Toxicology is trying to figure out the source now. We need to get on top of this right away. The media will be all over us by the morning. Can we have your permission to go in without a warrant?"

She knew if she didn't agree he would get a search warrant.

It would take a few hours, but the police would still go through the same procedure.

"Yes, of course. Besides, it's inevitable, right?"

"Yes, it is. We'll try to be quick . . . and not pull the place apart."

"That's some comfort," she murmured. Though not much.

"I hate to ask, but can you go over now and open the door?"

"There's a spare key hidden on the porch. Would it be all right if you open it yourself, with my official permission?"

"That would be perfect." Charles sounded pleased by the solution. And so was she. She didn't fancy getting out of her warm bed and driving into town at this hour.

"Very cooperative. I like that in a witness."

Maggie had a feeling he meant something more. She felt herself blush and was glad he couldn't see her.

"I almost forgot. I'd better let Phoebe know what's going on. She'll be frightened when she hears everyone go in. Can you give me five minutes to call her?"

"I'm at the station now. That will give me time to get over there."

Maggie agreed that was a good plan.

"Tell her we don't need to search her apartment, too," Charles said. "The film crew didn't use that space, did they?"

"No, no one went up there. I'm fairly certain it was locked the whole time. She'll be relieved to hear that," Maggie added.

Maggie was, too.

She told Charles where to find the spare key and then quickly dialed Phoebe. She hated to wake her at this hour, but was sure her assistant would appreciate the warning.

Phoebe was groggy and grouchy when Maggie reached her. Then shocked by the news. "Poisoned . . . with what?"

"The doctors found a certain chemical in his body. The

same that's found in heart medication. But it wasn't his pills and it was a very potent dose. So it nearly killed him."

Someone hoped it would, Maggie would easily wager.

"That's awful. I saw on the news that he was still alive."

"He's alive. But in bad shape . . . so now the shop is a crime scene and the police have to search the place. I just wanted you to know that they're coming over."

"Thanks for the heads-up. But I think they're already here."

She had run to the window while they were talking and reported that a slew of police cars were already waiting on Main Street, and the property was surrounded with yellow tape.

"They'll let me out of here in the morning . . . if they're not done yet . . . won't they?"

"Of course they will. We all have to give statements to the police. They'll have to let you out for that," Maggie teased her.

"I can't sleep now with all of them coming in down there. I guess I'll stay up and watch TV . . . and work on my knitting."

"Well . . . if you have to. But try to get some sleep," she advised. "They won't be very noisy."

"I know. It's just the idea."

Maggie understood Phoebe's uneasiness. She would have felt the same. She doubted the shop would be open tomorrow, and even if it was, she could muddle through by herself if Phoebe needed the day off.

Maggie finally shut the light and punched up her pillow, though it was hard to fall asleep. She tried not to think about her shop being picked apart during the next few hours.

What could the detectives possibly find at this point? Charles had practically admitted it himself. Though she knew they would go through the place inch by inch, the forensic team in their white suits, using magnifying glasses, sprinkling their gritty fingerprint dust all over the place.

Still, it was doubtful any trace of this crime remained. It wasn't a violent crime, where the scene could yield so much information. No, this attack was insidious and artful. So subtle and doubly sinister.

She hoped they worked quickly, without too much collateral damage. She'd already lost so much time with the movie crew, and she couldn't afford to keep the shop closed another day this week. Maybe she'd be able to open by the afternoon.

She realized she would probably see Charles again tomorrow, either at the shop or at the police station.

And I'm going to look like a zombie if I don't get some beauty sleep, she thought. That was enough for her to finally drift off.

"Tell me everything you can remember. Especially about Pullman and any conversations you may have overheard. Even if it doesn't seem important." Charles sat across from her with a large pad, pen poised.

The last of the investigators were leaving the shop. Charles had called her at home and said the coast was clear. He'd also told her that his boss had given him clearance to take her statement. Maggie was glad to hear that. Not that she would have minded talking to another officer, but it was easier talking to Charles.

"I'll try to remember everything. But I think it's possible the trouble started well before last night."

"What do you mean?"

"It could be a coincidence, but there's been an accident of some kind almost every day since the crew arrived. Last Saturday, even before they began filming, I saw a huge light fixture crash down and nearly kill Jennifer Todd. Well, maybe not kill her, but it would have injured her very badly if she hadn't jumped clear in time. These pieces of equipment are very heavy and there was broken glass everywhere."

Her beautiful face could have been cut to shreds, Maggie wanted to add. But she knew Charles wouldn't take her seriously if she overdid it. Though she did think the falling light fixture could have been lethal, if it had struck a bull's-eye on some target.

"Was anyone hurt?"

Maggie shook her head. "Jennifer was shaken but tried to act later as if it was no big deal. I think she dove under the table just in time. Nick was very concerned, as you'd expect. I remember that he examined her face very carefully . . . as if he was looking for scratches on a fancy car."

Maggie wasn't sure where that insight had come from, but it felt true. "I'm sorry to sound mean about the man while he's fighting for his life. I'm sure he was worried about her. But he seemed mostly . . . angry. Yelling at everyone to clean the place up. I guess he was annoyed at losing time in their schedule the very first day," Maggie reflected.

"He has a bad temper."

"Yes, he does. It's no secret. People seem afraid of setting him off. I've heard Jennifer refer to his touchy temperament more than once. Some people do show their concern by getting angry. It's an odd thing. But men especially."

"Yes, I suppose that's true . . . but no one was injured by the lights?"

"Jennifer's assistant, Alicia, cut her hand. She was picking glass off of Jennifer. The movie crew has medical help on site. A nurse practitioner, Nora Lynch. She examined both of them. She could tell you more."

"Okay . . . anything else besides the falling lights?" She could tell Charles wasn't impressed.

"Jennifer Todd is being stalked by a fan. A very persistent and creepy one," she added. "That might figure in somewhere." From the tilt of his head she could tell that tidbit had caught his attention.

Charles tapped his pencil on the table and frowned. "How do you know that?"

"Jennifer and her assistant came to the shop Monday night. She wanted to ask me some questions and see a knitting group in action. She was just about to leave when someone knocked. We thought it was the security guard coming to pick them up, but when I looked out, there was just a basket of roses on the porch. Someone had left it and run off. Not very far, it turned out. They were watching from a hiding place and called out when the door opened."

Charles recorded this information with interest. "What sort of roses were they, do you remember?"

"Yellow, long stemmed, in a wicker basket with a blue satin bow on the handle."

Charles made a note. "What did the person say? Could you tell if the voice was male or female?"

"A male voice. I'm not sure I can remember exactly. 'I love you, Jennifer. We can be together now.' . . . Oh wait. He said, 'You came back to me. I knew you would.' Something like that. Maybe one of my friends will remember?"

"I'll ask them about it. How did Todd react?"

"She was quite calm. It seems this happens a lot. Her assistant told me that the next day. Alicia said it's been more frequent since they arrived here. There are scary notes on Jennifer's fan page, too. I'm not sure if they think it's the same person, or if she has a number of crazy fans." Maggie paused. "I did think of reporting the incident myself, since it happened on my property, but Jennifer asked me not to. She said her husband hated bad publicity and their security guards would handle it. Again, she seemed afraid it would make Nick angry," she added.

"I'll check and see if he made a report. Maybe he was handling it with a security firm, or a private investigator. To keep the story away from the media."

Maggie hadn't thought of that. But it made sense.

"Alicia came to the shop the next day and said the stalker had left more flowers, right in front of Jennifer's hotel room door in the middle of the night. Pretty brazen, right? That must have been Tuesday night."

Charles nodded, his expression serious. "There might be security cameras at the hotel. We can check on that."

"Since Jennifer grew up around here, I thought it could be someone from her past. An old boyfriend, maybe. Or someone who had wanted to be her boyfriend . . . Wait—" Charles was about to say something but she continued. "I just remembered, yellow and blue. Newburyport High School colors. The Tigers, archrivals of the Plum Harbor Panthers. I know their colors well."

"That's possible." Charles didn't make a note about her brilliant revelation. "Anything else that could be related to Pullman?"

As much as he might have been concerned about Jennifer, his tone reminded Maggie that he'd been assigned to figure out who poisoned Nick Pullman. Though she had very fond feelings for Charles and respected him, she did know that police officers had a tendency to be left brained, comparing and contrasting and hardly ever looking or thinking outside their particular crime box.

Maybe that's because most people who broke the law were not very imaginative and performed their crimes in a linear, logical way. But sometimes, disparate, seemingly random events in these situations were connected. From what Maggie had seen.

"Yes, well . . . not exactly. But there was a fire on the set, on Wednesday. In Heath O'Hara's trailer."

"I heard about that. But I don't think the fire department suspected it was intentionally set."

"How did it start?" Maggie asked.

He shrugged. "I haven't read the report. But they don't have an arson investigator on it."

"You told me to tell you everything. Suzanne and Lucy were at the set the morning of the fire. They saw Heath O'Hara and Trina Hardwick coming out of a trailer in what seemed to be a compromising situation," Maggie said as un-sensationally as she could. "Later, Jennifer's assistant said she was relieved that Trina had not come out of Nick's trailer and embarrassed Jennifer. Or something like that."

Charles took a breath, looking a bit bogged down by the celebrity gossip and by Maggie wandering so far off track. "Did you ask what she meant by that? Are Hardwick and Pullman involved?"

"Alicia—Jennifer's assistant—seems to think they could be. She said Trina would do anything to have her role empha-sized. Including seducing Nick. But of course, that could just be Alicia's impression. She doesn't like Trina much. I did see Nick and Trina looking very familiar with each other last night on the set, in between the takes."

"Very familiar? How do you mean?"

"Well . . . let's see. He had his arm around her shoulder at one point and she whispered something to him. Their faces were very close, I thought. And he put his hand on her hip and sort of . . . pat her," she added.

The litany of observations sounded silly when she said it aloud. She couldn't tell if Charles was annoyed at her for wasting his time. He tapped his pencil on the pad a moment and looked up.

"Maybe that's just par for the course in Hollywood. Everyone acts chummy?" she added.

"So I've heard." He sighed. "Let's get back to your visit to the set, from the beginning, if we can."

"All right. But when you put it together with a premeditated poisoning, I think these other events are worth considering. That's all I'm trying to say."

"The incidents could be related. Or not. We don't know anything yet. Except that Pullman was poisoned."

"Yes, I know." She sat back in her chair and picked up some knitting. "Do you mind if I knit?"

"I like to watch you knit. It's relaxing."

Maggie was pleased to hear that. "Let's see, where should I start? We came to the shop at seven. There was very tight security. They checked the email Alicia had sent and checked our purses and knitting bags. Alicia showed us to our seats and told us the rules of visiting the set . . ."

It took Maggie a few minutes to recall everything she observed on the movie set and answer Charles's questions. "I did see him drink something. Just before they started filming the scene the first time. I remember because Lucy and Phoebe had gone to the snack table and ran back to their seats just in time. The lights had gone down, but I saw someone hand Nick a drink. It looked like a plastic bottle. He unscrewed the lid and drank a few gulps. Then he put it down on the floor, next to his chair."

"That's good. We can check the exact time he took that first drink against the film. The camera marks the date and time automatically. Then we can match it up with the presentation of his symptoms and stomach contents. To see if that bottle contained the tainted liquid."

Maggie nodded. That all made sense. Then the police would need to find the crew member who'd handed Nick the drink. And try to find out where it had come from. That could be a good lead.

She loved the logic of detective work. Even though it was usually a very slow process, like putting together a puzzle with thousands of pieces. And many missing ones. Or knitting a sweater . . . or filming a movie, for that matter. A pattern and story eventually emerged if you stuck with it long enough.

"Why did he drink so much of the poisoned liquid? Didn't it taste bad with that chemical in it?" Maggie made a face, imagining such a thing.

"It would taste a little bitter. But the drink or food it was hidden in must have masked the flavor. Maybe it was something that doesn't taste particularly good, so he didn't notice," Charles added.

"I think he's already had one heart attack. Maybe the person who poisoned him knew that."

"That's very likely. It should have killed him," Charles conceded. "I'd say someone fully expected it would."

Maggie nodded but didn't reply. Who could have done such a thing?

Powerful people like Nick Pullman must have lots of enemies. Maggie could imagine the many actors who might hold a grudge against him, feeling passed over for a part, or resentful about a performance that ended up on the cutting-room floor. Not to mention business rivals.

She hated to think it was someone in the crew who lurked close by, undetected . . . and remained near, waiting to see if Nick survived.

When Charles was finally ready to leave, she walked him to the door. "If I have any more questions I'll let you know," he told her. "But this is a very complete statement. You have a good eye for detail, and a good memory, Maggie."

Was he amused that she'd woven in so much gossip? She thought so, but didn't mind. "Thanks. I'll take that as a compliment."

"I didn't expect you to be a witness," he admitted again.

"It was fun to surprise you."

"You do keep me on my toes," he teased her. "Looks like I'm working tomorrow night. They have us scheduled around the clock. I don't know about our date."

They had plans to get together on Saturday night for dinner and a movie. Maggie had been looking forward to it, but she certainly understood.

"Don't worry. I understand," she assured him. "Maybe you'll solve the case by then."

He laughed. "You have a lot of confidence in me."

"I do."

He met her gaze and smiled. "I'll let you know how it's going."

Maggie smiled back, feeling a lightness in her heart.

She closed the door and went back inside, noticing that

Phoebe had come down from her apartment. She sat at the back table, looking sleepy, sipping from a giant mug of coffee.

"I wonder how Nick Pullman is. Did you check the news? I didn't get a chance to watch this morning."

Maggie was pleased that Phoebe didn't linger upstairs, watching TV. But she would have found it understandable this morning.

"He's still in intensive care. Charles thinks they might move him to Mass General once his condition is stable."

"Did you tell Detective Mossbacher about that fan who's stalking Jennifer? Maybe he was so jealous he thought if he knocked off her husband, she'd run into his wacko arms."

"I did. He said someone will look into that, if it hasn't been reported already. He said it could be related, but not necessarily."

Maggie found some skeins of yarn scattered on the table and returned them to their baskets. She had to straighten out all the stock in the cubbyholes too, all just jammed back inside by the police. She hated the way that looked. Had Phoebe downed enough caffeine yet to start helping? Not quite.

"What do you think will happen? How can they finish the movie without Nick Pullman?" Phoebe's gaze followed her.

"I don't know. Maybe they have to wait until he recovers before they can continue."

"If he recovers. Maybe they'll get a different director. Like bringing in a long-term sub, at school, if the regular teacher breaks her leg or something."

"I guess that's possible." Huge sums of money had been invested in this film. The salaries of the three big stars and director alone probably surpassed the gross national product of some smaller nations.

Nick Pullman was so entangled in the project—his wife,

best friend . . . and perhaps his girlfriend, in starring roles. His son a key writer, and his own production company taking the financial risk.

Tradition did insist the show must go on, but would the project really be turned over to a new director?

And who exactly stood to benefit by pushing Nick Pullman out of this picture?

Chapter Seven

Maggie was back to business as usual by Saturday morning. She'd been closed on Saturday the week before for the movie crew, which was the only day some customers could visit. She expected a wave of traffic today. Not to mention a wave of busybodies who wanted to see where the famous director had been poisoned.

She unlocked the door around eight, though she didn't officially open until half past nine. She and Phoebe had put the stock and displays back in order, but she wanted to poke around the flower beds. Spring bulbs were sprouting—hyacinth, tulips, and daffodils. Along with eager weeds.

She was yanking a clump of green invaders when she heard the gate creak open and someone called out to her, "Good morning, Maggie."

Lucy, she thought, who took her dogs for a walk into the village almost every day and always stopped for a chat. But when Maggie turned, she didn't face the familiar wet noses and panting tongues. Only a long black limo parked at the curb and the inimitable Victor, vigilantly scanning Main Street from behind a pair of wraparound sunglasses.

Jennifer Todd walked toward her, barely recognizable in even bigger sunglasses and a dressed-down look—worn jeans, sneakers, and a light canvas jacket with the hood pulled over her head. She might have been dressed for a walk on a breezy beach. Which would have done her good this morning if she'd had the time for it. The poor woman looked pale and tired, even under the camouflage.

Maggie came to her feet and tugged off her gloves. "Jennifer . . . what a surprise."

"I'm sorry to bother you so early."

"I was just weeding. These poor tulips and daffs managed to survive so far. I thought I'd give them a little encouragement."

Jennifer smiled. "I love daffodils the best, brave little flowers, pushing out of the cold, rocky soil at the first sign of spring."

"I love them, too. Isn't there a famous poem about daffodils?" Maggie knew there was but couldn't recall it.

"'I wandered lonely as a cloud, that floats on high o'er vales and hills, when all at once I saw a crowd a host of golden daffodils.'"

Maggie smiled with pleasure. "Very good . . . William Wordsworth."

Jennifer nodded. "I had to memorize it for school. One of my earliest dramatic efforts," she added with a wistful smile. "I have a big garden at home, but I miss the flowers you see in New England, especially this time of year."

"The blooming season here is brief, but worth the wait," Maggie agreed. "How's Nick? Any improvement?"

"He's holding on. The doctors say he's stable enough to move to Mass General. They're going to medAvac him by helicopter this morning. I'm on my way to Boston right now."

"That's encouraging," Maggie said sincerely.

"I have my fingers crossed," Jennifer replied, though she didn't sound very encouraged.

She had slipped off her hood to reveal a disheveled hairdo, her thick brown tresses pulled back in a ponytail, her face bare of makeup. She looked like one of those mean-spirited "stars without makeup" photos in the tabloids. Maggie hoped no enterprising, less-than-ethical photographer caught up with her.

"We had to pass the shop on the way out of town and I saw you. In all the confusion Thursday night, I think I left my knitting here. In a tote that you gave me, with the shop name on the front?"

Maggie thought a moment. "The place looked like a small tornado had passed through after the police search. I'm not sure if I saw anything like that . . . Wait. Yes, I did. I wasn't sure who had left it. Maybe it is yours. Let's go see."

Maggie turned and Jennifer followed her, up the porch steps and into the shop, where Maggie slipped behind the counter and pulled out the Black Sheep Knitting tote. She handed it to Jennifer and watched her peer inside.

"Yes, that's it." Jennifer finally smiled a bit. "I knew it was here somewhere." She took out the pattern and showed Maggie a small note Maggie had made for her. "See? You wrote that to help me remember the stitch."

"Oh right. I didn't notice that before. I would have remembered it was yours," Maggie agreed.

"I've been sitting next to Nick's bed since Thursday night.

He's barely said a word, of course. They have him on a lot of sedatives to keep him quiet. All I can do is read, or knit. And pray a bit," she confessed quietly.

Maggie's heart went out to her. "I'm so sorry for you, Jennifer. And Nick, of course. Why would anyone do such a thing? It's impossible for me to imagine it."

"I keep asking myself the same thing. Waiting to see if he'll live or die. I couldn't get the question out of my mind. Why? Why Nick?" Her eyes had filled with tears and she swallowed hard to keep from crying. "I . . . I blame myself, Maggie. It's my fault this happened."

"Your fault? How could that be?" Maggie asked gently.

"The fan who's been stalking me. I should have told the police right away. Especially once we came here. It got much worse." Her large blue eyes overflowed and she paused to dab them with a tissue. "Maybe if I'd ignored Nick and told the police, he'd be all right now. Not fighting for his life."

"Jennifer, you can't blame yourself for this. Even if the same person who's been harassing you did poison Nick." Maggie gently touched the star's shoulder. "It's the work of a twisted personality. Someone in deep pain who needs serious help. No one can blame you."

"That's good of you to say. But I don't feel that way. I told a detective about it, when I gave a statement to the police last night. He said I put myself and everyone involved in the movie at risk by not reporting it."

Maggie didn't reply. She wondered who had been so harsh with a woman who was going through so much, watching her husband fight for his life. She was certain it had not been Charles. He would never be that insensitive.

"I told a detective about the flower delivery here, and the

stalker, too," Maggie replied. "At this point, I thought the police need to know and they told me to be completely forthcoming."

"You did the right thing," Jennifer assured her.

"The detective I spoke to—who is a very smart man—said it might be connected, but it very well may not be. There's no way to know yet, and anyone who tells you otherwise . . . Well, they just shouldn't have said that. You can't hold yourself responsible for the insane act of some unhinged person. You're not being fair to yourself."

Jennifer's gaze was downcast. She sighed, but when she looked up again, she seemed a bit encouraged. "Thank you for saying that. I hope it's true."

"I know it is," Maggie said confidently. "What about the movie? Will you wait until Nick recovers to finish it?"

"Oh no . . . that's not an option. We're required by contract to continue, with a new director. Our executive producer, Regina Thurston, has been working on that."

"Who will it be, do you know?" Maggie didn't know the names of many directors, except for the very famous ones, but she was curious.

"I'm not sure I can tell you. Regina is very uptight about information moving through proper channels, publicists, and press releases. That sort of thing. She doesn't abide any leaks." Jennifer rolled her eyes. "Not that I consider you a nosy member of the media."

Maggie laughed. "I'd hope not."

"It wasn't easy to find someone good who was free and willing to take this on. But she jumped on a red-eye last night with a new director and they've probably landed at Logan by now. They might stop at Mass General before they come out here, to check on Nick," Jen added, glancing at her watch.

A grim meeting, Maggie thought. Of course, Nick Pullman could not communicate a word to his replacement. But it was respectful of his colleagues to visit.

She wondered if Jen was hoping to get to Boston in time to see them. Or maybe wanted to avoid them? It would be hard to see someone take over such an important, powerful position from your ailing husband. Would this affect her acting? The entire landscape of the movie had shifted with Nick Pullman swept off the scene, Maggie realized.

"It's not a very attractive opportunity," Jennifer said frankly. "To step in and direct a film that's already over budget and manage a cast and crew who have gone through so much. I'll be thankful to whoever shows up. I've been so distracted with Nick, I've hardly given that a thought."

"Of course not."

"I think the plan is to do some fast rewrites of the script, so we can finish up here quickly and shoot whatever's left at the studio. Theo has been working around the clock and taking meetings with Regina on Skype." Maggie wasn't that up on technology, but knew Skype was a camera connection on the computer. She talked to her daughter, Julie, at college that way from time to time.

"Ironically, this will be a help to Theo in the long run," Jen continued. "The more a writer contributes to a script, the larger his or her credit. Theo should get a very good credit out of this," she added.

She sighed again, the financial pressures bearing down heavily, as well as her worries about her husband's recovery.

Jennifer didn't add that she and Nick had a great deal of

their own money tied up in the production of the movie, but Maggie knew that from articles online and in the newspaper. "I hope the rest goes quickly and smoothly," Maggie replied. That wouldn't be too hard, considering the series of unfortunate events the group had faced so far. "And Nick recovers quickly."

"Thank you, Maggie. Thanks for listening to me. I feel embarrassed now, venting like that," Jennifer admitted. "It is a bit lonely being on location. Away from all your friends and connections."

"I understand. At least you have Alicia. Where is she today?"

Maggie didn't want to be nosy. But she'd rarely seen Jennifer without her assistant at her side.

"She's going to sit in on some meetings for me when the new director gets here. We'll probably read through the revised scenes tonight. She's going to work on the script, transpose all my notes and highlights, that sort of thing."

Maggie basically got the gist. And maybe Jennifer wanted to be alone with her husband at this serious time.

Maggie did wonder about Nick's son, Theo. She hadn't seen him leave for the hospital last night, unless he followed in another car. From what Jennifer had just said, Theo had been hard at work rewriting the script since his father fell ill.

But it was none of her business, for one thing. Nick's son would figure out how to visit his father when he could. And surely Nick would be thankful to his son for helping to hold the project together during this crisis.

Jennifer pulled up her hood and slipped her sunglasses back on, then said good-bye. Out on the porch, she clutched the bag of yarn to her chest and ran down to the car with Victor hovering alongside.

She had barely jumped inside and slammed the door closed when the car swooped away from the curb and disappeared down Main Street.

Maggie watched from the window at the front of her shop. A few early morning shoppers, joggers, and dog walkers were about, but there didn't appear to be any fans or media following the actress. Maybe that group was already camped out at the hospital, waiting to pounce on Jennifer there.

As Maggie went back to work, she was once again thankful for her own anonymous, relatively drama-free life.

Just as she expected, Maggie's friends converged at the shop around noon. Dana came in from a yoga class first and Suzanne arrived soon after, taking a break between appointments. They'd brought their lunch and knitting, and Maggie found them working busily on both when she walked up to the front of the shop after a morning class let out.

"Where's Lucy?" Suzanne asked between bites of a roll-up sandwich. She was suited up to run an open house in a black linen blazer, gray pants, and pale blue wrap sweater she had knit for herself.

She held her sandwich at arm's length, big gold bangles slipping down her arms as she avoided splattering juicy bits on her good clothes. Maggie wasn't sure what was in it—turkey and a refrigerator full of other ingredients. It looked like it might explode.

"She's at the police station, giving her statement. I just sent a text and told her we were here." Dana held a tall plastic cup with thick green liquid inside. Alternating sips between stitches.

"That looks healthy, " Phoebe said.

"It should be. There's probably a bushel of vegetables in

one glass of this stuff," Dana replied with a laugh. "I get one every Saturday at the farmer's market."

"I admire your courage. After watching Nick Pullman poisoned the other night, I'm sticking to my own homemade soup for a while." Maggie picked up her spoon and showed the others her humble lunch. "Good old chicken vegetable."

"Don't be silly." Dana swallowed another mouthful. "I don't think Nick's poisoning was a random act. I think it was carefully planned and directed at him."

"Most likely," Maggie conceded. "But you never know."

Dana smiled and put her cup down. "But you do . . . the police do anyway." Maggie could tell from her smile that she'd already heard something interesting about the case.

Dana's husband, Jack, was an attorney in town, but had once been a police detective for the county and still maintained close ties with the force. Dana was often privy to inside information on interesting cases, and though she really wasn't supposed to tell her friends, she usually couldn't help it.

Suzanne had put her amazingly sloppy sandwich aside and now held her hands out as she cleaned them with a wad of napkins.

"Spill it, pal. Did the police find evidence in Maggie's shop . . . or maybe in Nick's trailer? Or his hotel room? They must be searching everywhere for clues."

"They are," Dana confirmed. "And they're pretty certain they found the bottle that held the poisoned liquid—"

"Out in the trash next to my shop?" Maggie cut in, recalling what Charles had told her.

"You're warm. They found it in some trash collected at the park on the harbor. The label was torn off. But they're pretty certain it's the right bottle. There was a tiny, microscopic hole where a syringe must have been used to inject the poison into the drink, without disturbing the seal on the cap. Then the hole was sealed with a swipe of superglue. Ingenious, right? They're checking for Nick's DNA and anyone else's."

"How in the world did they pick that bottle out from the tons of trash generated by this town?" Suzanne asked with amazement.

"Good, old-fashioned, boots-on-the-ground—or rather, in the dump—police work," Dana replied. "They sent an army of officers to pick through the garbage, bit by bit."

"Charles said this is a very high-profile case and there's a lot of pressure on the Essex County Police Department not to flub it up and look amateur," Maggie said. "I think this is an amazing break. Don't you?"

"It is a good break," Dana replied. "But they were smart and methodical. They knew what type of bottle they were looking for and the time frame of when it would have been dumped. Jack told me they collected over a thousand bottles that exact size and shape, then had to narrow it down," she added.

Suzanne nodded her approval. "I always say, the harder I work, the luckier I get."

"Just think of all the plastic bottles we use and throw away . . . it's totally polluting the planet," Phoebe said sadly.

"Phoebe has a good point. I try to use my own containers whenever I can," Maggie told her friends. "But you can see why a traveling crew like this finds that inconvenient. If Nick drank the poison on the set, doesn't that mean it had to be someone in the cast or crew who poisoned the drink?"

"I'm sticking with the crazy-fan theory. Hell hath no fury like an old boyfriend scorned," Suzanne cut in. "He's obviously lurking around town. He could have planted the bottle on the set somehow."

"For instance?" Phoebe challenged her.

"I bet the crew and cast has stuff delivered all the time. I've seen pizza boxes, Chinese takeout, and UPS deliveries around the set. Haven't you?" she asked the others.

"Okay, so Crazy Fan disguises himself as a delivery guy. That's possible," Maggie conceded. "Then what?"

"He's outside with the fans when Nick gets poisoned. Waits for the trash to be put out by the crew, then finds the bottle and dumps it in the nearest public place, where there is always a lot of people and trash. Hey"—her eyes lit up— "maybe he was hanging around the inn, waiting for Jennifer to come back from the hospital. That park is right across from the Lord Charles. He could have been sitting there, doing his stalking thing, and that's why he dumped the bottle in one of those cans."

"Couldn't this crazy fan be a member of the crew *and* Jennifer's stalker?" Phoebe asked. "Maybe he isn't a local. Maybe this person was on the set all the time, and after Nick drank the poison, he or she picked up the bottle and just put it in their pocket or something. Then walked down to the harbor and dumped it. We were there, the place was insane and the lights were off for a while," she added. "Everyone was so focused on Nick, the culprit could have easily picked up the bottle and walked off with it."

"That's true," Maggie agreed. "It's certainly possible."

"But Jennifer said the attention intensified once she got to Plum Harbor. I have a strong feeling, too, that the stalker is someone she grew up with, or went to school with," Dana said.

Maggie had finished her soup and set up the yarn swift on

the little tea table. A class was coming in at two and she had to finish rolling their yarn.

"What if the crew had taken their trash? I think they were supposed to do that according to the contract I signed," Maggie recalled.

"He probably would have followed them to see what happened to the bags. They had to throw it out somewhere." Dana shrugged and picked up her knitting.

"Very true . . . and not even relevant, really. They did throw the trash out here, and it's very dark in that driveway if the light by the side door isn't on," Maggie added. "Charles told me that police officers were sent to watch the shop, in case anyone came back. He was especially concerned about the trash," she added with a smile, thinking that was clever of him. Or just showed his experience.

"But the police didn't know Nick was poisoned until at least an hour or two after he left in the ambulance. The doctors in the ER had to figure it out. Then report it. That would have given Crazy Fan plenty of time to dig the bottle out of the trash," Dana calculated.

"You'd think he would have thought of something a little sneakier than just dumping it in a public place." Phoebe gazed around at her friends. "He could have hid it somewhere, buried it . . . melted it—"

"Maybe he panicked and just wanted to get rid of it," Maggie cut in before Phoebe could go further. She did have a point, and the possibilities for disposing of the bottle were endless. "It's practically a murder weapon. Or maybe he thought removing the label was enough to render it useless as evidence?"

"It does seem too simple. But sometimes people have an unconscious wish to get caught," Dana said. "I'm just wondering who else stands to gain from Nick Pullman's death?"

But before anyone could offer their theory, Lucy walked in. She was smiling widely. Too widely, Maggie thought, for someone who had just been sitting in a dingy police station.

"Hi, Lucy, how did it go?" Phoebe was the first to greet her.

Phoebe had not gone yet to give her statement. She was the straggler, hoping a uniformed police officer would come to the shop to take a statement from her. A few weeks ago, during the investigation surrounding her friend Charlotte, Phoebe had spent many hours at the station, and understandably had an aversion to the building.

Lucy shrugged. "Surprisingly painless. Depressing decor, but the officer who took my statement was polite."

"Was he cute? There's a really cute one that has a desk in the front of the squad room, right after you get buzzed in," Phoebe recalled. "He was nice, too . . . for an authority figure."

Suzanne slid over on the love seat and made a space for Lucy. "We tried to wait for you, but we had to rush ahead and figure out who poisoned Nick Pullman."

"That's all right. I knew you couldn't resist. Did you break the case yet?" Lucy unwrapped a yogurt and fruit parfait. Probably also purchased at the farmer's market, Maggie guessed. But she held her tongue. She didn't have to make everyone nutty and neurotic about eating prepared foods . . . the way she was now.

"We've squeezed every drop from the crazy-fan theory," Suzanne replied. "My personal favorite."

"But Dana said the plastic bottle from the poisoned drink was found in a bag of trash that came from the park at the harbor," Maggie added, catching Lucy up. "So CF—Crazy

Fan—would have needed to come back to the shop to find it after the movie crew left. Then dump it down there."

"Or, this person could have been on the set and pocketed the bottle when no one was looking," Phoebe added.

"Now we're just wondering who else stands to benefit if the movie project is abandoned because Nick is out of the picture . . . no pun intended," Suzanne said.

"But the project won't be abandoned. A new director is arriving from California. Jennifer told me this morning, though she wasn't able to say who it is," Maggie said.

"This is where I come in." Lucy leaned forward as everyone turned her way. "I was leaving the police station when I noticed a lot of excitement out in the parking lot. A bunch of reporters with cameras and all that. Your *friend*, Charles"—Lucy said the word with special emphasis as she glanced at Maggie—"was leading a group of celebs inside, to take their statements, I guess. I recognized Trina and Heath, of course, but there was another man. He looked pretty cozy with Trina, her arm tucked into his and all that."

"A lot of men look cozy with Trina," Maggie noted.

"Very true. But this looked serious. There was another woman, too. Sort of severe looking, but well preserved, midfifties, I'd guess. And a guy with slick hair, a real expensive suit, and a briefcase."

"Obviously a lawyer," Dana noted.

"Yes, probably," Maggie agreed. "And maybe Trina's companion is the new director?"

"Ding . . . Maggie wins round one. I asked one of the reporters and they told me the guy with Trina is a director, Sam Drummond. And the woman is—"

"Regina Thurston, the film's executive producer?" Maggie guessed again.

"Ding. Two for Maggie."

"And Sam Drummond is Trina's boyfriend . . . Ding for me." Suzanne's tone was smug and satisfied. She whipped her knitting out of her tote with a flourish.

"I knew that," Phoebe mumbled. "My buzzer isn't working that well today."

"Let's see what the celebrity gossip experts are saying online. They must be blogging off their gel manicures over this story." Lucy picked up Maggie's laptop, which was sitting on the oval tea table, and tapped in a few words to search. "Here it is . . . posted an hour ago on Hollywood Buzz. 'Drummond to the Rescue,'" she said, reading the headline out loud. "And there's a nice photo of Trina greeting her honey at Logan Airport with a lip-locking smooch."

Lucy set the laptop down on the table so everyone could see. Then read aloud: "'Hollywood's hottest young director, Sam Drummond, landed in Boston this morning to replace Nick Pullman on the ailing film project *Love Knots*. Pullman was rushed to Harbor Medical Center Thursday night while filming the movie on location in Plum Harbor, Massachusetts. Reportedly, he is suffering from pulmonary and kidney damage, due to a near-fatal poisoning caused by ingesting a tainted beverage.

"'While local police investigate the attempt on Pullman's life, Drummond has been hired in a hurry to direct the rest of the filming. The movie stars Jennifer Todd, Heath O'Hara, and Trina Hardwick, who has been dating Drummond since they met last October in London. Trina told Hollywood Buzz, "Despite being united under these sad circumstances, Sammy and

I are thrilled to be working together. He's a brilliant director and I know he'll bring a special vision to this project.""'"

Lucy looked up at her friends. "Did you ever notice how everyone in Hollywood is brilliant? What are the odds of that?"

"Must be something in the water," Maggie said.

"Or the smoothies." Phoebe squinched her face, knowing she'd made a very bad joke. Her friends groaned in unison.

"You don't have to be a Hollywood reporter to see that Trina stands to gain big time by this switch. Wasn't Alicia telling us that she would do anything to get more time on screen, to see her role given more importance?" Suzanne reminded them. "Her significant other is the perfect person to do that for her."

"That's all very true, but is she so desperate that she'd poison Nick Pullman and risk having the movie sidelined for months, or maybe never finished? That doesn't make sense to me," Lucy replied, answering her own question.

"Jennifer told me that putting the movie aside was not an option. They were bound by their contracts to find a new director and finish it," Maggie said. She worked the swift quickly, creating small balls of yarn and snipping the thread every few minutes. She liked to see them piling up in the basket. It gave her a feeling of accomplishment.

"I guess we'll have to see if more physical evidence turns up. I'm sure the police are looking for Jennifer's rabid fan. He'd be my first choice, before Trina," Dana said. "No matter how ambitious she is."

"I have to agree," Maggie said. "I still wonder about the other events, though. Could the fan have caused the light fixture to fall, or set the fire in Heath's trailer? Were either of those events actually aimed at Nick? But he wasn't where the fan expected him to be, so he kept trying?"

"That would suggest that the person who poisoned Nick is close to the crew and cast . . . if not part of that group. Like Phoebe just said," Dana added.

"It does suggest that," Maggie agreed. "I don't know . . . maybe they were all random events. Just accidents. When you look at it logically, the light nearly hurt Jennifer and the fire could have hurt Heath. It would be a stretch to say Nick was the intended target in either of those situations."

"It would be a stretch," Lucy said around a spoonful of yogurt. "But it still seems odd that all these dangerous accidents have happened in such a short period of time. I think it's more than coincidence. But I can't see how the pieces fit."

Dana put her knitting down and placed tips on the needles, preparing to leave. "It's always fun to speculate with you guys. But I'm still glad we have the professionals to figure it out."

Maggie had to admit she felt the same.

She was even happier later that afternoon to learn that one of the professionals on the case was not obliged to work on the puzzle Saturday night, and was available for their date after all.

"Guess what, I don't have to work a double," Charles told her over the phone. "But I will be here late. What do you think? Do you still want to get together, have a late dinner or something?"

Maggie thought about it for only a moment. "Why don't I fix something for us at my house. That way we don't have to worry about being on time for a reservation. I'm sure you're tired and would like to relax."

"You got that right." Charles sounded happy but weary. "I'll bring some wine. Red or white?"

"White would be just right. I'm thinking fish."

"Sounds good to me," he said happily.

They set a time and Maggie planned the dinner. She was thinking fish, but was not even sure if Charles liked fish. Maybe he was just being polite. Though odds were, since he'd grown up in New England as she had, he did like it and ate all kinds without complaint.

Maggie wasn't sure what had come over her, offering the impulsive invitation. He'd been to her house, but she'd hadn't cooked for him yet. This would be the first time.

Weren't you supposed to fret and fuss a lot more over this dating milestone? Maggie hadn't dated all that much since her husband, Bill, had passed away. She did know she felt very relaxed with Charles, as if she didn't have to go out of her way to impress him. He always made her feel as if everything she did or said was absolutely charming . . . or at least intelligent. She felt as if he liked her just the way she was, no improvements or enhancements necessary. Maggie didn't need to date a parade of other men to know this was a special and rare thing.

Charles arrived a few minutes after nine. It looked as if he'd come straight from the office. With a brief stop at a wine shop. He opened the bottle and they sat down in the living room for appetizers—olives, cheese, and a fresh rosemary baguette, with a little bowl of herbed olive oil for dipping. Maggie had gone out of her way to pick up the bread at a special bakery, but it was well worth the trip and the calories.

"I know everyone is going gluten free. Jennifer Todd acts as if flour and sugar were poison now, too," she said. "But I do love a good piece of freshly baked bread now and again. It used to be called the staff of life."

"Everything in moderation. Including moderation," Charles

replied with a smile. "Thank goodness I'm not a movie star. I couldn't stand it."

"Me, either," Maggie agreed. "I heard that you had some very esteemed visitors at the police station today. Trina Hardwick and the film's new director."

"Oh right . . . Sam Drummond." Charles popped an olive into his mouth and chewed thoughtfully.

"Did you take their statements?" she asked curiously.

"We already got Hardwick's and Theo Pullman's."

"Theo Pullman was there? Lucy didn't mention him."

"Yes, he was in the delegation. Sort of a fifth wheel, seemed to me. They came to see how we were progressing with the investigation. I think it was more of a publicity stunt myself. But we humored them. The producer had a lawyer along. Not that she needed one. Just wanted to rattle my cage, I guess."

"Maybe she always travels with a lawyer. I don't think you should take it personally," Maggie advised.

He shrugged. "I knew they'd be on top of us. I wasn't surprised."

"But you have made progress. You found the bottle Nick drank from," Maggie reminded him.

He gave her a sharp glance. "Who told you that?"

A bite of bread nearly stuck in her throat. She covered her mouth with a napkin as she coughed. "I heard that in town . . . in the fish store," she fibbed, saying the first thing that came to mind.

Dana had told them not to repeat the information, or say where they'd heard about that evidence. Maggie was embarrassed she'd slipped.

"The fish store?" he squinted, not really believing her, she could tell.

"Everyone in town is talking about what happened. You must know that." Maggie shrugged. "I couldn't decide between shrimp or flounder. Maybe I should have asked if you were allergic to anything." A transparent bid to change the subject, Maggie knew, but he seemed to buy it.

His expression softened. "I'm not allergic to anything. Whatever you decided on smells delicious."

"It's almost done. I'll check it in a minute. Jennifer told me that Theo stands to get a larger credit for the screenplay, now that the script needs so much rewriting."

Charles selected another olive. But didn't reply.

"But he probably didn't poison Nick. That's just too obvious." She paused, hoping he'd jump in here and say if they suspected Theo, or didn't. But he didn't say a thing, just listened with a blank expression. "And why would he want to hurt his father?" she continued. "I got the impression Nick was giving his son a leg up on this project, trying to help Theo's career."

"Possibly," Charles said simply. His look suggested she could talk all night about the investigation, but he wasn't going to slip up and tell her anything.

"It is interesting, though, that Theo didn't go to Mass General today with Jennifer. Not that she mentioned it. And he wasn't there yesterday, either," Maggie added. "Jennifer told me that he's been working ever since Nick fell ill. But don't you think he'd want to see his father at some point? I didn't see him follow the ambulance on Thursday night, either. He didn't go with Jennifer—or in the car with Heath and Trina," she recalled.

"Maggie . . ." Charles shook his head. "You are a very

intelligent, observant, lovely woman. But I've been at this all day and was hoping for some diversion. Not shop talk," he said honestly. "You know I'm not allowed to talk about it anyway."

Maggie felt contrite. "I'm sorry. I get carried away. Let's not say another word. It was inconsiderate of me to go on like that. Let's see, there's a good film coming to the arts cinema. Nobody under investigation is starring in it. But it might be worth seeing. Next weekend maybe?"

He laughed. "That sounds like a plan. Provided this investigation is done." He paused and then sighed. "Okay. I will tell you one thing. The other night at your shop, Theo Pullman followed the ambulance in another car. He said O'Hara and Hardwick had left without him. Does that make you feel any better?

"Thank you. Yes, it does." She was grateful for at least one question answered. He smiled and shook his head, as if confounded by her interest in these details.

With all the flashing lights and activity in the street Thursday night, she obviously had not noticed Theo's car leaving. That was the problem with Theo. He was easy to overlook, so quiet and nondescript, easily blending in with the background. Especially among the flock of movie stars competing for attention. Lucy hadn't even noticed him walking into the police station today, eclipsed by the other celebrities.

Maggie didn't really suspect Nick's son of the heinous deed. Though it was true that most criminals hurt someone with whom they shared a close relationship, patricide required an awful lot of hatred and passion. Theo didn't really strike her as such a seething personality. Though it was often said that "still waters run deep" and she guessed it must have been hard to grow up in the shadow of a titanic figure like Nick Pullman, with his artistic sensibilities and hair-trigger temper. No wonder the young man was more comfortable laying low.

Who had poisoned Nick Pullman? Maggie only knew one thing for sure: She wasn't going to find out from Charles. Even if he did harbor some suspicions by now.

Chapter Eight

$\mathfrak{M}$ aggie had hoped to sleep late on Sunday. But the ringing phone jarred her awake. She peered at the clock on the side table as she fumbled for the receiver. It was barely six.

"Hello?" Her voice came out in a croak and she felt a dull headache, right between her eyes. The consequences of enjoying too much good wine and conversation with Charles. But they'd definitely enjoyed a perfect evening—after she'd stopped asking about his work.

"Maggie . . . did I wake you?" Suzanne was using her Minnie Mouse voice, a playful, apologetic squeak. Maggie could just picture her pinched expression.

"Of course you did . . . it's six in the morning. On Sunday."

"Is Charles there?" Suzanne asked in a mouse whisper.

"Suzanne . . . I can't believe you just asked me that." Maggie propped herself up on an elbow. "Wait . . . let me check . . ." She glanced over at the other side of the bed. "Nope. He's not here. I'll check under the bed, if you like."

"You know what I mean . . . sorry. I knew he was coming over for dinner, that's all."

Maggie sighed. "Is that why you called me? Sunday morning bed check? Did my house turn into a dorm in an all-women's college in 1952?"

Suzanne finally laughed. "I'm calling because Lyle Boyd is afraid of you."

"Afraid of me? Why on Earth would he be afraid of me?"

"Well . . . he's a nice guy and he knows how the movie using your shop as a location has not exactly gone as planned. And he knows how the contract said that they only needed it for one day and how that turned into two. But . . ."

"Saints preserve me, you're not trying to say that they want to come back to film again, are you? Please don't ask me that."

"They'd come over today and they'll leave by midnight. They really need to finish shooting that scene with Jennifer and Trina they were working on when Nick got sick, and two more they'd planned for the location shots. They'll be working at the beach house tomorrow and will leave town on Tuesday. Lyle said they'll pay you extra for the day," Suzanne added. "But if they have to shoot it back in the studio in California it will cost a lot to reproduce the interior—"

"You sound like an expert now," Maggie cut into Suzanne's speed-talk sales job. "Are you planning on ditching Plum Harbor for the Boulevard of Dreams?"

"Don't tempt me. The assistant director already told me I have 'unbelievable eyes.' He wants to use me in his next movie."

"They all say that. I'd watch myself."

"No danger. He looks about . . . thirteen," Suzanne clarified. "So, can I tell them it's okay? Think of Jen, all she's been through. She's involved in the business end of this movie, too. You'd be making it easier for everyone if you just say yes."

Maggie sighed and ran a hand through her bed-head hairdo.

"All right . . . do they still have a key?"

"I'm not sure. But I know where the spare is. I'll let them in. He said it's fine if you want to go over today and visit the set again. He'll put your name on the list. I might drop in around noon, after my appointment."

"I don't think so. Thanks. But you'd better warn Phoebe they'll be there. She's liable to wander down in her Hello Kitty pj's, snitching yarn for her sock orders."

"Will do," Suzanne promised.

At least she didn't have to make that call. Phoebe would be a cranky little cat, woken up at this hour.

"Thanks again, Maggie. You're a good sport."

"So they tell me."

Suzanne said good-bye and ended the call.

Charles walked into the room, carefully carrying a mug of coffee with two hands.

"I noticed you were up, so I brought you this." He handed her the mug and sat on the edge of the bed.

"Thanks. That was very thoughtful." Maggie smiled at him. She couldn't remember the last time anyone had brought her a cup of coffee in bed. "Maybe I will get up. It looks like a nice day. I can always take a nap later. I don't have much planned," she mused aloud.

"Good idea. I love to nap on Sunday. While reading the newspaper. Too bad I have to work, I'd join you." He smiled and flicked a curl off her forehead with his finger.

"That is too bad." She meant it, too. She smiled as he came

to his feet. Fresh from a shower, he had shaved and dressed. But hadn't put his tie on. He still had to run home and get some clean clothes. He was due at the station by seven for his shift.

"You can have a rain check . . . even though it's not raining."

"I'll remember that." He leaned over and kissed her quickly. Then smiled into her eyes again. "I'll call you later."

"Try my cell. I'm not sure where I'll be . . . Have a good day. Catch some bad guys," she added.

"I'll do my best."

She heard his footsteps on the stairs and the front door snapped shut. Then she heard him turn the knob, testing that it was locked. He was a police officer. Very security minded. Very caring, too.

She leaned back on the pillows and took a sip of coffee. Which was just right. He already knew how she liked it.

This relationship was advancing faster than she'd expected. But so far, it was just right, too.

Maggie had fully expected her friends to weasel that important information out of her via email or phone calls. Or even a surprise attack at the shop. But they must have been too busy on Monday to worry about her social life. Maybe because they'd all lost so much time the week before with their star gazing.

It was still cloudy on Tuesday morning, and a light rain fell. Maggie would have liked some sunshine, but reminded herself that her garden needed a good soak in order to bloom more.

Despite the wet weather, Lucy appeared with her canine pals in tow, marching down Main Street. The dogs were actually towing her. Nothing unusual there. Maggie watched from the porch as she unlocked the shop, then waited.

She and Lucy went inside together after Tink, the ever-panting golden retriever, and Wally, the three-legged chocolate Lab, were tied to a porch rail, and left to lap at a portable water bowl or snack on chew toys stuffed with treats.

Lucy was a sucker for the latest dog toys. The gadgets, most of them chewable, never failed to astound Maggie. Every possible contingency was covered.

Lucy followed Maggie into the shop. "Van Gogh isn't on the prowl this morning, is he?"

Van Gogh, Phoebe's cat, was a sweet-natured fellow, as felines went. But he had a habit of jumping into the window display to taunt the dogs through the glass. The dogs never failed to fall for his trick. You could hardly blame him.

"He's most likely still curled up on Phoebe's bed. Where she is still most likely curled up, too." Maggie glanced up at the ceiling, listening for Phoebe's light footsteps. Nothing yet. But it was barely eight.

Lucy followed Maggie into the storeroom and watched as she put on a pot of coffee. "I heard the movie people are leaving town soon. I'm sure you won't be sorry to see them go."

"No . . . I won't. But it was exciting having them here. In more ways than one," Maggie added. "Did you hear any more about Nick Pullman's condition? The TV news is already tired of the story. On to the next disaster, I guess."

"I did hear a sound bite. They say his condition is stable but still critical. Matt says his heart may be seriously dam-aged, especially since he already had a heart condition. And I spoke to Dana last night. Jack told her some interesting in-formation. The police lab has figured out that the drug found in Nick's drink, which reacted on his body like an overdose of heart medication, wasn't the typical compound produced by a pharmaceutical company. I think she said that medication is called digoxin, or digitoxin. It has a few names. Anyway, the digitalis they found in Nick's bloodstream was in a pure state." She tried to recall his exact words. "The way it's found in nature."

"Really? Digitalis is found in some blooming plants, like foxglove," Maggie said. "It's been used for centuries as a cure by the Native Americans. But it can also be deadly to people and animals."

"I didn't know that. I'll keep the dogs away from any foxglove plants."

"It's not blooming now, but it will come out later in the year," Maggie warned her. She shook her head. "That's an interesting and strange twist to the story. And Nick's poisoning has certainly cast a long shadow on this movie."

"I agree. I was here Sunday night to watch the filming again. I may have been imagining it, but the crew seemed very subdued, and the dynamics between the big shots was very different, too," Lucy said. "Suzanne didn't seem to notice," she added. "But I saw it pretty clearly."

Maggie smiled and sipped her coffee. "I love Suzanne . . . but subtle nuance in relationships is not her forte."

Lucy smiled. "Yes, she's more of a big love, or big hate, girl. That's for sure. But it seemed to me that when Jennifer and Nick were on the set Thursday night, they were the power center, calling the shots. Trina, and even Heath, were the second-string players. But with Nick gone and Trina's boyfriend directing, it looked like Jennifer has definitely lost leverage. It's hard to explain. It isn't as if anyone treated her disrespectfully," she added. "But I did see her disagree with the new director, and Regina Thurston had to smooth it out. He was also pushing through the script at the speed of light, compared to Nick."

"Interesting." Maggie cocked her head to one side, considering Lucy's observations. "Suzanne said they're on a super-tight schedule now. I'm not surprised he's pushing the actors. I'm curious to see how this film turns out. *If* it turns out," she added. "Seems to me, that's still a question."

"Speaking of questions and relationships, what's going on with Charles these days? Didn't you have the 'first time making him dinner at your house' date on Saturday?" Lucy's quick subject change threw Maggie a curve. She tried to hide her smile but really couldn't.

"We did. On the spur of the moment. We'd planned to go out, but he had to work late on the case."

"Oh right. Did he tell you anything interesting?" Lucy asked eagerly.

"Charles can be so tight-lipped. No fun at all . . . that way," she quickly clarified. "Dinner put him in a better mood. From the little he did say, it sounds like the police don't suspect Theo Pullman. Though I was going on about him. I made some flounder stuffed with shrimp," she continued, avoiding Lucy's impatient gaze. "I like to cook the shrimp a little first so they don't—"

Lucy made a time-out sign with her hands. "Enough recipe tips, Rachael Ray. How did the rest of the evening go . . . *after* dinner . . . and dessert?" she said with special emphasis. "Unless you came back downstairs for that?"

Actually, they did put dessert off, and came back down to the kitchen barefoot. Maggie smiled, remembering.

Lucy rarely hesitated sharing the private details of her life, but Maggie felt herself holding back. Not entirely fair, she knew. Natural shyness about these matters, perhaps. Or she was out of practice dishing on this topic; she was selective about her relationships reaching this stage.

Just as Maggie was about to disclose the whole story, the shop door opened. Suzanne flew in, a red trench coat swirling around her body, a black turtleneck and black jeans underneath. A very dramatic look, Maggie thought.

"I'm here . . . with news!"

"Quite an entrance."

"Thanks, I won't disappoint. I was just at the beach house."

"What was your excuse today?" Maggie cut in.

"I had to pick up *your* spare key . . . Thank you very much, Suzanne, for remembering," she mimicked Maggie's voice perfectly. "Lyle told me they'll be finished by five and I have to inspect the property and sign off before they leave . . . and guess what?"

Maggie couldn't imagine what she was going to say next. Clearly, neither could Lucy.

"There's a party tonight, to thank everyone they hired locally and give the crew and cast a morale boost. Lyle invited me and said you were invited, too. Since you were so nice to let them come back."

"So many times," Maggie added dryly.

"Is this what they call a wrap party?" Lucy asked.

"I think it's a prewrap . . . or a location wrap? They're not really finished with the movie. There are more scenes to shoot in a studio back in Hollywood. I wanted to go back today in time to see if they really say, 'It's a wrap!' You know, the way they always do in the movies?"

Maggie and Lucy nodded. Lucy was almost laughing.

"Though I do have other clients," Suzanne added.

"You'd never know it. I thought you went back to see your boyfriend, Heath. How's the romance going?" Lucy teased.

Suzanne shrugged. "Not that well. He was a little grouchy today. They were shooting that scene on the beach where he drowns. It was pretty cold in the water."

"Cold and dangerous, with the rough water in this weather. Don't they have stuntmen for that?" Lucy asked.

"For the long-distance shots, but he still had to jump in the water with his clothes on."

"And you were there for that . . . thoughtfully retrieving my key?" Maggie asked.

A dreamy look washed over Suzanne's face. She sighed. "Yes . . . I was. It's hard work, but somebody has to do it. Not only was he wet and cold, but he was also a little cranky from low blood sugar," she added. "Alicia said he's been terrified of eating anything since Nick was poisoned. Especially the food on the set. He decided it was a good time to try one of those liquid detox diets where all you can have is some lemonade drink you make yourself."

"I read about that. Looks like torture to me," Lucy confessed.

Maggie sighed. "I've read there's absolutely no need to 'detox' your body. That's why the good Lord gave everyone a liver."

"Believe me, I'm not about to try anything like that. I need something to chew on, or it's not pretty. I might feel differently, though, if I were a movie star," Suzanne mused.

"You fit right in with the beautiful people. No worries," Lucy assured her.

"Before we know it, you'll be moving to LA and selling zillion-dollar houses to celebrities," Maggie said with mock sadness.

"Please remember your friends back East . . . the little people?" Lucy added, jumping in.

"Don't worry, Little Person. 'No knitting pals left behind.' I talked Lyle into putting all of us on the guest list for the party. Isn't that great?" Suzanne practically clapped her hands with glee. "A real Hollywood party. Except it's not *exactly* in Hollywood."

"But not bad for our *first*," Lucy reminded her. "What time does it start?"

"Around six. They're going to be superstrict with the shooting schedule today. They have to get this in the can."

"As you film people say," Maggie murmured. Suzanne shot her a look, but was not dismayed.

"I'd say it's casual and quick. Drinks and appetizers. A few thank-you speeches. The big shots are heading to LA tonight."

"That sounds fun," Lucy said. "And I'd love to see the inside of that house."

"Worth the price of admission alone," Suzanne promised. She glanced at Maggie, in her sales mode again.

Maggie wasn't so eager to attend, but didn't want to disappoint Suzanne. "I'm a little tired for partying. Even in a spectacular house. Frankly, I'd feel out of my element. Are you sure it's all right for all of us to come?"

Maggie had gotten all the autographs she wanted, and she was supposed to see Charles after he left work, around nine. Though attending the party was still possible even with that complication.

But she didn't tell her friends about her date. She didn't

need to be double-teamed with questions. She'd just slipped out of Lucy's net.

"Maggie, stop acting so insecure. Lyle said there are going to be other local yokels there, too. Not that he used those words, exactly," she added quickly. "Some people from my office and others in town the crew has been doing business with. I bet you know a few."

"Oh . . . so the invitation isn't *that* exclusive?" Lucy cocked her head to one side. "I don't know. I'm not sure if I want to go now."

Suzanne glared at her with a fake mad face.

"Only kidding," Lucy promised.

Having closed that deal, Suzanne turned back to Maggie. "Maggie . . . don't be such a stick-in-the-mud. I thought you wanted to say good-bye to Jennifer."

"I do. That's true." The party could be interesting. Maybe they would hear more news about the investigation. More than she'd heard from Charles. She'd bet on that.

"All right. Why not? I've no doubts about Phoebe."

"Great. I already told Dana. She's in, too." Suzanne smiled, seeing all her ducks in a row. "Let's meet here. We all fit in my SUV. No sense taking ten cars."

That was a sensible idea. Maggie didn't even know where she was going. They arranged to meet at the shop at a quarter to six, so she'd have to close only a few minutes early.

As her friends left, Maggie felt cheerful, despite the rainy day. The local wrap party was certainly something different. She would have a good time with her friends, wherever they partied together.

Chapter Nine

By the time Suzanne's SUV had pulled up to the stunning beach house, the party was already in full swing. Maggie and her friends were checked by security, but hardly noticed as they slipped through the front door. Which was fine with Maggie. She felt gauche enough, attending a gathering that was really for the stars and crew. It was funny how Hollywood insiders considered it such an honor to let you socialize with them. And the locals tended to see it that way, too.

I'm being too harsh. It's my own insecurities, she reminded herself as she followed her friends into the crowd. She had to relax and have some fun. The people watching would certainly be worth the trip.

And so was the house.

Maggie had no idea why Suzanne kept calling the place a "beach house"—it was far from that. More of postmodern Taj Mahal by the sea. That's how she'd describe it.

They walked through a large, round foyer with a gray

marble floor to a main room with glass windows that must have been three stories high, framing a view of a large deck, and beyond that the blue-green ocean and rocky shoreline. The sun was setting later these days. Out over the sea, a dusky, lavender-gray light colored the clouds above the horizon. Mist and fog hung over the shoreline.

A large stone hearth and black marble mantel was set in between the windows in a swath of brown and tan stones that climbed to the ceiling. A curving staircase, set off by metal pipe rails, ran along the opposite side of the room and led to a balcony on the second floor, visible from the great room.

The space was filled with dark couches and chairs, a black lacquered baby grand piano, and a long, shiny black table that could have comfortably entertained . . . twenty?

"Look at that table. I could tweeze my eyebrows in the reflection," Suzanne murmured.

"Not that I'd want to . . . but it does seem possible," Lucy agreed.

Maggie didn't stop to consider the question. Her gaze darted around at the abstract paintings, sculptures, and other interesting touches as she and her friends wandered over to a table filled with food and drink.

The offerings were simple but expensive, just what she expected—a platter of cold seafood on shaved ice, crab claws and lobster chunks, raw clams and oysters, and huge shrimp. A tray of sushi and one of fancy cheeses and fresh fruit, artfully arranged.

Everything looked very tasty . . . but hardly a bite had been touched. Everyone was wary of falling to the same fate as poor Nick Pullman.

There was plenty of wine, imported beer, and sparkling water.

The screw tops on all the bottles were somewhat reassuring. Though reportedly, Nick Pullman's bottle had been sealed. Still, the bar was very popular and it took a few minutes to get a drink.

"This place does belong in a movie," Phoebe said under her breath as she daringly chomped on a cracker.

"If I had a house like this, I'd never rent it to a movie crew. They could have wrecked it," Lucy whispered back.

"But they didn't. Lucky for me," Suzanne said quickly. "I think Regina and Sam are going to say a few words, and then we can rub more shoulders with the stars again before they go. Like Heath. I love his shoulders. They're perfect." She gazed around, looking for her idol. "I haven't seen him yet, have you?"

Maggie hadn't spotted Heath O'Hara yet, either. She did see other familiar faces—Theo and Alicia talking by the window, Trina and Sam standing by a staircase on the other side of the room. And a few acquaintances from town—a guy who ran a car rental agency, and a friend of hers who owned a bakery. Helping her feel less of an interloper.

"Does everyone have a drink?" Sam called out in his booming, deep voice. He walked up a step or two, about to start his speech. "Regina and I want to take a moment to thank you all for pulling together to keep this production on track. No matter what was thrown at you." He shook his head in awe. "We can't thank you enough for the professionalism, focus, and going that extra mile, despite Nick's unfortunate health crisis. He's a greatly admired colleague and good friend," he added solemnly. "I know Regina shares my admiration and gratitude tenfold."

Was Sam Drummond actually Nick's good friend? News to Maggie, but it could be true. She did think the young director could easily jump in front of the camera. He was quite an actor and was putting this speech over in fine style.

He smiled and turned to Regina, who wore the same shapeless, but expensive-looking, black blazer and pants Maggie had seen her in since she'd arrived. The fabric did look as if it traveled well.

Her bobbed hairdo seemed particularly choppy tonight, going in a thousand directions at once. As if she'd stuck her finger in a light socket. Or maybe it was all the pressure she was under.

"But before she tells you that herself," Sam continued, "Jen, Trina, and Heath would like to say a few words."

He glanced around the room for the movie stars. Trina, who was never hard to find when a spotlight was shining, stood beside Regina. Maggie had not seen Jennifer in the crowd but noticed her now, standing by an arched entrance that opened to the foyer. Alicia stood next to her.

Theo wandered in from a doorway that led to the kitchen, a beer bottle dangling from one hand. He looked a bit windblown, his clothes damp, as if he'd been outside. A bit sullen and distracted, too. His usual demeanor—a moody writer thing.

Sam turned to Jen. "Would you like to start, Jen?"

Jen stepped forward, looking exhausted, Maggie thought.

"I don't have much to add. Except a heartfelt thank you for—"

Her speech was interrupted by a voice on the balcony. All heads looked up.

"Help, somebody! Call 911 . . . It's Heath . . . he's really sick . . . he's having a convulsion or something . . ."

Sam, still on the staircase, was the first one to rush up, followed by Regina and Trina, and finally Jennifer, who ran from across the room. Maggie pulled out her phone, but others had beat her to it, already calling for an ambulance.

"What happened to that first-aid person they had on the set?" Maggie asked Suzanne. "I don't see her here."

"I heard she left when the filming finished," Suzanne said. "Her assignment was over and she didn't want to stay for the party." She sounded scared.

"That's too bad. But help will come soon," Maggie said hopefully.

The waterfront community was far from the village and the fire station. It was even far from the fire department annex, built a few years ago so calls in the outer areas of Plum Harbor could be covered faster.

But help would come soon. Heath would be all right, she told herself. There was no reason to panic. Even though Nick Pullman's near-fatal poisoning shadowed everyone's thoughts.

"What do you think happened? What should we do?" Phoebe looked frightened as she turned to her friends.

"I don't know . . . Oh geez . . . I hope he's okay." Suzanne looked sincerely worried.

"Does anyone know if he has some chronic condition, like diabetes or epilepsy? It could be something related to that, a mistake with medication," Dana suggested.

"Or that stupid diet he went on. I hope it's that simple. But I've never heard he was sick," Suzanne replied.

"It wouldn't be widely known. Let's hope it's that simple." Maggie touched her hand.

The party had turned into a scene of confusion and panic. Lyle Boyd stood on the steps with his hand stretched out.

"Please stay downstairs. We have enough people up here now," he said grimly. "Everything's under control."

Despite his assurances, Maggie had a bad feeling, a queasy knot in her stomach. It didn't sound like things were under control. Not one bit.

She looked over at her friends, huddled together, not saying a word.

Finally, she heard a siren. The front door opened and two police officers rushed in. One ran upstairs while the other stood on the steps, asking Lyle questions.

Maggie tried to overhear their conversation. She couldn't help it.

Suddenly a bloodcurdling scream pierced the air.

Everyone stopped, then stood motionless and silent. The sound had come from the second floor, followed by heartbreaking sobs.

Maggie thought she recognized Jennifer's voice, choked with sobs as she spoke. "Oh my God, no! . . . Heath! . . . Oh God. Please . . . not Heath . . ."

Her voice was suddenly muffled. Maggie stood in shock as the sound level in the room rose instantly.

"What did she say?"

"Is he dead?"

"Is Heath really dead? That isn't possible . . ."

"I didn't hear her say *that* . . ."

Everyone was talking at once, asking the same question. Including her friends.

"He can't be dead." Suzanne looked dumbstruck. So did Phoebe. "There must be some mistake," she insisted.

"I don't even want to know. It's too sad." Phoebe covered her face with her hands.

Dana and Lucy both looked pale and shaken, but were holding up a little better. They glanced at her. Then Dana put her arm around Phoebe.

"We have to wait and see what's going on. We don't know yet if it's true. Though it doesn't sound good," Dana admitted.

Lucy stepped over to Suzanne and did the same, but she didn't say anything. Suzanne looked very upset, her dark head bowed.

Two more officers had entered the house and another ran upstairs. Maggie heard an ambulance siren and EMS technicians rushed through the open front door. A police officer stationed there directed them to the second floor and the crowd parted to let them pass.

Maggie released a long breath. The wait had been agonizing, though it had only been a few minutes.

Moments later, a police officer stood at the balcony. He spoke with grave authority and a thick Boston accent. "I'm sorry to announce that there's been a fatality on the premises. I have to ask everyone to remain here until an officer takes down your name and contact information. We'll be asking you all a few questions. We hope to get through this difficult situation as quickly as possible, with your cooperation."

"A 'fatality'? That means Heath is dead!" Suzanne was shocked to her core. "Poor Heath . . . That beautiful man. He's really gone. I can't believe it . . ."

She covered her mouth with her hand and stared into space with blank, glassy eyes.

Maggie didn't know what to say. She was completely shocked, too. And completely confused.

"Do you think the ambulance will take him away now?" Phoebe asked quietly. She was weeping. "I don't want to see that."

"It might be a while before they move him." Dana glanced around at her friends. "Considering what happened to Nick Pullman, I'd say the police are going to handle this carefully."

"I guess we're stuck here for a while. This house might be considered another crime scene before the night is over," Lucy guessed.

Maggie sighed, trying to remember why she had agreed to come to the party in the first place. But, looking over at her friends, she was glad in a way to be here with them, to share even this dark, sad moment.

Of course, none of them had really known Heath O'Hara. But they'd all felt as if they did. That was the funny thing about movie stars and other celebrities. It was so easy to be touched by their personalities and charisma, even at a great distance.

Long before they'd met Heath on the movie set last week, he'd won them over. And face-to-face, his charm was practically irresistible. Even the hardest female heart was not immune to a matinee idol of his caliber. Maggie knew that they all felt as shocked and mournful as if they'd known him well.

Her friends decided to look for seats while they waited for the police interview. That wasn't too hard, even with the large crowd. The room was nearly the size of an airport lounge, with just as much seating.

Maggie had just settled in when she saw the front door open again. Charles walked in and showed his badge to the officer guarding the door. Two other men in suits followed and did the same. Maggie guessed they were detectives on his team.

At first she was happy to see him. Then she wondered if he'd be happy to see her.

He clearly didn't like to mix business with pleasure, and liked to leave his work in the squad room when they were together. He'd been trying hard to discourage her interest in this case, and here she was, a potential witness to another tragedy. This one, even more serious than Nick Pullman's poisoning.

Maybe her natural attraction to crime scenes was going to give him second thoughts about their relationship?

Golly . . . she hoped not.

"Look, there's Charles." Lucy, who sat beside her on the couch, gave her a nudge.

"Yes, I noticed . . . and things between us were going so well," she sighed.

"Why do you say that?"

"Let's just say he's not wild about my interest in his work," she said simply. "First man I ever met in that category. Usually, you ask one question and they'll go on for hours."

"He can't blame you for being here. We were all invited."

"Yes, I know. And I don't mean to make him sound so rigid," she said, trying to explain. "It's just a little awkward . . . or could be."

Charles had gone straight upstairs with one of the other detectives. Meanwhile, a woman at the door in a white contamination suit showed the police officer her badge, then carried in a large black case. She had an assistant, a younger man who also showed his badge and carried in more equipment.

"The medical examiner," Dana told them. "She'll try to determine the cause of death. If it's natural causes, this won't turn into another investigation."

"Or dovetail into the search for the person who poisoned

Nick Pullman," Lucy said. "They haven't made much progress with that."

"True . . . but they've got some leads," Dana whispered back.

Maggie wondered if Dana knew anything more than she did, about the uncommon purity of the digitalis found in Nick's body. Jack was certainly more chatty at home than Charles was. Then again, he and Dana were married. She and Charles might not even be dating after tonight.

An officer who had been working his way around the room with a pad and pen reached their corner and they each spoke to him in turn, giving their name and address and contact information. And explaining how and why they were at the party.

Maggie had just finished when she spotted Charles coming down the stairs. He spotted her, too, and she stood. Their eyes met and his widened. Not a good sign, she thought as he walked straight toward her.

"Maggie . . . What are you doing here?" he asked quietly.

"Don't you mean, *again*?"

His head tilted to one side as he waited for a serious reply.

Maggie sighed and explained how Suzanne had been invited by the location manager and she'd persuaded him to include her friends.

Charles looked down at the couch, noticing the group, sitting like birds on a wire, huddled together as they waited for the rain to stop.

"What a terrible night. What a tragedy," she said to Charles.

"Yes . . . it is. No question."

"How did he die, do you know yet?" she asked quietly. Wondering if he'd tell her.

"The ME isn't sure. Even if we had any information, I couldn't say," he reminded her.

"Yes . . . I know. Didn't mean to put you on the spot," she said quickly. "We'll probably hear something on the news later."

"You might," he agreed. Charles rubbed his forehead. "Considering Nick Pullman's situation, we can't rule anything out right now."

"Yes, of course. It's awful. No matter how it happened. Heath was really very sweet. Despite all his fame and movie idol image." Maggie covered her mouth with her hand. "He was so nice to us at the set last week. He didn't have to be," she reflected sadly.

Maggie had the impression that Heath's good points far outweighed any flaws. His untimely death, no matter what the cause, seemed so unfair.

Charles touched her shoulder a moment. She got hold of herself quickly. He was about to say something more when he turned to look at the stairs. Regina, Sam, and Trina were coming down, followed by a police officer. Jennifer, Alicia, Theo, and Lyle followed with another officer walking behind them.

"I have to go. That group is going to the station to give statements."

"Of course. Another long night," she said sympathetically.

"It will be," he sighed. They had plans to get together at nine, when he got off work. But it wasn't even a question anymore.

"I'll call you tomorrow." He briefly touched her hand.

Maggie met his glance. "Whenever you get a chance. I'll be around."

"You'd better get out of here as soon as you can. I think we're going to be pounded by a horde of reporters any minute."

"Okay, we will," she promised.

Charles said good-bye and left to consult with another detective in the foyer. Maggie joined her friends.

"A police officer said once we give our information, we can go," Phoebe told her.

"Charles said we'd better go, too," Maggie told her friends.

Suzanne was crying, dabbing her eyes with a tissue. "I guess there's nothing left to do here. I still can't believe it . . . Poor Heath."

No one answered. Maggie knew they all felt the same.

As Maggie and her friends headed to Suzanne's SUV, they encountered a flow of reporters coming toward the house. The media had already gotten hold of the story.

Guests at the house must have gone online using their phones and posted news of the tragedy on Facebook, Twitter, and other social media. It didn't take long in this information age for news like this to spread.

When the group reached Suzanne's vehicle, a man with press tags hanging around his neck stopped Dana. Another with a video camera on his shoulder trotted close behind. "Were you just inside, ma'am? Did you see anything? Did you see Heath?" he asked bluntly.

"Not a thing," she said shortly.

"Go away. We don't want to talk to you," Suzanne shouted at them.

The question had started her crying again.

The reporter showed no reaction to her harsh tone. Just waved his hand at his burdened companion and continued toward the house.

They climbed into the SUV and shut the doors.

"I can drive if you want me to," Lucy offered.

"I'm okay, just give me a minute." Suzanne took a deep

breath and wiped her eyes. "Poor Heath . . . Who in the world did this to him? It's so senseless. Such a waste."

"He was so young and strong. And beautiful," Lucy added.

"This is so wrong," Dana sighed.

Maggie felt the same. Heath O'Hara was a beautiful bloom, in the height of his glory.

Had he died a natural death? Or had someone cut him down much too soon?

Chapter Ten

ℳaggie watched the late-night news before she went to sleep Tuesday night, and flicked through the stations showing early news the next morning. The airwaves were full of stories about Heath O'Hara's surprising, tragic death and reactions from his fans, fellow actors, and movie business colleagues.

The video footage showed the big house at the beach. Piles of flowers, signs, and candles had already appeared on the side of the road, all along the yellow police tape.

But there was scant information about the precise cause. Some reporters made a glancing connection to Nick Pullman falling ill from poison just a few days before. With no hard evidence or facts, they could only raise a big question mark as to whether these events were connected. Or whether it was just a case of the most unlucky movie project in the history of Hollywood.

"Three Penny Productions could not be reached for comment, but it is widely speculated that the filming of *Love Knots*, the project O'Hara was working on when he died, will be suspended indefinitely."

The movie . . . that seemed the last thing on anyone's mind right now. But that was true—how could they finish the film without a key star? It was Maggie's understanding that many scenes were left to finish in the Hollywood studio. Even drastic rewriting and computer magic could not fix this situation. News had leaked to the press that Heath O'Hara had been on a liquid detox diet—the homemade lemonade "cleansing" drink Suzanne had mentioned. Some news outlets were speculating that the diet brew had inflicted fatal consequences. Hence, a parade of medical talking heads were interviewed, cautioning the public on the dangers of fad diets.

Maggie clicked off the TV and headed to town. The diet sounded like self-inflicted torture. But deadly? She doubted it.

If Heath had died from this liquid regime, he'd be the first confirmed case, after hundreds of thousands, possibly millions, had tried it.

That didn't seem plausible. More plausible, the frightening thought that along with the lemonade diet drink, Heath had swigged down some poison. Just like Nick Pullman. Maybe even the same type?

Even if the news outlets were not free to connect the dots here, she hoped the Essex County detectives did.

The weather had cleared and a bright, breezy, classic spring day greeted her. As she parked by the shop, she didn't find Phoebe's yellow Bug in its usual spot on the drive next to the shop, then remembered Phoebe had an early class on Wednesdays. But her assistant would be in the shop later, which was good. Maggie didn't feel her usual energy today.

She headed up the path to the porch, the scent of blooming hyacinth nearly overwhelming, their dark purple heads bobbing alongside the bright daffodils.

Pansies. Definitely needed now to brighten up the beds—blue, purple, yellow, peach, and white, to complement the flowering bulbs. Maybe some in the window boxes, too, though they didn't last long when the weather turned warmer.

Maggie felt cheered, despite dark thoughts about Heath that lingered like smoky clouds in the corners of her mind. Life goes on, as they say. But this poor boy's life was cut short so quickly.

Just as she expected, Lucy appeared a short distance down Main Street, pulled along by her dogs. Suzanne had just pulled up in her SUV and both arrived at the gate together.

Lucy looked as if she'd processed the loss of her movie star crush. But Suzanne still seemed deflated and blue. She was dressed in a dark blue sweater and gray slacks, with her hair pulled back and hardly any makeup or jewelry. A very un-Suzanne look.

Maggie waited for them on the porch and they walked into the shop together, then headed straight to the back. Suzanne and Lucy settled in at the table while she made coffee.

"What a nightmare this deal turned out to be," Maggie heard Suzanne moan. "The owners of the house are calling every minute. They wanted the property to get some publicity. But they weren't thinking of a movie star dying there." Her tone was dry and sarcastic . . . and annoyed.

"Who would?" Lucy said. "I thought you might be here. I brought you something from the bakery." Maggie came in just in time to see Lucy push a small white bag across the table.

"A chocolate croissant? Lucy, how sweet. My favorite breakfast." Suzanne looked inside and sighed. But surprisingly, closed it again. "I'll have it later. I've lost my appetite."

Maggie was worried now. Lucy seemed so, too. "Are the

police still at the house? Are they saying it's a crime scene?" Lucy asked.

Suzanne sighed. "They called me in the middle of the night. But they didn't release the news yet. I guess because he's so famous, they're trying to keep a tight hold on the case. They said Heath definitely did not die of natural causes."

"Wow . . . you're like the first person in town to know. That's a big secret to keep," Lucy said in awe.

"Yeah . . . I know. I didn't even tell Kevin yet. But I had to tell you guys, right?"

"What about the movie people? Where are they? What about all their equipment and trailers, and all that?"

"The trucks and trailers are still parked right in front of the house. Where they left them. The neighbors are loving that." Suzanne rolled her eyes. "But the police won't let them move anything yet. They have to search every inch of everything. And the movie people have to stay in town. I bet they're all out at the inn, hiding out from the press."

"What did the police find . . . did they say? Maybe we should turn the TV on?" Lucy asked.

Dana had come in so quietly no one had noticed her. "Hi, guys," she greeted them.

"We were just talking about Heath. Suzanne says it was foul play. But the police haven't told the press yet."

"Yes, I know." Dana sat down with a large coffee cup and took out her knitting. She seemed the only one interested in stitching this morning. Including me, Maggie realized. Though she did need to get supplies ready for a class.

"Chief Nolan, is giving a news conference at eleven," Dana told them. "But Jack just sent me a text. It wasn't the diet drink. It was—"

"Poison," Maggie finished for her. "Sorry. I stole your thunder, right?" she said in a quieter voice.

Dana smiled, not caring a bit. "It was poison. But nothing ordinary, like arsenic, or chlorine. His body reacted to a concentrated dose of something called . . ." She had to pull out her phone to get the chemical name straight. "Lycorine. Jack says it's an 'alkaloid that affects the digestive and nervous system.'"

Dana looked up again. "I had to call him to get the whole story. Apparently, it's not a fast-acting poison. But Heath must have mistaken the early symptoms of the toxin for effects of his juice fast—dizziness, nausea, stomach upset . . ."

Suzanne sat up and waved her hands with excitement. "Heath was sick, just like that, when I was at the set yesterday. Sam was really angry because Heath kept running back to his trailer. He must have been sick all day and thought it was from the diet drink. 'Where the hell is Heath? He's making us fall behind schedule,' Sam kept yelling." Suzanne did a very good imitation of the substitute director. "But at one point, both Heath and Trina were missing in action. Neither of them came back from a break. I wondered if something was going on again." Suzanne paused to give her friends a meaningful look. "But maybe she was just resting. Alone. Sam Drummond was putting those actors through their paces the last day of filming. They could have read the phone book. He would have shouted, 'Cut! Great job! Brilliant!'"

"He was obviously hired to finish the picture quickly and stay on budget. No matter how it turns out." Lucy sipped her coffee and glanced out at her dogs. Maggie could see their furry heads by the window. At least they weren't making marks with their noses. Not yet.

"I'm going to search it. Lycorine . . . Let's see what we find." Lucy happily took hold of Maggie's laptop, which was sitting on the table alongside the coffeepot. She typed for a moment, then peered at the screen.

"Wikipedia says it's 'a toxic crystalline alkaloid.'" She looked up at her friends. "Whatever that means. I avoided chemistry in high school at *any* cost."

"And hid out in the art room?" Maggie guessed. She'd always had a circle of art room groupies hiding out there.

"How did you guess?" Lucy answered without looking up.

"What else does it say? Anything in plain English?" Suzanne peered over her shoulder. She was eager to know what had killed her true love.

"Yes, it does. Listen. ' . . . found in various'—three-inch Latin term here I can't even pronounce, sorry—'species, such as cultivated bush lilies, surprise lilies, and daffodils, also called narcissus . . . highly poisonous or lethal when ingested in certain quantities. Symptoms include diarrhea, vomiting, convulsions, and paralysis . . .'" Lucy's voice trailed off. She seemed suddenly sad, not nearly as eager to read the rest of the entry.

"I think we have the idea," Maggie said softly.

Lucy shook her head, pushing a strand of hair behind her ear. "It's all right. There's more. 'Daffodil bulbs are sometimes confused with onions. Leading to accidental poisoning.'"

She looked up at her friends again, her expression bleak and drained. "What do you think? Did the same person who slipped digitalis in Nick's drink somehow feed Heath daffodil bulbs?"

"It would have been harder than drugging a drink," Dana pointed out. "But possible."

"The diet drink is made of fresh lemon juice, maple syrup, and cayenne pepper," Suzanne recalled. "I think a flavor combo like that could cover up nail polish remover."

"I suppose. But even if someone managed to sneak into

Heath's trailer and tamper with his spicy lemonade brew, wouldn't he have noticed chunks of daffodil bulbs floating around his glass? It's clear liquid. Not a hide-all-sins, smoothie sort of drink," Dana argued.

"Did you ever try one of those do-or-die diets?" Suzanne paused. "You're looking at the champ. I can't even read the guidelines before I'm craving a big, fat cheeseburger, smothered with mushrooms and onions. What if he fell off the detox wagon and secretly called Burger Heaven, for a cheat meal delivery?"

"Or ordered onion rings. Perfect diet cheat food," Lucy chimed in.

"The poisonous bulbs could have been slipped into his food that way," Maggie agreed. "But that sounds too compli-cated. Was this killer standing around with a secret container of sliced and sautéed daffodil bulbs . . . and slipped a few spoonfuls on this secret hamburger?"

"I think Jack said his stomach was pumped and it appears Heath was no diet cheater. Nothing else was found but the ingredients of the lemonade . . . and the poison."

"So somehow the poison was extracted from the bulbs?" Maggie pondered aloud.

"I only read aloud one article about it. Maybe there were never any actual daffodil bulbs involved. Maybe this diabolic person got the poison someplace else. In a bottle or something." Lucy looked around at her friends to see what they thought.

"In a poison store, you mean?" Suzanne asked with a small smile.

"Lucy's right. The actual flowers didn't have to be involved. Nick was poisoned with digitalis, which is also found in cer-tain flowers," Maggie reminded them. "But it's extracted for heart medication by pharmaceutical labs."

"So are we looking for someone who's a chemist or knows about that stuff?" Suzanne asked.

"I don't know . . . I think a knowledge of chemistry would be helpful. But people who like gardeners know a lot about flowers," Maggie replied. "And flowers are used so much in paintings and literature as symbols."

"The Victorians even communicated with one another following something called *The Language of Flowers.* Gifts of bouquets and cards with flower illustrations carried a special message from the sender to the person who received it," Lucy recalled. "Violets, for instance, meant faithfulness and purity. Roses meant love, of course."

"What do daffodils mean?" Suzanne asked.

"I'm not sure . . . but I can look it up," Lucy offered quickly.

"I have a thought," Maggie said while Lucy typed quickly. "Daffodils are also called narcissus, from the Greek myth. Let's see . . . Narcissus was a beautiful but very vain young man, who rejected a wood nymph, Echo. She was in love with him, but he had no sympathy for her. So he was condemned by the gods to fall in love but never have his loved returned. He looked into a pool of water and fell in love with his own reflection, and lived the rest of his life in torment, trying to grasp the false image, while it melted in his hands."

"Hence the psychological term narcissistic personality disorder," Dana added in a far less poetic tone. "It's hard to explain the term in a few words, but basically, people who are narcissists are grandiose, attention seeking, lack empathy, and are focused only on satisfying their own needs."

"The way you might expect a movie star to be?" Lucy asked quietly. "Acting like the world revolves around them?"

"Yes, exactly," Dana answered.

"But Heath wasn't that way at all," Suzanne insisted.

"No, he wasn't. Not with us," Maggie recalled. "Though I did expect him to be much the way you just described, Dana," she admitted.

"I bet a lot of people did," Dana agreed. "It's impossible to say from briefly meeting him, but I didn't get the feeling he was extremely self-centered."

"What happened to Narcissus? Did he just hang out at the edge of the pond, staring at himself? Or did he jump in and go for it?" Suzanne asked.

"I don't remember." Maggie turned to Lucy, who had found an entry for the term.

"This entry says, 'He didn't move. He didn't eat or drink. He only suffered. As he pined, he became gaunt and lost his beauty and died. His body disappeared and in its place, flowers grew. The wood nymphs mourned his death.'"

Suzanne was glassy eyed again and sniffed into a tissue. "I'm sorry now that I asked."

"I'm sorry I read it aloud," Lucy admitted. "But it does tell us something. I'm going to look up the poison that was in Nick's drink."

"Digitalis," Maggie reminded her.

"Right . . . got it." Lucy looked up at them. "It not only comes from foxglove, it's also found in lily of the valley. Highly toxic. Every part of the flower, especially the red berries. But just like foxglove, they aren't in season around here now. Not until May."

"And it's very expensive if you try to order it at a florist. Brides sometimes choose it for wedding bouquets. It's very traditional. It was in Princess Kate's bouquet, I think," Dana recalled.

"You can find it, I suppose. If you're willing to pay . . ." Maggie's voice trailed off. Was she the only one who remembered the big bouquet of lily of the valley in Jennifer's trailer?

Why wasn't she reminding her friends of that? And Jennifer's knowledge of gardening . . . and the way she'd recited the poem about the daffodils?

But before she could speak, Dana said, "Jennifer Todd had a bouquet of lily of the valley in her trailer, remember? She said it was her favorite flower and people sent her bunches of them."

"Yes, I remember," Maggie said firmly. "She said Regina Thurston had sent her that one, to wish her luck with the movie. She knows a lot about flowers, too," she added. "She was talking to me about gardening the other day."

Maggie hated to cast aspersions on Jennifer. She wasn't sure why; there was just something about her that she liked, a genuine connection. Still, these connections were undeniable, too.

"Everyone in the world knows she likes flowers. You just have to read one interview. The stalker sent her bouquets all the time," Suzanne reminded them. "Maybe he's behind all this, trying in some twisted way to send Jennifer a message. Maybe he thinks he's a Victorian gentleman?" She offered the joke in a halfhearted tone.

Dana put her knitting down. "You might be on to something. Nick and Heath were the two most important men in Jennifer's life. The stalker must have seen them as rivals for Jennifer's affection. Anyone who leaves anonymous notes and gifts is certainly a passive-aggressive type."

"It makes sense that he would try to get all his competition out of the way, in order to have Jennifer all to himself."

Suzanne's voice rose, excited by the theory. She looked around at the others. "Do you think the police see this? That could be it."

"I think it's someone from Jen's past. Someone she knew while growing up around here. The flowers he left on the porch that night were yellow and blue, the colors of Newburyport High School. I told Charles," Maggie added. "I hope he took me seriously."

"I know they're looking for the stalker," Dana assured her. "It's definitely an important line of investigation."

Suzanne sat back but didn't seem entirely satisfied. If she could go out and find Heath O'Hara's killer herself, Maggie knew she would. A lot of his fans probably felt the same.

"I've got some information on digitalis . . . want to hear it?" Lucy's head popped up again. She was eager to share her findings.

"Go on. But you'd better hurry. It's getting late." Maggie glanced at the shop door. The sign still said "Resting our needles now . . . Please come see us again," though it was almost nine. They'd been so engrossed in their conversation customers might have knocked already and she wouldn't have noticed.

"We already know about the physical effects of the drug," Lucy said, skimming down the page. "But there are two legends, both interesting. A Christian legend says that the flower sprung up from the tears of Eve when she was driven from the Garden of Eden. And another, that it grew from the tears of the Blessed Virgin Mother when Jesus Christ died." Lucy looked up at her friends. "Two very dark tales for such a light, fragrant flower."

"I'll say," Suzanne agreed.

"I just thought of something else," Dana said. "Remember when I said I saw Jennifer play Ophelia in *Hamlet*? During

Ophelia's famous soliloquy, she hands out flowers to her family and says what each symbolizes—'rosemary for remembrance, pansies for thoughts.' That's all I can remember," Dana admitted. "When she's done speaking, she drowns herself."

"Ugh . . . no wonder I can't stand great theater . . . or opera," Suzanne added.

"A lot to ponder," Maggie said quietly. "I will say that I'll look at my Spring Fling: Felted Flowers Class much differently now. I didn't realize my students were sending secret messages with the finishing touches on their projects."

Dana had gathered up her knitting and coffee cup and was getting ready to go. "It is a lot to consider, and we don't even know if the person doing this has any knowledge of all these symbols and legends. Maybe they picked toxic ingredients they knew about and found handy."

Lucy stood up and looked outside, to make sure her dogs were all right. Still there. Maggie hoped they hadn't preferred the wicker chairs to their chew toys.

"Maybe. But I think these toxic ingredients are too obscure . . . and eccentric," Lucy said. "The digitalis would be ordinary, if it had been smashed-up pills. But it wasn't in that form, right, Maggie?"

"No, it wasn't. Charles told me it wasn't from a pharmaceutical lab. It was in a pure state."

"And the other poison is just bizarre," Lucy concluded. "Daffodil bulbs? I think there's some meaning here. Some special message."

Maggie felt the same. "A repeating theme of love and loss, if you think about the subtext of all these myths."

"Oh boy . . . you guys are just too literary and highbrow for me. I feel like I'm in a college lit class again. But I can't stay for extra help," Suzanne said with sigh. "I have to call the house owners and report in. And hope the police don't tear the house apart. Who knows when they'll be done? The movie company did such a good job of keeping everything nice and clean . . . and unscratched. I thought I was home free."

Maggie felt sorry for Suzanne. Not just because of her work pressures. Anyone who had been to the gathering last night would find it very hard to return to the grand house on the beach, which she was bound to do, eventually. She was fairly certain that's what Suzanne was really upset about.

Lucy seemed to sense that, too. "Hey, want me to take a ride out there with you?"

Suzanne was surprised at the offer. "Would you? . . . You're probably too busy . . ."

"I can come. Honest. I just turned in a project and I'm looking for excuses to get out of my office. I'd just be cleaning the house or at the gym . . . Maybe we can take a walk on the beach or something, if you don't have to rush back to town."

"That might be a good thing for me," Suzanne admitted.

"Oh . . . if you don't mind the dogs in your car?" Lucy added.

"Are you kidding? The dogs would be an improvement over the groups I'm usually carting around. Did you ever chauffeur an entire soccer team of eleven-year-old boys? Maybe the dogs can clean up all the stale fries on the floor back there."

"I'll ask them to work on it," Lucy promised.

Maggie was glad Suzanne would have company. It had been sweet of Lucy to offer. She was a sympathetic soul. Maggie would have offered herself if Phoebe had been around to cover. As it was, just as her friends left, knitters in the morning class drifted in: Booties, Bibs, and Beyond. A perfect class to teach in the spring, she always found, when new life seemed to be bursting all around.

Phoebe returned from school just as the group left. She came straight into the shop and dumped her knapsack onto the counter.

"Did you hear? The police chief is going to hold a press conference in like . . . two minutes. Want to watch upstairs? Or I could DVR it for you."

Maggie hated to lose even one customer, but this situation was too tempting. The shop was empty; maybe it would stay that way for a few minutes more.

"Okay, you turn on the TV, I'll be right up."

She locked up the register but decided to leave the shop door open when she ran upstairs.

"It's starting!" Phoebe called to her.

Maggie hustled up the back stairway just in time to see the Essex County chief of police, Rusty Nolan, behind a podium and microphone. Maggie wondered if she would catch a glimpse of Charles. Was he there with the other detectives? Maybe not; maybe they were working steadily while Rusty got all the glamour.

Chief Nolan quickly reviewed the specifics of Heath O'Hara's death. No news there, since they were both on the scene. "Toxicology tests have confirmed a high level of a chemical compound, lycorine, was present in Mr. O'Hara's body at the time of his death. Lycorine is a highly toxic substance that affects the digestive and nervous system. Early reports of the medical examiner state that Mr. O'Hara suffered convulsions and paralysis, brought on by lycorine poisoning, resulting in his death."

He added a short coda about the investigation, how they were working around the clock with a team of detectives on several leads and expected to have more news to release soon. "That's all I can report at this time, due to the delicate nature of this case. We will report any significant progress as soon as we're able, believe me." He paused and looked to the side, as if waiting for a sign. "All right . . . I can take a few questions."

Rusty didn't seem that happy to be making the offer, but Maggie suspected he'd been advised to put himself on the hot seat. She could hear his pants sizzle.

"So, you're changing the cause of death and stating now that Heath O'Hara did not die from a diet drink. Is that so?"

"We never said O'Hara died from the diet drink. Some of you folks in the press said that." Rusty could be tough when he needed to be, Maggie had to grant him that. "The investigators said they didn't know. We know now and I just told you."

His Boston accent grew more pronounced when he got agitated, that was for sure.

A hundred hands or more immediately shot up in front of the weathered police chief.

"Has the investigation connected the poisoning of Nick Pullman with O'Hara's death?"

"We have no evidence to connect the incidents. Of course, we're looking into every possibility . . . Next?"

"Can you tell us something about Jerome Nesbit?" the reporter shouted out. "Is he the prime suspect now?"

Rusty's face turned fire engine red. He cast a sidelong glance at someone standing next to the podium, just beyond the frame of the camera. A press secretary for the department? His flustered expression said, "Who the heck leaked that?"

Then he coughed with his hand over his mouth, his expression blank.

"Mr. Nesbit is considered a person of interest," he replied, leaning into the microphone. "He's being interviewed this morning at the Essex County Police Station . . . Thank you, ladies and gentlemen. No more questions," he added gruffly. He ducked his head and hurried off.

Phoebe and Maggie stared at each other. Phoebe clicked off the TV. "Wow! I bet that Jerome guy is Crazy Fan! Who else could he be?"

Maggie had the same thought. She hoped he was. That would make it all simple and easy. Heath's family, friends, and fans could continue their grieving and have a sense of closure.

"I guess we'll know soon. It doesn't take long for the police to find enough evidence to make an arrest, once they focus in on the guilty party. Maybe he'll confess."

"He might. I'm picturing a really nerdy guy with pale skin. Probably lost most of his hair already, though he's not really old. Oh, and a weak chin," Phoebe added.

Maggie had to smile. "I guess we'll see . . . I'd better go back down. The shop can't stay empty all day."

"I'll be right there. I just want to Google this guy's name . . . see if I can find a picture."

Maggie wished that Phoebe would come down and help now . . . and pay a little more attention to her official schedule. But Phoebe often worked overtime and put in lots of extra effort in different ways, so Maggie was rarely a clock-watching manager.

Luckily, no one had wandered into the shop while she was upstairs. Two young women with toddlers in strollers did roll in moments after she returned. Close call, she thought.

They both wanted to learn how to knit, but weren't sure where to start. Maggie showed them some projects from her beginner classes, including the summer tank top that her knitting group and Jennifer Todd were making, and the felted flower totes. She left the women in the little alcove to chat and decide.

Phoebe had come down with her laptop and set it on the counter. "Look at this . . . I searched 'Jerome Nesbit Newburyport High School.'"

Maggie glanced at the screen. It was a website for alumni who graduated in 1995.

"You can't get into the site if you're not a member," Phoebe explained. "But I bet this is his graduating class. The same year as Jennifer Todd's. She's thirty-eight years old, right?"

"Yes, that's right. It's just what I expected. A spurned boyfriend. Or maybe someone with a secret crush who's been pining for her all these years?" Maggie looked up at Phoebe. "I'll bet Captain Rusty is up at his podium with an announcement very soon."

"I bet I can find a lot more about *Jerrr-ooome*," Phoebe said, drawing out his name. She typed away as quickly as an airline attendant changing a reservation.

"Please save that for later?" Maggie said. "Or for the police and the reporters, who get paid for it? I think you already have a job."

Phoebe looked up with a Cheshire cat smile. "Right . . . nearly forgot." She turned away from the screen. "Okay, gonna hop to it now, Mag."

"Great. Could you hop back to the storeroom and start unpacking the deliveries?"

Phoebe complied with a short salute as she passed. Maggie returned to the young mothers and found they had chosen Knitting 101 and were eager to buy the supplies in advance. It was nice to have a decent sale before lunch.

When Maggie went back to the storeroom, she was pleased to see Phoebe had made good progress with the new inventory, but had also found a few minutes to sneak peeks at her laptop, eager to unearth more information about Jerome Nesbit.

"You won't believe this . . . it's soooo perfect. Guess what he does for a living?"

"Owns a flower shop?" Maggie was half joking.

"Almost. He's teaches *biology* at a high school in Beverly. So he'd know all about poisonous plants and all that."

"I guess he would." Maggie glanced at the man's picture again.

"He's like a *Breaking Bad* bio teacher," Phoebe said, excited by her discovery. "That show with the high school chemistry teacher who's really a drug dealer?"

Maggie shuddered at the plot line. She'd heard of the show but it wasn't anything she'd ever watch. "Not a fan. But I get your point."

"He's even in one of those old high school photos of Jennifer that was in the newspaper last week. I fished this out of the recycle bin . . . look."

She showed Maggie the two-page article, folded to the place where the photos were inserted. "This one, where she's posing with the Science Club. Doesn't that kid on the end look like . . . this guy?" She quickly brought up Jerome Nesbit's photo on the computer.

Maggie slipped on her glasses. "That does look like an older version of the boy in the photo. Though it's very blurry."

"It's got to be him. He hasn't changed at all. Just gained a little weight and lost a little hair. He's even wearing the same glasses."

"Yes . . . he is."

Jerome Nesbit was much as Phoebe had imagined

him—a lank man with stooped shoulders, a droopy mustache, and a thin neck. A pair of aviator glasses were balanced on an angular nose, the same style eyeglass frames in both pictures. His reddish-brown hair had thinned on top and a few lines had formed around his small eyes and mouth. But otherwise, he looked the same.

And very much like a high school science teacher. One who was possibly afraid of the students, their vitality and energy, who hid behind lesson plans, long tests, and a grading rubric. Or maybe he was the most popular teacher at Beverly High.

Maggie scolded herself for jumping to conclusions; it was impossible to tell from a picture. Or to tell if he was Heath O'Hara's killer.

Phoebe had no such scruples about jumping to conclusions.

"He looks like the kind of guy who would get all lovelorn over a movie star and sneak around at night, leaving love tokens." She had brought down her lunch from her apartment and heated it in the microwave—half of a leftover burrito that originally must have been as large as her head. She bit into it with gusto. She had a passion for Mexican food, though Maggie wasn't sure where she put it. No matter how much the dear girl ate, she remained rail thin.

Maggie looked back at the photos. "It's not fair to judge anyone from a photo. But he doesn't look to me like the type of person who could poison two people within a week, and even kill one of them. I'd never pick him out of a lineup."

"That's the genius of it. From his point of view, I mean," she added. "Mild-mannered bio teacher by day. Killer by night. Or whenever he slipped the poison into their foods. No one would suspect him, skulking around."

Maggie sighed. "I guess we have to see what the police say."

"I bet the next thing they say is this guy is the one." Phoebe spoke around a mouthful of burrito, hardly noticing, she was so excited about her discovery.

Maggie could have played devil's advocate. But for one thing, she didn't want the poor child to choke. For another, what did she know? She was well aware that many innocent-looking people were capable of truly awful deeds.

Much later that day, she was alone in the shop, about to close, when Charles walked in. He had called her late the night before, but they'd both been very tired and didn't talk long. She was happy to see him and hoped the case was wrapping up after the interview with Jerome Nesbit.

"Good, you're still here. I was hoping to catch you."

"Here I am, you've got me." She raised her hands in surrender.

He smiled and leaned across the counter to kiss her quickly. He seemed happy to see her, but also looked very tired.

Maggie put away a pile of Black Sheep Knitting Shop totes and came out from behind the counter. "Working hard?"

"Very."

"I saw the chief on TV. It sounds like you'll be back to regular hours soon." When Charles gave her a puzzled look, she added, "Jerome Nesbit? I heard his name mentioned on TV. He's the one, isn't he?"

His gaze slipped away from hers. She realized he wasn't able to tell her yet.

"Oh . . . sorry. I can wait for the official announcement. You don't have to give away any secrets," she said quickly, not wanting to be a pest.

He cocked his head to one side and smiled. "I can tell you. It's okay. Jerome Nesbit is not our guy. He was stalking Jennifer Todd and had delivered at least two flower arrangements. One here to your shop," he clarified. "But all the rest of it didn't pan out. We couldn't place him anywhere near the movie set for the time frame of the poisonings." He hesitated, then added, "And there's some physical evidence that didn't match up, either."

Maggie's heart sank. She'd thought this was it, victory. And a solution to the puzzle that made sense to her and her friends.

"So you let him go?"

Charles shrugged. "We know where to find him if anything else comes up. Frankly, he didn't seem to have the stomach for an attempted murder and a successful homicide. All we could get him on is harassment, and Ms. Todd didn't want to press charges. She remembered him from high school and felt bad. She said she didn't want to embarrass him."

"I could see her saying that. She has a soft heart."

Charles didn't reply. Though she didn't notice a change in his expression. As if he wanted to say something but held back.

"Now what?" she asked. "Back to square one?"

"Not quite. We're working on some other leads." He didn't seem discouraged. Just tired. "What do you think of going out for a bite on Saturday night? Got my schedule today. I'm off for the weekend. If we close this case," he added.

She smiled. "Saturday sounds perfect."

Maggie was ready to go and Charles walked her out, waiting while she locked up. "I'll bet those movie people are getting restless. Are they all still in town?"

Charles nodded. "Barely. We can't keep them here much longer."

"Do you think it was one of the cast or crew? Oops, sorry, I shouldn't have asked you that. Just forget it. Besides, I know what you're going to say," she added in a teasing tone as she unlocked her car door.

"What am I going to say?" he asked with a smile.

"'We don't know yet, but we're looking into all possibilities.' Or something like that."

Charles laughed. "You're right. That was my answer and it's true."

Maggie kissed his cheek. "Keep calm and search on. The sooner you crack this case, Mossbacher, the better for me."

She slipped into the car and shut the door, leaving Charles laughing as he waved from the sidewalk.

That night after dinner, when Maggie finally settled in front of the TV with her knitting, she found even more coverage of Heath O'Hara's death. An older brother, Daniel, had come from the West Coast to take Heath's remains back to California. He looked a lot like Heath, though not quite as dashing. His eyes lacked the movie star's sparkle, she noticed.

Or maybe Daniel's grief had robbed them of that light. Maggie felt sad for the young man, who spoke to a reporter only briefly. Heath's family was shocked and devastated, as one might expect. Daniel was waiting in Boston, at an undisclosed location, to avoid unwanted attention from Heath's fans.

A cremation and private memorial service had been planned. The service would take place at Heath's estate and Maggie expected throngs would line the road outside the gates, waiting and watching. The police had not released the body yet but were expected to shortly.

There wasn't much more that could be said about the star's cause of death, or even the investigation. But there was an endless stream of photos, film clips, and biographical information, and a vast number of people claiming to have known Heath at different stages in his life, and happy now to be in the spotlight, reminiscing about him.

Maggie did not give the broadcast her complete attention, but was still curious enough not to change the channel. She dialed Lucy's number and put the phone on speaker so she could knit and talk at the same time.

"I'm just calling to see how you're doing. Are you watching any of the coverage about Heath O'Hara?"

"We're switching . . . between that and the Red Sox." Lucy sounded a little annoyed, but not seriously. Maggie recalled being peeved at sharing the TV with her late husband, but had often realized since then that she would have given anything to have the problem again.

"I'm not really *watching* watching . . . just have it on in the background. How did it go with Suzanne? You were so sweet to keep her company."

"She couldn't get into the house yet. We waited awhile and took a walk on the beach. It was good for her. For both of us," she added. "But when we went back they still weren't done. She didn't want to wait, but something interesting happened. Jennifer Todd was there, with Alicia. She wanted a few things from her trailer, but the police wouldn't let her go inside."

"Oh . . . well, I guess all the vehicles have to be searched. All the equipment trucks and trailers. That makes sense."

"I guess. She was surprised but didn't make a fuss. She said hello to us," Lucy added.

"She's not the type to rant and make demands and she does have wonderful people skills."

"She looked very sad. First her husband and now Heath."

"It's a lot," Maggie agreed, "and it's not over yet. Nick's recovery is still touch and go, I've heard on the news. And it appears the film will be scraped or put on a shelf . . . or whatever they say when a movie isn't finished."

"I heard that, too. I guess she and Nick will lose a lot of money. On top of everything else."

"I guess they will." Maggie's gaze slipped back to the TV. An image had caught her eye. She quickly raised the volume so she could hear what the commentator was saying. "Hold on a second, all right?'"

"Sure," she heard Lucy say as she put the phone aside.

A few moments later, she picked it up. "That was interesting. I've been watching a show about Heath's life and career, sort of a retrospective. They just showed an old photo of him and Jennifer. Did you know they were at the same acting school in Hollywood together?"

"No, I'd never heard that."

"Yes, that's where they met, and this reporter said they even dated for a while. Until Jennifer met Nick. It seems Heath introduced them."

"That's interesting. So she had to choose between the two?"

"The reporter didn't say that exactly. Nick was older than both of them, at least ten or twelve years. It seems he was married when he met Jennifer. Or on the verge of a divorce? That part wasn't clear."

"What channel are you watching? I want to see the rest." Lucy sounded intrigued.

Maggie told her the channel, then said, "What about the Red Sox?"

"We'll tape that. Matt can watch the ninth inning before he goes to work tomorrow morning. That's the most important one."

"Not necessarily. But it's a good compromise." Sometimes that's the best we can aim for in life, and in love, Maggie realized.

Chapter Eleven

When Lucy left the cottage with her dogs Wednesday morning, she decided to take the long way into town, a curving route down to the water, a path along the harbor and up Main Street, then toward Maggie's shop.

It was a beautiful morning, and they all needed the exercise. Whenever she was digging in, trying to finish a project on time, she sat like a slug stuck to a rock in front of her computer. When she finally got up, she felt the stiffness all over her body . . . and the snugness of her jeans.

"That's the way it goes, my friends. Lean and mean going into the project, tight jeans going out. What can I say? Maybe I should get a treadmill in the office and balance my computer on top? They say the number-one health hazard as you get older is sitting too much. You guys need to think about that," she added.

She often talked to the dogs. Matt didn't seem to notice. Since he was a veterinarian, it was actually one of the things about her that had attracted him.

"When they start answering, I'll worry," she told concerned friends.

They had reached the harbor and Lucy had to be mindful of staying to one side of the path; there were many joggers, bikers and groups of power-walking seniors out at this time of day. A light wind whipped up whitecaps on the water and the air smelled rich and salty. Lucy inhaled a deep, cool breath.

"I'm feeling more fit and toned already. How about you guys?" she asked her shaggy companions.

Tink turned her head at the sound of Lucy's voice and sort of smiled. Or maybe she was just panting. It would be good to get to Maggie's and give them a drink.

Wally didn't turn. He needed to keep up his momentum and balance. Lucy suddenly stopped and he nearly tipped over. "Wally . . . sorry!" she said aloud.

Poor old hound. She stooped to pet his head, her gaze fixed on the Lord Charles Inn, where a blue-and-white police cruiser and another car that looked like an unmarked police vehicle stood parked in the elegant curved drive. A uniformed officer stood by the cruiser and two men, plainclothes detectives probably, stood talking to him.

Lucy led the dogs up from the harbor and across the green to get a better look. She was not the only person standing and watching. But the police presence had not drawn a huge crowd yet.

She stood there for a few moments observing. Nothing seemed to be going on. Her dogs tugged on their leashes, one on each side of her body. They were bored, too.

She was about to give up, when the hotel doors opened and Jennifer Todd came out, flanked by a bodyguard Lucy had seen on the set, and Charles Mossbacher.

Several men and women carrying bulky cameras with long lenses ran forward and started photographing, dropping to their knees or darting around the fenders of parked cars. Lucy hadn't even noticed them. Where had they been hiding?

"Jennifer," yelled one. "Where are they taking you?"

"Hey, Jen, what's up?" another called. "Are you going to the police station?"

Her face covered by huge sunglasses and a scarf tied around her hair à la Jackie Kennedy, the star walked at an even pace down to a long black car, driven by one of the film security staff. Lucy saw Regina Thurston climb into the car with her.

Charles Mossbacher spoke to her briefly through the window, then climbed into the passenger seat of an unmarked car with his colleagues. The caravan pulled out of the inn driveway, cameras snapping furiously. Lucy noticed some of the photographers dashing to their own cars, in order to meet the entourage at the police station, and get even more photos.

Photos of what? she wondered. Was Jennifer going back to the station to be interviewed again about Heath's death? Or talk with the police about the investigation into Nick's poisoning? Or about a connection between the two?

Lucy didn't stop to ask the dogs. She just steered them up Main Street toward Maggie's shop. This was a conversation for humans.

She found Maggie on the porch, planting pansies and vinca vines in the window boxes. She greeted Lucy happily. Gardening always improved Maggie's brain chemistry, almost as much as knitting.

"These were expensive, but I had to buy a flat," Maggie said. "If there are any left over, I'm going to stick some in the beds with the tulips and daffs." She finally glanced up. "You look winded; want some water?"

Lucy took a breath. She was winded; she'd run nearly all the way. "I was just at the harbor. I saw Jennifer leave the inn, escorted by Charles and the police. It looked like they were going to the police department."

Maggie frowned and put her shovel down. "Oh? I guess they want to ask more questions. Maybe about Jerome Nesbit. Or maybe about some other leads they have on Nick's poisoning."

"Maybe." Lucy tied up the dogs and gave them water. She was thirsty, too, and opened her own water bottle for a quick swallow. "I don't know why, but I have a bad feeling. Why don't they just ask her questions over the phone, or at the inn? Why at the police station? Regina Thurston was with her and that guy I saw last week, with the fancy suit and big briefcase."

"You said he looked like a lawyer."

"That's the one."

Maggie shrugged again. "I really don't think she's a suspect. She was close to both men. She was a business partner with both of them, too. She's definitely a good source of information. Maybe she knows something important that ties these events together, and she doesn't even realize it."

"Maybe." That was a good possibility, Lucy thought. Maggie usually had such a sensible point of view. She was so grounded—like a lightning rod at times for the rest of them.

"You know how discreet Charles is about his work? He did let it slip that the police have some physical evidence or something they feel significantly ties a suspect to at least one of the crimes."

"Like fingerprints? Something like that?"

Maggie shook her head and laughed. "Please . . . I knew he wouldn't tell me what it was, so I didn't even ask. I have to be extra careful not to press him for details. I understand his situation and respect it. But of course I'm dying to know the details," she added with a sigh.

Lucy could tell that Maggie really liked Charles, maybe more than any other man she'd dated since her husband passed away.

Their relationship was so new, and hadn't quite jelled yet. Lucy understood why Maggie was being so cautious.

"It's good not to ask too many questions, if that's the way he feels. But what did he say exactly, do you remember?"

Maggie pressed the last clump of pansies into the soil with her fingertips, then grabbed her watering can. "He said they had to rule out Jerome Nesbit because they couldn't place him anywhere near the set—in enough proximity to get poison into Nick's and Heath's food, I guess he meant. And because something else didn't match up."

"Match up?" Lucy echoed. "Maybe it's a fingerprint or a strand of hair?"

"I was thinking the same. Something with a DNA marker."

"Interesting . . . I did look up more online about Jennifer and Heath last night. After you told me that they had dated."

"Really? What did you find?" Maggie glanced at her as she brushed some soil from her gloves.

"Not too much more. They met in a small acting school in

LA. It didn't say much more than you heard on TV. Heath was friendly with Nick, who had started his career as an actor also, then got into directing later. He's older than Nick and Jennifer and had already had his first big success by the time he met her."

"A lot of actors jump to the other side of the camera, as a director or producer, or even a writer," Maggie said, turning to her. "Speaking of writers, I haven't seen Theo interviewed on TV about his father at all. Have you?"

Lucy thought for a moment. "No, I haven't. But maybe he didn't want to give any interviews. He's sort of shy. I tried to talk to him on the set the night Nick got sick. He would barely make eye contact with me."

Maggie waved the can over the flowers, giving the pansies a drink. Lucy took one, too. Then noticed the time and stood up.

"Got to head back. Are we meeting tomorrow night? I wasn't sure whose house we're at. I hope it's not my turn," she confessed, suddenly realizing it might be.

"I don't think so. Technically, I think it's *mine*. It was Suzanne's last week, but we met at the movie set instead. When we met last Monday at the shop, to help Jennifer with her role, that was all out of order." Maggie shook her head and tugged her gloves off. "I think it's just easier if we meet here and start the rotation from scratch again."

They weren't that good at keeping track of their turns. Luckily, no one was a big stickler. They often volunteered as needed.

"That's nice of you," Lucy said. "I'll have you all over next week. I should have the house back in order by then," she added, rolling her eyes. "You'd think the police searched *our* place."

Maggie smiled. "Funny, but . . . don't say that too loud."

She hefted the window boxes up to the wire holders on the porch rail and fit them in. She stood back admiring her handiwork. Lucy did, too.

"There . . . what do you think?"

"Very nice. A good job and it isn't even nine."

"Thanks. On to the rest of my day. Talk to you later."

The pansies did look pretty and brightened up the shop, Lucy thought as she headed down the path. I should get some, too.

Maggie had a way of improving everyplace she passed through. It was a gift, Lucy thought, one she admired. She waved briefly to her as she headed home down Main Street.

Maggie didn't give much thought to Jennifer Todd's visit with the Essex County PD. She expected to hear the basic details on the TV news . . . and any really interesting tidbits from Dana, maybe at the knitting meeting Thursday night.

The shop wasn't busy in the morning but picked up around noon.

Phoebe had classes all day and Maggie was left to fend for herself, scurrying from one side of the store to the other helping customers.

Quite a few of the customers asked her about the movie, what it was like to have all the movie stars there, and of course there was gossip and speculation about all the dreadful events of the past week. Maggie tried to stay neutral, not offering an opinion one way or the other. Talking to customers was different from talking to good friends, she had long ago discovered. Best to stay away from religion, politics, and gossip.

She was sorting out her sales for the day, trying to keep the inventory accurate, when two men walked into the shop. She immediately sensed they were detectives, and may have even recognized them from the beach house or news on TV.

"Mrs. Messina? I'm Detective Howard Craft, with the Essex County PD, and this is my partner, Detective Joe Mazursky." The officers both showed her their badges.

She felt a little nervous, but smiled. "Yes, what can I do for you, Detectives?"

"We need to ask you a few questions regarding Jennifer Todd. This has nothing to do with you personally or your store," he added quickly. "We're just looking for some information."

Maggie had heard those assurances before. But in this case, she felt she had to trust his promise. "I'm happy to help if I can."

He didn't quite smile, but she could see his expression relax a bit, as he realized he wasn't going to have to pressure her.

"Good . . ." He took out a pad and checked a handwritten note. "Did Ms. Todd visit the shop at all between last Thursday night, when the film crew was here, and Sunday, when they returned?"

Maggie thought a moment. "Yes . . . she did. She stopped by on Saturday morning. On her way to Boston to see her husband in the hospital. He was about to be transferred to Mass General."

The detective made a note but didn't react.

"Can you tell me exactly what transpired?"

Maggie was starting to feel nervous; her heartbeat quickened. This seemed . . . serious. She was afraid she would say the wrong thing and get Jennifer in trouble. But all she could do was tell the truth. Though in her experience, that was not always a foolproof protection, even for an innocent person.

"Let's see . . . She was being driven in a car by a security guard. I think he stood outside of the car, watching the street. She's always surrounded by fans," Maggie added.

"Yes, go on," Detective Craft said.

"I was outside, working on the flower beds. I asked about her husband," Maggie recalled. "And we talked about gardening a little, too. Oh . . . I don't know if this is important. She knew a poem about daffodils by heart. She recited it." Maggie felt silly adding that detail, but he'd said to tell him everything.

He made a note. "All right. Then what?" He glanced at his partner; they seemed to be waiting for her to say . . . something. Maggie wasn't sure what.

"Let me see . . . ." She felt nervous and her mind went blank for a moment. "She said she thought she had left her knitting here. She had come with her assistant on Monday night," Maggie explained, "to get more information for her role in the movie. She was playing the owner of a knitting shop."

"Yes, we know. Go on," he prodded her.

"My knitting group was here that night and we were starting a project. Jennifer started it, too. She liked to knit. I gave her the yarn and pattern in a little recycle-type tote I've had made up for my shop. It's black and it has the store name and logo on it. She told me that she'd had it with her Thursday night, on the movie set, but couldn't find it. She thought she'd left it here."

He nodded, clearly interested in this part of the long, rambling story.

"What happened next, Mrs. Messina?" his partner leaned forward and asked.

"The shop was messed up a bit after the police searched it Thursday night. I'd expected that," Maggie added, not meaning to complain. "On Friday, I'd found a knitting bag with the type of yarn I'd given Jennifer and the pattern. I wasn't sure who it belonged to and I put it under the counter." She stepped back and pointed. "Right here."

The detectives looked at each other. "All right, go on."

"I thought it might be hers, so we went inside to look. She said it was and she was happy. Her husband was pretty much unresponsive and she was going to sit with him all day. She wanted something to do to distract her, calm her down."

"Yes, we understand," Detective Mazursky said quickly.

"Did you look inside the bag yourself and see the contents? The entire contents?" Detective Craft repeated.

"Yes, I did. I even put my hand in to check for any personal belongings—an eyeglass case or something that could identify the owner. There wasn't much to see. Just a few skeins of yarn that I'd given her. There was also a set of needles with a few rows done. Oh, and the pattern sheet. Jennifer recognized that it was all hers," she added, not sure what they were getting at with all these questions.

"And you were sure, too?" Detective Mazursky asked.

"Yes, absolutely." Maggie met his glance.

"All right. What happened after that?" Detective Craft asked her.

"We said good-bye and she left."

Maggie felt confused. She squinted at them but knew they wouldn't tell why they were asking these questions. "Is there anything else?" she asked them.

Craft shook his head and put the pad back into his pocket. "That's it for now. Would you be willing to sign a statement?"

A signed statement that might be used in court, Maggie

realized. They were asking if she was willing to be witness in the case. But she wasn't sure if this strange bit of information would be used to help Jennifer Todd or to hurt her.

Maggie let out a breath. "Yes, I would. It's the truth. That's all I can say," she added with a shrug.

The detectives glanced at each other, then looked back at her. They seemed a bit deflated. Detective Craft said, "Thank you for your help, we'll be in touch.'

Maggie had her cell phone in hand before the duo closed the shop door behind them. She quickly dialed Dana; if anyone would know why the police were interested in Jennifer Todd's knitting projects, she would.

Luckily, Dana picked up quickly. "Hi, what's up? I'm between patients, but I can talk for a minute."

Maggie quickly explained that the police had just came by the shop and asked her questions about Jennifer, about any visits she'd made there and what happened.

"I told them she came on Saturday morning, looking for the Black Sheep Knitting tote I'd given her. She told me that she'd left it here Thursday night, in all the confusion when Nick fell ill."

"Interesting," Dana said. "I was chatting with Jack today. When I heard that Jennifer Todd was being questioned, I couldn't help calling him," she admitted.

Lucky girl, to have a husband willing to divulge the nitty-gritty. But Jack was not on the police force anymore. It was different for him.

"Did he know why the police took Jennifer in? They don't suspect her of anything . . . do they?"

"I think they do. It seems they're trying to connect her to Nick's poisoning. Isn't that awful? It's the plastic bottle they found. There were fibers, stuck to the glue where the label had been torn off. The forensics lab has traced the fibers to the yarn that you gave her. So they're theorizing she put the poison in the bottle and picked it up after he collapsed, then hid it in the knitting bag before she was able to dump it at the park on the harbor. The one right across from the Lord Charles Inn, which makes it a likely place, I guess."

Maggie felt a jolt of shock. She swallowed a lump in her throat. "But she must have told the police she'd left the bag here and didn't retrieve it until Saturday morning. All the yarn I gave her was in there. I had to look through it and I noticed. So that scenario doesn't work out with their timing. They found the bottle in a collection of trash from Friday, didn't they?"

"That's right. It doesn't fit." Dana was silent a moment. "Jack wasn't really supposed to tell me this but . . . there was also some other physical evidence on the bottle. A microscopic bloodstain. It might not hold up in court. But it's enough for the police to pin a suspect and build a case from there. Investigators are so desperate now, they're trying to see if they can make a match to anyone involved. DNA tests haven't come back yet, but they do know the blood type."

Maggie was afraid to ask the next question. But she did anyway. "Did it match Jennifer's blood type?"

"Yes, it does. But it's not a rare type, so it doesn't prove anything definitely."

"But it would sound bad in court," Maggie mused.

"Yes, it would, and will sound bad if the newspapers get hold of the information. But it's privy to the investigation right now. A DNA match would be conclusive. Jack said Jennifer was already lawyered up and advised not to give a DNA sample. Legally, she doesn't have to."

Maggie had heard that. But reluctance to cooperate tended to cast a shadow of guilt. Then again, many were known to cooperate and incriminate themselves. There were risks either way.

"I guess her lawyer doesn't want to dignify the whole thing," said Dana. "And see the newspapers pounce all over it."

"I can just hear the TV commentators now," Maggie said.

"I think you helped her, Maggie. You backed up her claim."

"I just told the truth. But I really don't believe she's involved in any of this . . . do you?"

Dana didn't answer right away. "There was something else. I was going to tell everyone tomorrow night, but you might as well know now. They found some text messages on Heath's phone and emails in his computer. Between him and Jen. Of an intimate nature, you'd have to say."

"They were having an affair?" Maggie said. "I know they dated when they were young, but I thought she and Nick had a good marriage."

"The messages weren't that recent. Jennifer didn't deny it. But said it had been over for a while. Before they started the movie. She told the police that she and her husband had hit a rough spot in their relationship and she'd turned to Heath for sympathy. He'd always been such a good friend. But she was sorry afterward and had ended it."

Maggie's head was reeling with this last disclosure. She did have a certain image of Jennifer Todd as a "nice" person, not the type to fool around on her husband. But it wasn't fair to judge anyone about such matters.

"I guess in the eyes of the investigators, that ties her to Heath's murder, too, doesn't it?" said Maggie.

"Yes, it does. But they aren't speculating how. Not openly."

"I did see some tension between Jennifer and Nick. He wasn't that . . . warm to her, somehow. Do you know what I mean, Dana?"

"I do. I don't think it was easy to combine two high-powered careers and also direct, star in, and produce a movie together. The pressure would wear on anyone's relationship." Dana paused. "There's my patient. I have to run."

"Yes, of course. I'll see you tomorrow night."

By tomorrow night's knitting meeting, Dana would surely have more juicy details to share. But no more evidence mounting up against Jennifer Todd, Maggie hoped. She didn't know why. She just didn't feel that Jennifer was responsible for any of this. Though she had no idea who might be.

Maggie wished she could talk to Charles about it. But she wouldn't be able to disclose all the specifics Dana had told her.

She hated keeping secrets. But she didn't want to get Dana and Jack in trouble.

She'd just have to wait. Maybe the case would be solved by Saturday when she met Charles for dinner. He'd be free then to share all the details without compromising his ethics. But before the case was solved, she really couldn't put him in that position.

Although Maggie expected Charles to call her Wednesday night, she didn't expect to find him at her front door. It was half past seven and she was just about to have dinner.

"Mind if I come in?" he asked politely.

"Not at all. I was just warming up some leftovers. There's plenty. Would you like a bite?"

"Knowing your cooking, that's very tempting. But I have to

get back to the station. I just wanted to say hello. I know you had a visit from the police today. I was just wondering how that went. Are you okay?"

He followed her into the living room and they sat down on opposite ends of the sofa.

"It was fine. The questions they asked me seemed odd. But . . ." She shrugged. She didn't want to add that Dana had told her what the police were really asking about. "I told them the truth. Everything I could remember. What else could I say?"

Charles nodded. "I'm sure you did."

She met his glance, confused about what he was getting at. Or why he'd really come. "Aren't you able to read accounts of people who are interviewed . . . like me? I thought it was one big case, all the information shared."

"I did read the report of your interview."

"And?"

"Well . . . I'm wondering if you're really sure it was *her* bag. I think you told Craft that you weren't sure who had left the bag."

"I did say that. I wasn't sure at first. But when I took a better look with Jen, she saw a note I'd made on her pattern sheet. That's how we knew it was definitely hers."

"Oh . . . that wasn't in the report."

"I just remembered. They only asked if I was sure, and I said that I had been very sure it was hers . . . and that there was nothing else in it besides the yarn, pattern, and knitting needles," she added. But quickly regretted that.

His gaze narrowed. He was sharp; no wonder he was a detective. "Nothing else as in . . . what?"

Maggie shrugged again, trying to act as if she didn't know what he was getting at. "They asked me about the contents. It seemed important to them. I told them I'd put my hand in to feel for any personal belongings that could identify the owner. That's all I meant."

Well . . . that was a lie. But she couldn't help it, she decided.

He sighed and leaned forward, then glanced at his watch.

"All right, I'm sorry to have bothered you. I was concerned about you, getting a visit like that. I wanted to call you to give you a heads-up, but—"

"—you weren't allowed," she finished for him. "I know that. It's all right. I was glad to help."

It was nice to know he'd been worried about her.

"You did help," he assured her. "But I just need to say one thing. I hope you don't take offense."

She braced herself, trying to look as if she was totally open to anything he might say . . . though she was suddenly deeply worried.

"Go ahead. I won't take offense," she promised.

"We know things that you don't. That's all I can say. We see the players in a much different light. I know Jennifer Todd is a very charming woman. Absolutely charismatic. She could charm a dog off a meat wagon," he said bluntly. "But she's an actress. An award-winning, professional actress. She's not your friend, Maggie. You'll never hear from her, or see her, again, once she leaves town."

Maggie felt stung. "Are you trying to say that I'm . . . star-struck? That I'm trying to protect her?"

Charles looked immediately sorry for being so forthcoming. "I don't think that you're intentionally holding back any information. But I'm afraid if you did know something, you might not come forward with it. I'm sorry, I have to be honest with you. I know you have an interest in the investigation—you and your friends. But it does no good to meddle and poke around and try to figure things out, as if this was a parlor game. It's practically a double homicide," he said, his voice rising a notch. "Trying to find out details of the case and interfering with the investigation doesn't help us. It can only help the person who is really guilty. Whoever that may be," he added quickly.

Maggie sat for a moment, considering his words.

"I'm sorry, Charles. I know you're under a lot of pressure right now. I certainly don't want to add to that. The problem is, I'm just so curious about all this. It's only natural for me. Everyone in town is talking about it. But I hate to feel a certain tension when we're together, as if you're afraid I'm going to pressure you to tell me things you can't say . . . and then I'm all self-conscious and tiptoeing around it. And then there's a huge elephant in the room," she concluded, her tone a bit more emotional than she'd hoped it would sound. "A poisoned elephant," she added.

Charles sat back, looking surprised at her reaction. He frowned but didn't say anything.

Were they having their first fight? Seemed so.

"Yes, there is some tension about my work. I noticed that, too," he said quietly. He glanced up at her, then looked down again.

"Maybe we should take a little break, until the case is over? You've already told me it was a problem for you to be on this case because of our relationship, after Nick was poisoned."

That was the first time he'd mentioned it. He didn't say anything about her being at the party where Heath died, but that probably wasn't good, either.

He looked surprised at her suggestion. "I just had to

disclose it to the chief and let him decide. He was all right with it. But if you're comfortable with this idea, I guess it's for the best."

Now he was hurt, blaming it all on her. That wasn't fair. Had she not explained this clearly to him?

"I'm thinking of you. I don't want you to be . . . all uptight and on your guard when we're together," she insisted.

But he still didn't seem to understand. She could tell from his expression. He looked even more upset.

"I didn't realize I seemed 'uptight.' All I'm asking is for you to leave all this to the police. To sit back and be like everyone else in the world. Not so involved."

Maggie shrugged. "I'm not doing anything on purpose." She didn't like his tone now. Or his attitude. "I like you, Charles. I think you know that," she reminded him. "But I don't like feeling that I can't exactly . . .be myself. That's not me." She shrugged. "The case should be over soon. Let's talk then."

She wasn't sure why she'd said that. It had just come out.

But she couldn't take it back now.

She couldn't tell what he was thinking. He seemed about to say something, then stopped himself. He stood up and quickly met her gaze.

"All right. If that's what you want."

Maggie felt annoyed. It wasn't her, it was him. But she held her tongue.

"I like you, too, Maggie. I like spending time with you. But I'm working so much, it's hard to make plans anyway. I'll call you when the case is over."

Maggie didn't answer. She felt like she might cry, but tried hard not to. Not in front of him.

She walked him to the door and said good night. He seemed about to lean forward and kiss her. Then he stopped himself.

She closed the door behind him and wondered if that was good-bye.

Chapter Twelve

𝕸 aggie felt terrible after her fight with Charles. She couldn't stop herself from going over and over it in her mind. The argument had seemed to bubble up from nowhere. But it must have been simmering under the surface for some time. That's the way these things worked, gushing up when you least expected it. Why hadn't she been calmer and not so easily upset? Why hadn't she stopped herself from saying all those stupid things? She wished now she could hit some invisible rewind button and get a second chance to act calm and wise . . . and not nearly so touchy. But of course, she could not.

She wanted to talk it over with her friends, and hear their advice. And sympathy. But for some reason she wasn't ready to confess her troubles. It felt like such a defeat. She felt so sad . . . and embarrassed. She'd been so hopeful about this relationship, and what had happened? She'd somehow tangled it all up . . . like a ruined knitting project. She was the champ at repairing mixed-up stitches, but wasn't sure if this situation was could ever be sorted out.

After dinner, which she hardly ate, she sat in front of the TV with her knitting, as usual. Is this all she had to look forward to?

The thought was depressing, even with complete control of the TV remote.

There was some news about Jennifer Todd being questioned by the police and released. Video clips of her going in and out of the station, in her big sunglasses and head scarf. Just as Lucy had described her.

"Ms. Todd would not speak to reporters directly," the newscaster said, "but a statement issued by her attorney, Richard Novak, emphasized the movie star has not been named a person of interest in the case. She was interviewed by the police in regard to information that may help the investigation of the poisoning of her husband, Nick Pullman, and close friend, the actor Heath O'Hara . . ."

Well, that wasn't entirely true. The police were looking for more than mere information. But Maggie guessed the police department would not rebut this account. They had bigger things to worry about and had to walk a fine line when building a case against a celebrity. They'd be sued into the next galaxy if they made a misstep. That was for sure.

"Heath O'Hara's body was released today by the Essex County Police," the newscaster continued. "A private memorial service will take place at his Beverly Hills estate on Saturday."

Maggie wondered if Jennifer would attend the service, or if she had to stay in the area. Perhaps she would remain near Nick, who was still too sick to be moved.

Was Charles right? Was she just dazzled by Jennifer Todd's attention and didn't want to see that she could be the guilty one? Maggie had to wonder about that now.

If Jennifer was not behind these poisonings—and it wasn't Jerome Nesbit—who could it be? Someone in the cast or crew who the police had overlooked so far?

Maggie guessed the movie people were all free to leave by now, or would be very soon. The police could only keep them in town for so long. They would all disperse, making it even harder to find the culprit.

As Maggie puttered around the shop Thursday morning, she was looked forward to seeing her friends that night, so she could tell them all at the same time what had happened with Charles.

She would be deluged with opinions and advice, she was sure. All well meaning. She'd just have to weather it. She had not slept well, feeling blue about the situation, as if she was the one who had derailed such a promising start.

Was this some unconscious wish to remain alone, to avoid a close relationship with a man? Did she feel a threat to her independence? Or was she afraid that if someone got close enough, they'd reject her? So she did it to them first?

Maggie decided to leave those questions to Dana. She knew best about such things.

She heard a light tap on the door before nine and suspected one of her friends had dropped by. Certainly not Charles . . . dare she even hope?

She opened the door to find Jennifer Todd, wearing her incognito glasses and hooded windbreaker again. The shiny black car waited by the sidewalk, just like the last time.

"Jennifer . . . good morning." Maggie couldn't hide the surprise in her tone.

"May I come in, for just a minute?"

"Of course." Maggie stepped aside to let her in, then shut

232 / Anne Canadeo

the door. Jennifer seemed relieved to slip off her hood and took her sunglasses off, too.

"I just wanted to thank you," she said. "My attorney heard that you confirmed what I told the police. About the tote bag."

"I just told the truth. You don't have to thank me for that."

"I know it was the truth. But you never know what some people will do or say when they're confronted like that. There are people who would take advantage of the situation. I know you're not like that. I don't mean to say I *ever* thought you would do such a thing," she rushed to add. "But it's just the way the world is."

Her world, perhaps. Maggie did realize that. There were unscrupulous souls, lying in wait to take advantage of someone rich and famous.

Expecting money to give the "right" story. Expecting some money now, perhaps. Maggie thought that's what she was getting at. But didn't want to go there.

"The thought never occurred to me," she said honestly. She quickly tried to change the subject. "Are the movie people able to go back to California?"

"Oh yes. Many gave their statements and left. Practically everyone else is leaving today. There's a memorial service for Heath in California on Saturday," she added.

"I heard that on the news. Are you going, too?"

Jennifer looked away and shook her head. Maggie saw a flash of sadness cross her eyes. Whatever she and Heath had been to each other at the time of his death, they had been lovers once, and she clearly had deep feelings for him.

"No . . . I can't make it. I feel very badly about that. I have to stay here, with Nick. There are complications. He's still in ICU. I'm planning on moving to a hotel in Boston. Probably tomorrow." She paused and sighed. "The police have asked me not to leave the area yet. They haven't told me I can't, but my attorney thinks it's better if I cooperate. I can't believe they suspect me . . . of all people." She gave an incredulous laugh. "It's a nightmare, from start to finish—Nick being poisoned, Heath killed . . . And now I seem to be the prime suspect."

"The police haven't said that exactly, have they?" Maggie asked in alarm.

"Not in so many words. But they don't seem to be talking to anyone else." Jennifer looked up and met her gaze. "Someone is trying to frame me. I don't know who," she said quickly, her voice distraught. "And I don't know why. I told the police that. They don't believe me."

"I believe you," Maggie said quietly. And she did.

Though Charles's harsh warning suddenly echoed in her mind—*Jennifer Todd is charming. Charismatic. But she's an actress. She's not your friend.*

Was she acting now? What would be the point? What does she have to gain by winning over my good opinion? Maggie didn't think there was any hidden motive. Jen was just lonely and had no one to talk to.

"What about Alicia? Where's she?"

"She's still in town. But I told her to go back to LA with the others. There are some things at the house she can take care of for me. And I know she wants to go to Heath's service. I don't want to deprive her of that, just because I can't be there. And Nick isn't able, either, of course. Theo will have to represent us," she added.

Theo was not exactly sitting a vigil at his father's bedside, was he? But of course she couldn't say that to Jennifer.

"Will Theo come back to be with Nick, too?"

"He said he would. He's very upset and concerned about his father," she assured Maggie. "Even though they haven't had the easiest relationship." Maggie wondered what she meant by that but didn't ask. "Alicia will come back, too, after the memorial. Probably on Sunday. She'll meet me in Boston," Jennifer added.

Jennifer offered a small, brave smile, then leaned over and impulsively hugged Maggie. "I might not see you before I go back. Thanks again."

"No thanks necessary," Maggie said honestly. "Take care."

Jennifer put her camouflage back in place and ran out the door with a small wave. Maggie waved back. She did not envy Jennifer Todd one bit, for all her fame and fortune.

At half past five, Maggie wondered if she should close early. There hadn't been any customers in the last half hour or more. That's just the way it was some days. Her friends were coming in about an hour and she wanted to start setting up for dinner and put the finishing touches on the meal she'd made. Crostini with chopped plum tomatoes, fresh basil and other herbs on top, for a starter, along with some olives and cheese. She was serving pasta primavera with a pink sauce for the entrée—in honor of spring arriving. Suzanne was bringing the dessert—something horribly decadent and delicious, she had no doubt.

Just as she locked the door and turned the sign around, a text message arrived on her phone. It was from Dana. Maggie guessed she'd be late with a patient. It happened all the time.

Jennifer picked up by police. About to charge attempted murder and homicide. Will find out all I can asap.

Maggie was stunned and stood staring at the phone. Phoebe came in from the storeroom. "What's wrong? Bad news?"

"Jennifer Todd was just arrested. The police believe she tried to kill her husband . . . and did kill Heath." Maggie looked up at Phoebe. "I wonder what they finally found to tie her to the crimes? I won't believe it until I hear," she added.

Suzanne and Lucy had both heard by the time they arrived. They sat at the oak table, waiting for Dana with the inside story. Maggie had already set out the starters and her guests helped themselves. She poured a glass of wine for herself and told them about Jennifer's visit.

"She came here this morning, to thank me for helping her," Maggie said. "By confirming her statement about the tote bag. I told her I'd just told the truth. But she's used to people looking for angles, profiting from some celebrity's problems or pain." Maggie paused. "She was very worried. She said someone was out to frame her."

"Looks like they succeeded," Suzanne replied. "Unless— I know you don't want to hear this, Maggie—unless she is guilty?"

"I think we ought to wait until Dana comes and see what she's found out. That should tell the story one way or the other," Lucy said evenly. "I will say, I'm with Maggie. I don't think Jen is guilty. I think the police just aren't seeing something . . . something outside the frame of this picture."

An apt way of putting it, Maggie thought. She agreed.

Before anyone could say more, Dana sailed through the door.

"Sorry I'm late, but I had to catch up with Jack. He knows a lot about the investigation, some breaks in the case that happened just today."

Maggie took a breath, bracing herself. To find out I'm a bad judge of character after all, she thought. And I've missed the best chance I've had lately—and possibly the last chance I'll ever get—of finding a really good relationship, because I'm so stubborn sometimes.

Dana settled in and Suzanne poured her a glass of wine.

"There's some physical evidence," Dana said, "nothing that totally nails it, but they're hoping all together it builds a case against her."

"Go on." Suzanne had bitten into a crostini and dabbed her chin with a napkin.

"First, we already heard that the digitalis used to poison Nick was from some pure, organic source. We were right with our guess about flowers. The police lab narrowed it down to lily of the valley, a certain variety grown only at a few flower farmers in the U.S., but the same type used by the online flower order service that sent out Jennifer's delivery—the bouquet from Regina Thurston. They believe a solution of the ground-up flowers was injected into the green health drink. Which would have masked the flavor. The intent, to kill," she added. "Though it didn't quite kill him."

"So they linked her to the lilies . . . What about the daffodils? We didn't see any of those in her room," Phoebe said.

"No, but there were banks of them growing around the beach house," Suzanne said. "I guess you didn't see them the night of the party."

"I didn't notice any," Maggie said. "But it was raining and almost dark." She didn't feel happy about hearing any of this. It was a bitter pill to swallow; a bitter bulb, more precisely. But she sat still and quiet, listening. Trying to keep an open mind.

"The police say a few bulbs had been dug out of the

garden. And they found a pot in the kitchen of Jennifer's trailer with residue of lycorine, which leads them to believe daffodil bulbs were boiled or cooked in it. Cooked down, they think, so that the water was highly toxic. It would have had a bitter flavor. But the lemons in Heath's drink would have masked that."

"Diabolical," Suzanne said quietly.

"Isn't it?" Dana agreed. "And there was something else. It took time, but technicians traced the threatening emails sent to Jen's website, over the past few months. The police say the transmissions came from a computer in her own house, and an email account set up specifically for that purpose."

"So she created a fake stalker?" Lucy asked, sounding confused. "But what about Jerome Nesbit? He admitted coming here and sending her flowers."

"Yes, he did. But Jennifer—or someone—took advantage of that and made it seem like more. And more threatening than Jerome ever was," Dana explained.

"Trying to throw suspicion off of herself and make someone think a crazed fan killed her husband?" Phoebe asked. "That was dumb. Everyone knows how easy it is to trace emails."

"Yes, that seemed odd to me. If you were smart enough to plan out the poisonings, it seems you wouldn't slip up like that," Lucy said. "There are ways to hide the source of emails. And it's relatively easy to find out how to do that," she added.

"I think that supports her claim of being framed, don't you?" Maggie piped up. Though she was also starting to doubt Jennifer.

"Possibly . . . but what really put the police on Jennifer's trail was Trina Hardwick's statement," Dana told them.

"Did she see anything that proves Jennifer is guilty?" Lucy asked quickly.

Dana shook her head. "It wasn't that. But she told the po-lice Nick and Jennifer had serious problems in their marriage. They were no lovey-dovey power couple. They had knock-down-drag-out fights all the time. People on the set confirmed it, too."

"I could see him mixing it up," Suzanne broke in. "That guy has a bad temper. You don't need to be with him more than five minutes to figure that out . . . But Jen doesn't seem like a screamer."

"No . . .anything but," Lucy agreed.

"And a lot of couples argue. They were under a great deal of pressure, making that film together," Maggie said. She be-lieved that was true. But still felt upset by the turn in the con-versation. She got up and went over to the buffet to bring her guests more napkins.

"That's true. But there was more than bad arguments," Dana added. "Trina claimed that Jennifer wanted a divorce, but Nick wouldn't let her out of the marriage. Nick had a string of flops lately and had lost a lot of their fortune on stupid in-vestments. Jennifer was tired of being his 'cash cow' and the big money earner. She knew she was getting older. Actresses don't get very good roles after forty . . . if they get anything. That's why she wanted to get away from him. But he'd some-how persuaded her to stay and make this film, to make back some of their losses. She agreed to it. As long as Heath signed on."

"And we already know about her and Heath," Suzanne sighed.

"Trina said they always had a thing for each other. Even after Jennifer married Nick. And Nick was no angel, either," Dana added. "So Jennifer must have justified her dalliance.

Heath was her only affair, but Nick liked variety. That's how Trina claims she knew all these intimate details of their married life. She and Nick . . . well, you get the idea."

"I'll say we do. Too much information, thank you," Maggie said as she returned to the table.

"It's better than *Hollywood Insider*, I'll say that," Suzanne admitted.

"I think it's interesting that of the four principal people involved in the film—Nick, Jennifer, Heath, and Trina—Trina is the only one who *wasn't* the target of any accidents. Or poisoning. Even Jennifer nearly got hit by that falling light fixture," Maggie pointed out. "How do the police explain that? Did she try to throw suspicion off herself by having her face cut to bits by broken glass?"

"The police think that was a bona fide accident. Just a coincidence."

"What about the fire in Heath's trailer? How do they connect that to Jennifer? They say they know how she killed him . . . but why would she kill Heath?" Lucy asked Dana. She looked around at the others, too.

"I agree with Lucy. I think she loved Heath. I don't see any reason why she'd hurt him. She probably hoped to be with him after she divorced Nick," Suzanne said. "Why kill him?"

Dana sat back and sipped some more wine. "They're a little bit fuzzy on that one. But they are building on the money motive—in addition to the financial stress in the marriage, Nick had a big insurance policy, and Jennifer is the beneficiary. In regard to the movie, that's a little stickier, but Jack heard the movie is insured, too. If the film can't be finished due to something called force majeure, the partners—Nick, Jennifer, and Heath—stand to recoup their investment. And in this agreement, the remaining partners get the share of any other who is not alive to claim it."

"So they think she just wanted to undermine the movie to collect the insurance? I don't buy that, either," Maggie said. She thought it was time to serve the pasta and headed back to the storeroom to get it. But she could still hear the lively conversation quite clearly. And still felt a heaviness inside, feeling the urge to defend Jennifer, but wondering now if she truly was guilty.

"Wait, what's force . . . margarine?" Phoebe asked.

"Force majeure: an act of God. It's a clause that frees someone from fulfilling the terms of a contract if there's a flood or a war. Or an alien invasion," Lucy explained.

"So Heath's death made it impossible to finish the picture. That's an act of God . . . even though God didn't poison him," Suzanne added, sounding angry all over again at whoever did.

"That's all very interesting," Maggie said finally. She set the hot pan of pasta in the middle of the table and began serving her friends.

"What about Theo, how does he stand in the will?" Suzanne asked.

"I don't know," Dana replied, accepting her dish. "Hmm, this looks good," she added quietly.

"Jennifer said he was very concerned and upset about his father," Maggie told them, "but that they haven't had the easiest father-son relationship. I wonder what she meant by that?"

"I know," Lucy piped up. "I've been reading a lot of old celebrity gossip news online about all these people," she admitted. "It's been sort of addictive."

"What's the story with Theo and Nick?" Dana asked curiously.

"It seems that they didn't have much of any relationship until the past few years. Nick's first wife was so angry at Nick when he left her that she kept Theo away from Nick for about ten years or more," Lucy reported between bites. "I think Theo was about nine when the family broke up and he didn't see Nick again until he was in college. Nick probably reached out to him and he was out of his mother's influence by then. One article I read played up a cozy father-son reunion and said Nick had taken Theo under his wing and was teaching him the business. I think Theo even lives with Jennifer and Nick now."

"Interesting," Dana said. "Did Nick leave his family to be with her? If he did, Theo would still have a strong reason to resent her."

"It's hard to tell from the clippings I found. I think it's possible. They met when Jennifer was about twenty-three and he sort of swept her off her feet."

"Stole her away from Heath," Suzanne clarified, chewing thoughtfully.

"Or maybe Jennifer was attracted by an older, successful, established man. A man who could help her career. Heath wasn't famous yet. They were both still in acting school," Lucy reminded the others.

"She lived to regret that move," Suzanne noted.

"Maybe," Lucy agreed. "But somehow they all remained friends. But right before you find any mention of Nick and Jennifer dating, it seems that Nick was involved in a scandal. Or maybe you could just call it an unfortunate incident that happened on his property? Dana, you were telling us about that a while ago. Right before the film crew came to town."

"Yes, I remember. But the details are a little foggy now."

"There was a young actress who died after one of his

parties," Lucy filled in. "She drowned in the swimming pool. A combination of too much alcohol and nobody noticing. Practically all the guests had gone by then. I think only Heath and Jennifer were still at the house. One of the articles I found said that Heath found the body."

"How awful. I've never heard that," Suzanne said quickly.

"She was only nineteen. She'd come to LA right after high school. She was still underage for drinking alcohol. I'm not sure how Nick Pullman escaped any legal punishment for that, but he did," Lucy added.

"We can understand his phobia about bad publicity now, I guess. That was the start, but he was very adept at keeping it quiet. He settled with the girl's family out of court. The best thing for everyone's career, including Heath's," Dana added.

"So Nick was the one to fix it," Suzanne concluded. "Heath had no money then, right?"

"Right," Lucy said. "All he had was his talent and good looks. Which proved to be plenty. He must have felt indebted to Nick after that," she speculated. "They did several films together that were all big hits."

"So they both benefitted from the alliance, however it had been forged," Maggie noted. She'd served herself last and sat at her place. But didn't have much appetite.

"What was the girl's name? The actress who drowned? Was she well known?" Dana asked.

Lucy shook her head. "Not at all. Her name was Lana Lambert. She'd come to Hollywood from someplace in the Midwest for her big break. That's what makes it so sad."

"This is all very interesting, but I still don't see how it fits together," Maggie said honestly. "Or helps us figure out who might be trying to frame Jennifer Todd."

She knew she sounded disappointed, but couldn't help it.

"I know it sounds bad for Jennifer. But she's able to hire the best lawyers in the country," Dana reminded her. "So much of the evidence linking her to these crimes is circumstantial. The police still haven't come up with an eyewitness or any DNA evidence that links her to either poisoning."

"That's true," Maggie said quietly. "What about that drop of blood on the plastic bottle?"

"She didn't give a DNA sample. But maybe she will now," Dana added.

"That might tell the story." Suzanne shrugged.

Maggie didn't reply. She glanced around at her friends. "Well, let's have a bite and do some knitting. Better minds than ours have been trying to crack this nut."

Including Charles's mind, she wanted to add. But she felt too tired and drained now to tell her friends what happened between them. Or to hear all their well-meaning advice.

On Friday morning, Maggie flicked on the morning news. Just as she expected and dreaded, she heard it reported that Jennifer Todd had been arrested and charged with the attempted murder of her husband, Nick Pullman. And that further charges related to the homicide of actor Heath O'Hara were expected to follow.

"Ms. Todd remains in custody but is expected to be released on bail later today," the newscaster said.

Maggie felt sad and turned off the TV. Maybe it was true and she was really starstruck. Even worse than Suzanne.

She sincerely liked Jennifer Todd, and was surprised at this turn in the case. But she could get over that. What really hurt now was Charles. The case was closed, but she hadn't

244 / Anne Canadeo

heard from him. She had to assume she'd damaged their relationship beyond repair.

When she reached the shop, the flower-lined path did not cheer her as it usually did. The daffodils in particular seemed to be mocking her. She recalled the way Jennifer had recited the Wordsworth poem—"I wandered lonely as a cloud"—and felt foolish, taken in, by the actress.

Had she been taken in? Or was Jennifer Todd being framed by some dreadful enemy?

Luckily, Lucy stopped by before the coffee had even finished brewing. Maggie was glad for the distraction. Surprisingly, she was without her dogs. Though she had brought her laptop, Maggie noticed.

"No four-legged friends today? Did they decide to sleep in?" Maggie asked as she poured them each a mug.

"Matt had the day off. He took them for a jog on the beach."

"You didn't join the family? I'm flattered." Maggie actually was. She knew how Lucy loved to go running with Matt and the dogs.

"They're having some one-on-one time with their 'dad,'" Lucy replied. "Besides, I wanted to come here first thing. After the meeting last night, I couldn't resist noodling around on the Internet again. I tried to find out more about that situation with the actress who drowned at Nick Pullman's house. It seems that Jennifer was at that party, too."

Maggie sat down with her coffee across from Lucy. "That's interesting. So the three were tied by this incident?"

"It seems so. Remember last night you said why wasn't Trina a target of any accidents on the set? You probably meant maybe she was behind all this mayhem, right?"

"Yes, I did. Though she doesn't have much motivation, except wanting more time on screen in the film. And that's not enough. Even having her boyfriend take over the movie wouldn't justify *all* these events."

"I agree." Lucy nodded. "But what if three of them—Nick, Heath, and Jennifer—were all targets of one person? Someone who wanted to destroy all three of them and even undermine their film project? Nick and Heath were poisoned, and Jennifer made to look like the culprit."

Maggie considered this theory. "It sounds plausible . . . but who's behind all this? Who wants to see the three of them ruined that badly?"

Lucy had turned on her laptop and typed a bit. "I did a search for Lana Lambert. You can find out a frightening amount of information about people these days. Especially if you're willing to pay a small fee."

"You *paid* to find out about her?" And Charles thought *she* was obsessed with these police investigations.

"It wasn't much. About twenty dollars. The results came this morning. She was about the same age as Jennifer and attended the same acting school in LA."

"The same school as Jennifer and Heath?" Maggie said.

"That's right. They were classmates and were all at that party. Chances are that Heath, who already had some acquaintance with Nick, got the invitation and brought both of the girls. After Lana died, Nick said he didn't really know her and had not invited her directly. That she'd come with Heath O'Hara. Heath was dating Jennifer at the time, and maybe Lana was a mutual friend from acting classes."

"That sounds possible. I can imagine young, unknown actors eager to go to a party at some successful director's house. Trying to do each other a favor by bringing a friend along."

"Exactly," Lucy replied. "Lana Lambert was a stage name, which is why it was hard at first to find out anything about her."

"What was her real name?" Maggie asked curiously.

"Eileen Litowinsky. Sort of a mouthful. You can understand why she changed it."

"Absolutely. Lana Lambert is much more glamorous. Where did she grow up—did you find that out, too?"

"There was quite a list of prior residences before California. I guess her family moved around a lot. She had one sibling, a sister, Ava. About five years younger. Her father died recently but her mother is still alive. I'm not sure where she lives."

"That's all very interesting, but I'm not sure how it fits in. Except to give a more detailed picture of the poor girl." Maggie had a class coming soon but had already sorted out the yarn and other supplies. She set the basket on the middle of the table alongside some number-five needles.

"I'm not sure, either," Lucy admitted. She was about to close her computer but opened it again. "You just reminded me. I found a picture. Sort of blurry, but you might want to see."

She clicked a few times and a picture came on the screen. It was unclear, black and white, but looked professional. Maggie fumbled with her glasses and leaned toward the screen, peering over Lucy's shoulder.

"It's probably a head shot, the type actors send with their résumés when they audition for a role," Lucy said.

"She's flat-out gorgeous," Maggie murmured. "With some talent, she might have gone far."

"I thought the same," Lucy agreed.

Lana was a beautiful girl with thick, dark hair, high cheek-bones, and large dark eyes. She had an exotic look, simmering with sex appeal, even at that young age.

"I'm not sure how this connects, if it does at all. But it is a situation that Jennifer, Nick, and Heath shared, and a dark shadow on their past." Lucy closed the computer and looked up at her. "Do you think the police have made this connection yet?"

"I imagine so. I can't say for sure. Who knows what the police are thinking . . . except Dana, perhaps," she murmured.

"I thought you should call Charles. He might not have found this stuff yet. He might be interested."

"That's very considerate of you, Lucy. I would call Charles . . . but I'm not sure that we're speaking to each other."

Lucy sat back, looking shocked. "Why? I thought every-thing was going so well. Did you have a fight?"

"Not exactly . . ." Maggie tried to explain what had hap-pened without getting upset. But it was hard. "So I thought I was being considerate of him. And he thought I was being . . . I don't know, willful or something? It just got so fouled up. And we decided we wouldn't be in touch until the case is over. But this case is over, it seems. And he hasn't gotten in touch with me. Either way, I doubt it will be a very happy reunion. More like a second breakup," she said.

"Oh, I don't know about that. You can work it out. He's under a ton of pressure right now."

Maggie sighed. "Unfortunately, I added to it. I guess we'll just have to see what happens. I'm not sure how it will go," she added honestly, trying to sound far more sanguine about the situation than she felt.

"Maybe I should tell them," Lucy said. "It might be helpful. I don't even have to tell Charles. Any of the detectives would hear me out. For a few minutes," she added.

"I hope they do. They might not be interested, since they think the murderer is behind bars. I feel doubly sad for Jennifer. I think she's innocent, and now she's all alone here, with no one to support her but some attorney she probably doesn't even know. Her husband is in a hospital, still in intensive care. One of her very best friends, and possibly her lover, is dead, and even Alicia is in LA by now. Jen told me yesterday that everyone had left for Heath's memorial service."

"Maybe Alicia will come back . . . or maybe Regina Thurston?" Lucy offered.

"I hope so. Maybe her family will come to help her. She should be out on bail soon, but she might have to stay in Massachusetts," she added. She looked back at Lucy again. "I'm not sure how all this information about Lana Lambert can help her. But if there's any possibility at all, I think you should bring it to them. Even if they do brush you off, at least you tried."

"That's what I'm thinking, too." Lucy stood up and tucked the computer case under her arm. She glanced at her watch. "But I can't go right now. I offered to ride with Suzanne out to the beach house. The police said she can finally do her walk-through. I'll go right after that. She can drop me at the station."

"You're a brave woman, Lucy Binger. I applaud you. You know how the police always scoff at *amateurs*. They say we're crackpots and busybodies."

"But we know that we aren't either. And a Black Sheep knitter's got to do what she's got to do."

Maggie could not argue with that.

* * *

Lucy met Suzanne at Prestige Properties, a few blocks down Main Street. They were soon cruising past the Marshes and heading for the Beach Road in Suzanne's SUV. Suzanne seemed uncommonly distracted and anxious.

"Thanks for coming with me, Lucy. You're a pal." Suzanne turned to her briefly, with a thin smile. "I just want to get this over with. I don't know what's rattling me more—visiting the spot where poor Heath died or waiting to see if the cops trashed the house."

"Maybe both? I feel sad going back there, too," Lucy admitted. It was impossible not to think of Heath today. "If I saw all of this in a movie—everything that's happened to these Hollywood people this past week—I'd say, that is totally unbelievable."

"I hear you. Has it only been a week? It feels like a freaking month," Suzanne moaned.

They drove in uncommon silence for a few minutes. Suzanne turned on the road parallel to the beach and the house soon came into view.

The trucks that transported the movie equipment were gone, but Lucy was surprised to see the big white RVs still parked on the side of the road, a few strands of crime scene tape drifting in the wind around them like yellow streamers.

"I didn't think the trailers would still be here," said Lucy.

"The police didn't release the crime scene until late last night. I guess nobody dealt with removing the trailers yet. Jennifer is in jail, Nick is in the hospital and . . ." Suzanne didn't finish. They both knew the rest.

Suzanne parked on the side of the road, a short distance from the trailers. They climbed out and she paused, fishing through her big black leather purse for something. "Drat . . . I must have the keys to this place in here somewhere . . ."

While Suzanne searched, Lucy gazed around. It was so quiet and empty here now. So different from the night Heath died. She could hear the waves rolling into the shore, a hollow, crashing sound. A few birds swooped and dipped above the tall beach grass, chirping to one another, as a light breeze shifted the reeds.

Then she heard another sound, one she couldn't quite identify. Like a hammer striking wood. *Crunch, crunch.* Then it stopped.

Suzanne had found the keys and sighed with relief. "If I had forgotten these babies, I was just going to scream—"

"Shhhh . . ." Lucy touched her arm. "Did you hear that?" She turned and met her friend's surprised, puzzled frown. "That sound."

"I don't hear anything . . ."

Suzanne had not even finished speaking when Lucy heard it again. She could tell from Suzanne's expression she'd heard it, too.

"It's coming from inside this trailer." She spoke quietly, pointing to the nearest vehicle. Lucy already recognized it. It was Jennifer Todd's, and they were standing at the back end.

"Maybe it's someone from the movie company. Here to drive the trailers somewhere." The explanation was logical, but Suzanne whispered also.

The hammering got louder and faster now. Whoever was inside, handling the tools, was intent. They probably didn't even hear us drive up, Lucy realized.

"Let's walk up to a window. Maybe we can see what's going on," Lucy suggested quietly.

She led the way, walking close to the trailer, on the side opposite where the hammering sound was taking place. They had reached the middle of the long vehicle and could see the door. The glass on the door window was shattered.

Someone had broken in.

Suzanne saw it, too, and nodded. They stood at the middle of the trailer, not as far as the sitting room where Jen had entertained them. Probably near the bedroom Lucy had noticed when they were inside, having tea.

"There's a window up there." The shade was pulled down but Lucy thought she could see a little through that space near the sill. "Give me a boost," she whispered to Suzanne.

"Are you kidding? I can't walk around with a bad back all week. I have a life," she hissed back.

Lucy gave her a look. "Hey, this is my adventure, okay? I'm calling the shots today. I always do the stupid things you tell me to do."

Suzanne seemed shocked, then nearly laughed out loud.

"Whoa . . . hear her roar," she whispered with uncommon respect. "You have a point. What do you want me to do?"

"Cup your hands so I can jump up and look in the window. I can hold myself up after that."

Suzanne sighed and leaned over as Lucy slipped off her shoes. "Cirque du Soleil, here we come . . ."

Lucy jumped up, clinging to the side of the RV. There was a wheel well nearby and she stuck one foot on a big tire and the other in Suzanne's hand. She reached the window and held on with both hands, her fingers curled on the narrow ledge as she stared inside.

The window was in a bedroom, as she'd guessed. She couldn't see anyone in the room at first. Then she saw a figure reflected in a large mirror at a dressing table. Of course a star would have a gigantic mirror framed by large lights in her movie location trailer.

Someone was squatting on the floor in the corner, at a large wall-to-wall closet, the folding doors pulled open. Lucy couldn't tell if it was a man or a woman. They wore a sweat-shirt with a hood pulled up. The person held a sledgehammer in one hand and a large metal chisel in the other. Tools used to break up bricks or concrete. They leaned into the closet and seemed to be working with the hammer at the back wall, which was covered by wooden paneling.

"Gonna drop you in a minute . . ." Suzanne gasped. "Hope you're okay with that?"

"Wait . . ." Lucy hissed back as the hammering began again. "Just a—"

The intruder stopped hammering and suddenly tossed the tools aside. Lucy held her breath, expecting the intruder to come to the window. But the mystery figure jumped up and impa-tiently grabbed at clothes on a rack above the spot where they worked, pulling everything out of the closet and flinging it to the floor. Then pieces of wood came flying across the room as well.

Lucy saw the prize in the closet, a safe that was hidden in the wall. The intruder seemed frustrated and angry. But dou-bly determined. The hammer and chisel was grabbed up again and as the thief set to work, the sweatshirt hood fell back. Lucy finally saw the thief's face and gasped.

But before she could say a word, Suzanne groaned and Lucy felt the bottom drop out of her support. She was sud-denly falling to the ground and only managed to soften her landing by clinging to the side of the RV and sliding down.

She practically landed on Suzanne, who was squatting close to the ground, breathless and grumpy.

"It's Alicia . . . she's trying to break into a wall safe in Jen's bedroom. She probably knows the combination, once she gets to it." They sat on the ground, side by side, checking for bodily damage and searching for a second wind.

"Alicia? I thought she went back to LA for Heath's memorial service."

"I guess she had some business to take care of here first," Lucy said quietly, rubbing a bruised knee. "We'd better call the police."

"I know . . . but we can't let her get away. That little rat . . . and she always acted so devoted to Jen. What a phony!" Suzanne had seemed exhausted a second ago but was suddenly totally energized.

"Suzanne, she might be dangerous. We can't go in there."

Suzanne frowned. "Oh right. She might hammer us?"

"Be serious. I'm calling 911." Lucy waved her hand. "Let's go down toward your car. So she can't hear us."

Lucy led the way on tiptoe and Suzanne followed. She heard the pounding hammer, slow and steady. Alicia was hard at work on the wooden wall. But Lucy was still cautious and spoke to the emergency dispatcher in a whisper. She reported the address and a robbery in progress and gave her name.

"The police are on the way, ma'am. Where are you now?"

"On Plum Beach Road, right across from house number 107."

"You need to leave. Find a safe place," the operator advised. "Do you want me to—"

The call suddenly broke up. Lucy stared at the phone as the line went dead.

"Bad cell service out here," Suzanne observed.

"She said to find a safe place. Let's go. We can drive down the road and wait for the police in your car."

Suzanne put her finger to her lips and pointed. Lucy saw a

little motor scooter leaning next to the other side of the trailer. There was a bike and scooter rental shop in town, right next to the Lord Charles Inn. Alicia must have picked it up there.

"That's why we didn't see a car. Let's hide it so she can't make a fast getaway," Suzanne whispered.

Lucy nodded. "Good idea."

They tiptoed toward the scooter. The hammering had stopped and Lucy winced at every crunch of sand under her feet.

The scooter was right under the window. It was a light scooter, little more than a bike with a motor on it, but they soon found the rear wheel was locked and it could not easily be rolled away.

"Great," Suzanne said. "Now we need Houdini, too, to unlock this darn thing. Maybe Alicia will loan us the hammer."

"Just pick up your end. We can slide it," Lucy whispered harshly.

Suzanne grabbed the back end of the scooter and started walking backward, toward the rear of the trailer again. "Let's put it in the marsh grass. Where she won't see it."

Lucy nodded, holding the handlebars and rolling it along as best she could.

Suzanne turned her head to see where they were going, then looked back at Lucy. Her expression went slack. "Oh . . . crackers . . ."

Lucy turned to see what Suzanne was staring at. Though part of her brain already knew.

"Drop that scooter, damn it!" Alicia ran toward them. The hood was up again and she wore big sunglasses. She had a huge pack on her back, bulging with booty, Lucy suspected. And in one hand, she brandished the big sledgehammer.

Lucy stood back against the trailer, every nerve ending tingling. But didn't let go of the scooter handles. Suzanne dropped her end, but crouched down, in a squared-off, bulldog stance.

Lucy didn't think Suzanne knew martial arts. But she sure looked like she did now.

"You little punk . . . You cheap, two-faced little rat," Suzanne shouted at Alicia. "Jennifer trusts you. Don't you have a shred of conscience?"

"Shut up. What do you know about anything? Why don't you ask Jennifer Todd about her conscience? Or any of them." Alicia scoffed. She tried to grab the scooter away from Lucy, but Lucy held on fast, without saying a word. "Let go, you idiot."

Lucy didn't answer, just bit her lip and tightened her grip. Alicia pulled a slim key from her sweatshirt pocket and snapped open the ignition lock. The rear wheel was free now. Alicia started the motor with a twist of the handle bar, even with no one on it.

"Let go of the damn scooter, or you'll never knit again. I promise you . . ."

Alicia aimed the sledgehammer at Lucy's knuckles. Lucy stared into her eyes as she swung back the metal head to take a solid swing.

"Ava . . . stop. I know you loved Eileen . . . but none of this will bring her back."

Alicia stared at her in shock. Lucy knew her wild guess had hit a bull's-eye. Alicia's face turned beet red, her eyes narrowing with anger.

"They deserved to die. They all do. I hope Jen rots in jail and all over again in hell," she screamed as she focused again on Lucy's hand, and began to lower the hammer.

Lucy braced herself, about to let go of the scooter. But Suzanne had snuck behind Alicia, and suddenly pounced. She grabbed on to the pack and pulled Alicia back, the hammer dropping from her hand. Alarmed and caught by surprise, Alicia clung to the straps of the backpack with both hands. She wasn't going to let go of her prize so easily.

Taking full advantage of Alicia's greed, Suzanne pulled with all her might, standing solidly in one spot as she swung Alicia around in a circle. For a moment, it looked like Alicia was on a carnival ride. She screamed, her feet flying out from under her, turning in a full circle and finally coming to a stop. Alicia staggered, looking dizzy and drunk; Suzanne pounced on her, pushing her facedown on the ground. Then quickly straddled her body, leaning over the pack to grab Alicia's flailing arms.

It all happened so quickly; Lucy stood there dumbstruck.

Alicia twisted and squirmed, while Suzanne held her down, as if riding a bucking bronco.

"Help me, for pity's sake! I feel like I'm wrestling an alligator!"

Lucy let go of the scooter and it crashed to the ground, motor sputtering. She grabbed one of Alicia's kicking legs and held it to the ground while Suzanne continued to hold down their captive's arms.

"Let me go . . . I can't breathe!" Alicia managed.

"Stop moving . . . and I'll let you breathe. Just a little. You're lucky the police are on the way. Every time I think about what you did to my Heath, I can't trust myself," Suzanne growled at her. Obviously, from what Lucy had said and Alicia's reaction, Suzanne had put the pieces together, too.

Lucy wasn't sure if Suzanne was serious. But she sounded

serious enough to put a scare into Alicia—Ava Litowinsky, actually.

Suzanne was a tiger when cornered. Lucy had no idea what a street fighter she was. Though she'd never doubt her friend would be fierce defending—or avenging—anyone she loved.

Finally Alicia's body went limp. She was exhausted and knew she wasn't getting away. Lucy felt relieved but still held Alicia's leg with both hands. Suzanne was vigilant, too, as they heard the siren in the distance grow louder.

The police car pulled up to the trailer and two officers jumped out. Not brandishing firearms, but looking ready to, Lucy noticed.

"We got her, Officer," Suzanne called out. "She was trying to escape on that scooter, but we nabbed her."

The police officers stared at the scene in amazement. Lucy had to admit, they must have made a strange sight, Suzanne on Alicia's back and Lucy holding her leg, the fallen scooter with its motor still chugging.

"Get her off me! My ribs are broken!" Alicia squirmed under Suzanne like a bug, calling for help.

"It's all right, miss. We'll take it from here." One of the officers stood beside Suzanne and spoke in a calm tone.

Lucy let go of Alicia's leg and Suzanne slowly stood up as the other officer took charge of their captive. He removed the backpack and cuffed Alicia quickly.

"This weighs a ton," he told his partner as he led Alicia to the cruiser. "Check it out."

The officer near Lucy picked up the pack and unzipped it a few inches. "Whew . . . nice haul. Cash, jewelry, trinkets."

"Jennifer Todd's trinkets. She's Jennifer assistant and everyone thinks she's in California," Lucy told them.

"You know her?"

Lucy and Suzanne nodded. "It's a long story," Lucy said.

"I had a feeling. Let me take your names and contact information." He took out a pad and pen. "I guess you should both come down to the station to give your statements."

"I'd be delighted. I have a lot to say," Lucy replied, brushing herself off.

"Me, too. We're a team." Suzanne straightened her blazer and the badge from her real-estate office, then brushed the dirt from her knees.

"So I noticed," the officer said dryly.

It was about half past noon when Maggie went outside to water the window boxes and flower beds. Even the taunting daffodils deserved a drink, she thought. She had her back to the street and didn't notice Charles until he was right behind her. She turned quickly and nearly soaked him with the hose.

"I'm sorry . . . I didn't see you there."

He smiled sheepishly. "That's all right. I deserved that."

Maggie had to smile, though his unexpected visit made her nervous.

They went inside and Maggie brought him a towel. She didn't know what to say. She wondered if Lucy had gone to see him at the station. Plenty of time had passed since Lucy's trip to the beach house with Suzanne. Though she hadn't heard from either of her friends since.

"Did Lucy come to see you today? She's been nosing around the Internet about the movie stars," she admitted.

"I did see Lucy. And Suzanne," he added. "And Ava Litowinsky. Also know as Alicia Littel."

Maggie suddenly realized the case was solved . . . and the police had been wrong about Jennifer. She felt so relieved she wanted to jump up and give Charles a huge hug. But decided not to. She had no idea how he'd react.

"So she told you her theory. How did you put it together? Alicia looks nothing like Lana Lambert—Eileen Litowinsky, I mean."

"No, she doesn't. Not now. We had been looking into the Lana Lambert lead, too. And came up with photos of Lana— Eileen Litowinsky—and her younger sister, Ava. There's the head shot of Eileen that Lucy found. And one of Ava from a high school yearbook. But we still didn't figure it out. Ava changed her appearance so drastically, along with her name. Intentionally, of course," he added.

"Of course," Maggie agreed. "So she could get close to Jennifer, Nick, and Heath, without them noticing a resemblance . . . How did Lucy's information help?"

"It didn't. But Lucy did. And so did Suzanne. They caught Alicia cleaning out a safe in Jennifer's trailer. I don't know how the police search missed it. But it was well concealed. And we did come up with the daffodil bulbs, hidden in a coffee can in the closet, and the pot that Alicia cooked them in. Planted there for us to find," he added with chagrin. "Alicia didn't have the key to the hiding panel but did know the safe combination. But your friends managed to hold her there until the police came and took her into custody."

Maggie's jaw dropped. "You're kidding! When was this?"

"An hour or so ago, I guess." Charles glanced at his watch. "I was called down when the arresting officers brought Alicia in and your friends gave their statements. That's when Lucy pulled out her laptop," he said with a small smile. "She told me that I should be the one to bring you the news that the case was solved." He gave her a look, knowing she'd confided their relationship problems to Lucy. But understanding, too.

"I suspect they'll be calling soon with all the gritty details," he continued. "They were real heroes, both of them. Alicia was armed. Just a sledgehammer," he added when Maggie nearly gasped aloud again.

"I can't believe it." Maggie shook her head. "I can't wait to hear the whole story. So you had both photos, and Alicia . . . and figured out the connection and her motive?"

"When Lucy confronted her, she just about admitted everything. She's being held on robbery charges now," Charles explained, "but she broke down quickly once we started questioning her. She said she did it to avenge her older sister Eileen's death. She blamed the three of them—Nick, Heath, and Jennifer.

"That night at Nick Pullman's house," he continued, "when Eileen drowned, Alicia believes that Heath and her sister were alone at the pool and he encouraged Eileen to drink too much, trying to seduce her. Then he fell asleep, while Eileen fell into the water and drowned."

"So all the flowers and poetic references to Narcissus and lost love did make sense," Maggie said. "Is that true?"

"Well, she was an English major in college. But the statements taken during the investigation of Eileen Litowinsky's death don't match her scenario. However, Nick and Jennifer were in the house and Heath was alone outside with Eileen. That part of her story is confirmed. I doubt we'll ever know for sure," he added. "But Alicia was also angry that Nick bought her parents off to save his own career . . . and protected Heath and Jennifer. Alicia hated her parents for that, too."

"So she'd planned this revenge scheme her whole life. Or ever since her sister died," Maggie murmured.

"Looks like it. She came to LA after college and wrangled her way into the job at Jennifer Todd's house, starting as a dog walker, drawing Jennifer and Nick into her confidence."

"She did a good job playing the role of devoted assistant," Maggie mused. "She has some acting talent herself."

"Undoubtedly. When Jennifer and Nick teamed with Heath to make the movie, the three of them were sitting ducks for Alicia. She saw her chance to finally get revenge. To undermine the production they'd all invested in so heavily. And to physically harm them, any way she could. The combination was too tempting for her to resist."

"I can see now how it all falls into place. I didn't for the longest time," Maggie admitted.

"Neither did we," he said. "The case is closed and the guilty party is behind bars. We just dropped all charges against Todd and are about to release her."

"I'm glad to hear that," Maggie said sincerely. She wondered if she would hear from Jen before she left town. She'd probably run straight to Boston, to be with Nick, she realized. "What a shock for her, to hear it was Alicia, who she truly trusted. Even loved. What a painful betrayal."

Charles nodded. "Jennifer was shocked. It was a blow. Alicia had tricked us all. Operating in clear sight, flying right under our radar. She had a one-way ticket to Brazil in that pack, and was ready to fly out of Logan this afternoon. Fake ID and passport, the works. We would have never found her, if not for you and your friends. They took a big personal risk this morning . . . Not that I'm encouraging it," he added quickly.

262 / Anne Canadeo

Maggie laughed. "Believe me, I know. But it's good of you to say."

He paused and gazed into her eyes. "I'm sorry we had words over this."

"I'm sorry, too," Maggie said quickly. "It wasn't worth it. I shouldn't be so stubborn. And touchy."

"I was being a little stubborn myself. Too macho or something?" He made a face that was very endearing.

She reached across the table and took his hand. "Maybe. But I can deal with a little macho . . . or something . . . from time to time. Not a problem."

"Show us again how you took Alicia down, Suzanne. Please?" Phoebe sat back in an armchair near the fireplace, ready for a show.

Lucy was just coming into the living room with a tray of appetizers: fresh feta cheese and cucumber and tomato chunks with red onion and dill. She'd also made her friends hummus and tzatsiki dip with crudités and pita slices. It was her turn to host their weekly meeting and for once she was ready on time and all her friends had arrived promptly, too.

Which was a good thing, because she and Maggie had cooked up a little surprise for them that did require careful timing.

"Come on, Phoebe. Nobody wants to see that again." Suzanne shook her head, but Lucy could tell she was tempted to demonstrate their amateur "collar" of Ava—alias Alicia—again.

"I'd like to see it one more time, and I was there," Lucy encouraged her.

Dana sat smiling and looked up from her knitting. Maggie took a bit of humus and feta salad on her plate. "I bet you could teach us all a class in self-defense, Suzanne," she said. "That might be useful someday. If we don't have any knitting needles handy." Maggie added. Of course, that would be her weapon of choice.

Suzanne didn't need too much coaxing. "Okay, one more time." She came to her feet and stood in the middle of the room. "It was a simple, playground, bad-girl move. I need a volunteer."

Phoebe jumped up and raised her hand. "I'll be Alicia."

"You need something on your back, for a pack. Use your knitting bag—perfect," Suzanne said. Phoebe did use a backpack for her knitting and slipped the straps onto her shoulders.

Suzanne positioned Phoebe and faced her toward the door. "She was yelling at Lucy, about to spill her guts about the murders. So I just snuck up behind her, grabbed the pack, and whirled her around like this . . ."

Suzanne demonstrated her heroic move. But Phoebe was light, much lighter than Alicia, and was caught by surprise with little motivation to hold on to her knitting bag. Hardly the treasure trove Alicia had clung to so fiercely.

Almost as soon as Suzanne spun her, the straps of the pack slipped off Phoebe's slim arms and she flew across the room, screaming with glee. "Whoa!"

Everybody stared, dumbfounded, as Phoebe landed on the couch, like a surfer washing up onshore, across Maggie's and Dana's laps. Maggie grabbed hold of her flying assistant's shoulders to slow her momentum, as a glass of wine tipped over and the basket of pita pieces fell.

The dogs quickly jumped up to gobble the bread and even lapped a few drops of wine.

Everyone gasped and ran to the couch..

"Phoebe . . . are you all right?" Dana pushed Phoebe's hair back so they could see her face. Suzanne and Lucy hovered over them.

Phoebe slowly lifted her head. "I think so . . ." She squirmed out of Maggie's hold and sat in the middle of her friends. "Thanks for catching me," she murmured.

"Happy to help. You were really moving," Maggie said sincerely.

Suzanne was upset. "I'm so sorry! I didn't mean to throw you across the room . . ."

"That's okay. It was fun," Phoebe insisted, in a bit of a daze.

Lucy shook her head and laughed as she quickly dabbed up the wine with some napkins. "Enough of our glory days in law enforcement. I would like to hear more about how Alicia managed all her heinous deeds. Since Charles has been sharing the inside story, Maggie."

Lucy had not meant to embarrass her friend, but the meaningful note in her voice did make Maggie blush.

"He knows how to get on my good side. What can I say?" Maggie replied. "The DNA tests on the blood droplet on the bottle came back. Alicia's blood is a perfect match. Along with a bit of iodine mixed on the stain, which came from the scab on her hand from the cut she got when the light fixture fell." Maggie turned to Phoebe and caught her glance. "You were the only one who wondered why the person who poisoned Nick dumped the bottle in such an obvious place and didn't try to hide it better, or destroy it. Now we know why. She wanted it to be found easily and had rigged the bottle to be linked with Jennifer."

"How did she manage that?" Dana asked.

"Remember when she came to the shop Tuesday morn-ing, after she and Jen had visited the night before? She said Jen needed more yarn for her project. I didn't think much of it at the time, but had been pretty sure I'd given Jen the right amount for the pattern. I thought maybe she knit with a very tight stitch. Or was making the pattern for someone with a larger size. Anyway," Maggie said, "Alicia kept that skein for herself, planning to use it to frame Jen. It didn't matter where the tote actually was. She had her own yarn and rubbed it on the bottle before disposing of it. She wanted to make it look as if Jennifer had picked up the bottle and hid it in the tote. But Alicia's plan was fouled up when Jen left the tote at the shop the night Nick was poisoned. No one saw Jen touch the tote, from the time Nick was poisoned to the time she got into the ambulance. In fact, all the video on the news confirmed Jen's story. And the tote was here, under police protection from Thursday night until they found the bottle," Maggie explained.

"But Alicia still thought she'd get away with it," she added, "since the police suspected Jen and were building a case against her. But when the police finally compared the yarn in the tote with the fiber on the bottle, the fibers turned out to be from a different dye lot than Jen's. One that matched a skein they found in Alicia's belongings. And the police couldn't find any trace at all of the bottle or the liquid in the knitting bag after they took Jen into custody and had it back. Though they examined every inch microscopically."

"So, when everyone was panicking about Nick's attack, Alicia took the bottle, hid it somewhere—in a pocket or in her purse—and rubbed the gluey part with her own yarn before she dumped it," Lucy said, trying to get the specifics straight.

"Yes . . . and dumped it in an obvious spot, in a trash can on the village green, right across from Jennifer's hotel," Dana added.

"Wow, is she diabolical or what?" Suzanne had gotten over nearly flinging Phoebe through Lucy's bay window and was enjoying the appetizers. "What about the light fixture? How did she manage that one?"

"Oh, that was pretty simple. Remember when we walked into the shop, we had to speak to a girl who was taping down the extension cords all over the floor?" Maggie asked.

Suzanne nodded, her mouth full.

"Alicia pulled up the tape that was under the table, attached to that big fixture, then ran a thin wire from the base of the fixture to the spot where she was sitting. She said it wasn't hard to do, with all the confusion of the crew putting the set together. No one even noticed her. She maneuvered Jen to sit there and go over the script. She thought Heath was going to be sitting there, too. But he was late for the meeting."

"I remember that," Suzanne cut in. "Jen was asking Alicia to text him. So she didn't care who she killed first. She was painting with a wide brush."

"Yes, she didn't care who she hurt with that part of the plan. I saw her stand up and say she wanted a bottle of water," Maggie recalled. "She had wound the wire around her foot and was pulling down the metal tripod with the lights as she walked away."

"Like a magician on a stage," Phoebe remarked.

"Exactly. When the fixture fell, like a big metal tree, and all the broken glass sprayed everywhere, no one noticed a stray wire in the mess," Maggie added. "Though she admitted that she cut her hand on the wire, not a piece of glass, pulling it off the tripod stand, so no one would find it. Later, the gaffers thought the equipment, which they'd rented in Boston, was just old and had not been assembled correctly."

"And there she was, getting so much sympathy for hurting herself, trying to clean the glass off Jen, and she was just covering up her own dirty work," Lucy said.

"Exactly," Maggie agreed.

"The fire in Heath's trailer," Suzanne reminded them. "That was a good one."

"Alicia had access to all the trailers. She was constantly in and out, delivering laundry, scripts, food. She knew all the combinations to the door locks. Heath told everyone he was taking a sleeping pill to take a nap. He claimed that he hadn't slept well the night before and had to shoot a scene that night at the house. Alicia snuck into his trailer and set a fire in a wastepaper basket with some of his own cigarette butts, which she'd found in his living room. She slipped open his bedroom door a crack and left it there, thinking he was in bed and wouldn't wake up because of the pill. But she never looked to make sure he was there."

"Ha!" Suzanne laughed out loud. "So she was surprised, too, to hear the sleeping pill story was just a cover for a tryst with Trina, in her trailer."

Maggie nodded. "Yes, she was surprised. And annoyed that plot had failed. So she moved on to the poisonings— the digitalis from the lily of the valley arrangement in Jen's trailer. She tossed it into the juicer and added it to the special health smoothies. She injected the poison into the plastic bottle with a syringe and sealed the hole with glue," Maggie reminded them. Lucy did remember that Dana had told them that, too.

"And the daffodil bulbs were cooked up in Jen's trailer, right?" Suzanne asked.

"That's right. She left the pot unwashed at the back of a closet in the kitchen and some bulbs in a coffee can, in a closet as well. Again, she had no problem at all slipping the potion into Heath's diet lemonade. He was carrying around a plastic bottle full of the stuff and drinking it all day. Anyone could have tampered with it." Maggie shrugged.

"But all her heinous handiwork on the set was just the last act of a long, complicated plan," Maggie added. "She'd been working on this scheme for months. While the movie was being planned, she was planning these murders and how to frame Jen. Creating the fake online stalker, leaving notes on Jen's fan page, using Jen's own computer. So that Jen would be accused later of trying to create a cover for herself."

"Alicia . . . Ava, I mean, has amazing intelligence. Imagine if she'd channeled it toward something worthwhile, like medical research or inventing things," Dana said wistfully. "What a waste."

"I guess she'll spend a long time in jail now," Lucy said.

"Yes, most likely. She'll have years to figure out how to channel that genius toward something constructive. Though I doubt that she will," Maggie added.

"What about Jennifer? Has anyone heard from her since she went back to LA?"

They all knew that after Jennifer had been released from custody, she went to Boston to be with Nick. His condition had improved and they were able to return to California on Monday. That news had been reported on TV.

"I heard from her," Maggie said. "She called from the airport, just to say good-bye."

"Too bad she couldn't come back and say good-bye in person, but I'm not surprised," Suzanne said with a shrug. "I bet she's not in any hurry to visit Plum Harbor again. It wasn't exactly a happy experience."

"She is a big movie star. We tend to forget that," Dana added. "She was very sweet to us when we spent time with her, but I doubt we'll hear from her."

"To the contrary, Dana. She really did want to come see us again. She even wished she could come to another meeting," Maggie insisted. "In fact, she's coming here tonight, on Skype. Lucy is going to set up the computer right now," she added, glancing at her watch.

"Really?" Phoebe, who had been very quiet since flying across the room, suddenly sat up. "She's going to knit with us again?"

"She'll be here in one minute," Lucy promised, picking up her laptop. It was on the lamp table, safely out of the way of her flying guests. Lucy flipped it open and brought up the Skype program and Jen's contact information.

Jen was already at her computer, waiting for them, and her lovely, smiling face soon filled the screen. "Hi, everyone!" She waved to them.

The knitters all waved back. "Hi, Jen!"

Not much was visible, aside from Jen's face and shoulders. But in the background Lucy could see a hint of Jennifer's house, a spacious living room with a simple but luxurious-looking decor.

"Thanks for coming to the meeting. This is so cool," Phoebe said sincerely.

"It is, isn't it?" Jennifer laughed. "Maybe I can be a regular and tune in from LA or wherever," she added. "Nick is really improving. We have a live-in nurse and of course Theo is here. He's got an idea for a movie based on everything we've just been through. They're already taking meetings by the pool," Jen added, glancing over her shoulder.

"I'm not surprised," Lucy said. "What about the movie, will you continue to work on it?"

She wondered if she should have asked that, but she was curious.

"Yes, we will. We're going to finish it. They've decided they can finish without . . . Heath." She sighed, her gaze lowered for a moment. "We'll have to see how that works out. Nick and I are trying to work things out, too. With the movie . . . and our marriage," she confided.

Lucy was happy to hear that, too. It would take time, but Jennifer sounded as if she was getting her life back on track, after these awful and tragic events had swept through like a tsunami. Lucy hoped Jen and Nick would have the privacy they needed to mend their relationship and their lives.

"I just want to thank you all for . . . for what you did. The way you helped me," Jennifer added. "I still can't believe what happened. It was a nightmare. Or like playing a character in a very dark drama. Except that I didn't know the ending and could never walk off the set. Nobody believed me. Except all of you."

Lucy knew that there were moments when at least one or two of her friends had their doubts. But by and large, it was true. They had believed her and had helped to track down the real murderer.

"We knew you were innocent. It just wasn't right. We had

to find the person who did," Suzanne replied. "I hope you don't think badly of Plum Harbor forever."

"On the contrary, when I think of Plum Harbor, I know I have friends there. *Real* friends." Jennifer's smile beamed warmly. Lucy knew for sure she wasn't acting.

"That you do," Maggie promised her. "Friends who knit together *stick* together."

"I agree," Jen said wholeheartedly. "So . . . let the knitting begin. What are we working on tonight?" she asked brightly.

"I have a lacy summer shawl pattern to show everyone. But first we're going to show off our tank tops. Did you finish yours?" Maggie asked.

"I haven't blocked it yet. But I have it right here."

Jennifer turned away from the camera for a moment and soon held up the tank. She had chosen a shade of sea-blue yarn that matched her eyes, Lucy thought. "I was wondering if I should add some embellishment to the neckline, to perk it up a bit? Maybe just an edging in a contrasting color."

"That's a great idea," Maggie encouraged her.

"Look what I did to mine," Phoebe said proudly. She held up her finished project. Which was about six inches shorter than the pattern called for, Lucy noticed, with ribbing on the bottom about three inches long. "I made a crop top, instead of a long tank. It's a little hipper looking, I thought." She shrugged.

"It definitely is and you can wear it, too, kiddo," Suzanne said. "With my hips and top . . ." She shook her head. "I don't think so."

Everyone laughed, including Jennifer. It was good to see

her so lighthearted, Lucy realized, after all she'd been through. It was great fun to know that the Black Sheep knitting circle could boast a real celebrity member now, too.

Jennifer must have picked up on her thoughts. "It's so much fun to hang out with you. I'd almost forgotten," she admitted. "Maybe sometime we can have the meeting at my house."

Lucy and her friends exchanged looks and smiles. "My bags are packed, Jen," Suzanne answered for all of them. "Hollywood, here we come!"

Notes from the Black Sheep Knitting Shop
Bulletin Board

Dear knitting friends--

Sorry for the delay posting a new pattern on the board. I don't know about you, but I'm just getting back to my unglamorous but peaceful life. It was very exciting to have the movie crew in town . . . though not all the excitement we expected. But as Shakespeare once said, "All's well that ends well."

And yes, it's true—the famous Jennifer Todd is now an honorary member of the Black Sheep Knitters. She had a great time knitting with us, and even finished our latest project—an easy, ribbed summer tank top. She's sending a photo soon, modeling her creation. In the meantime, I'm posting links to two summer tank patterns. I think you'll enjoy making and wearing both of them.

Please feel free to post a photo of your finished project on the board, too. That honor is not reserved for Hollywood celebrities. I think you're all rare and wonderful.

Happy knitting!

Maggie

Link to Ribbed Tank Top:
http://www.free-knitpatterns.com/detail.html?code=FK00461&cat__id=382

Link to Lacey Shoulder-Tie Tank Top:
http://www.allfreeknitting.com/Tanks/Lilac-Lace-Tank

Dear Friends,

I'm still not sure "the way to a man's heart is through his stomach." And I don't think I'd admit it, even if I did believe it was true. (The old adage is certainly not very flattering to our male friends, is it?)

I do know that it's very satisfying to cook for someone you really care for, and enjoying a delicious, relaxing dinner with others is a wonderful way to end the day and nourish any relationship.

So, here is a favorite, easy recipe for Flounder Stuffed with Shrimp. Charles really loves it, and since you can set up the fish ahead and stick it in the refrigerator until it's time to cook, I make it for dinner parties, too.

Maggie

Flounder Stuffed with Shrimp

Serves 2–4

2 to 3 wide slices of flounder fillet—about 1½ lbs.
(If the slices are narrow, you'll need more slices,
    about 4.)
8 to 9 medium to large shrimp, cleaned and deveined,
    tails removed
4 Tablespoons of flour, divided
4 Tablespoons of unsalted butter
4 Tablespoons of olive oil
½ cup fresh parsley, chopped
¼ cup fresh dill, chopped
1 to 2 lemons
toothpicks

Preheat oven to 375 degrees.

Line a rimmed cookie sheet with parchment paper.

Rinse shrimp, pat dry. Spread 2 to 3 tablespoons
white flour in a flat dish.

Heat 1 tablespoon butter with 1 to 2 tablespoons
olive oil in a large, flat heavy skillet until butter is just
foamy.

Lightly dredge shrimp in flour and place flat on one
side in skillet, a few at a time. (Don't add too many shrimp

to the pan at once, or pan will cool down and fish will release too much liquid.)

Cook shrimp on each side until they are white/opaque, but not cooked through. Set aside as they are done.

Spread 1 to 2 tablespoons of olive oil evenly on cookie sheet, or spray lightly with cooking spray.

Spread flounder slices flat on the cookie sheet, smooth side facing the pan.

Place 2 to 3 shrimp at the widest end of each slice and roll flounder around the shrimp, securing with toothpicks .

Line the flounder rolls up in pan, evenly spaced apart. Pat each very lightly with some flour.

Melt 1 to 2 tablespoons butter and drizzle over fish. Place pan on middle rack in the oven.

After 5 minutes, lower heat to 350 degrees.

Cook about 5 minutes more. Test for doneness with a sharp knife. Flounder should be flakey and cooked through, but not dry.

Remove from oven and squeeze fresh lemon over all the slices, then sprinkle some parsley and dill on top. Garnish with thin lemon slices and serve immediately.

Enjoy!

Dear All--

Rumors are still swirling around me. Comes with the territory of being semifamous, I guess. I decided to answer your top questions here, instead of holding a press conference :)

Yes--I did capture Alicia Littel, as she was fleeing town on a motor bike. After allegedly (pul-leeze . . .of course she did it) fatally poisoning Heath O'Hara and nearly fatally poisoning Nick Pullman. To give my good friend Lucy Binger credit, she did assist me.

No--I have absolutely no plans to move to the West Coast . . at this time. (Though an assistant director did tell me that I have "fabulous eyes." Wasn't that sweet?)

Yes--I did bake some awesome cupcakes for our group the night Jennifer Todd visited Maggie's shop and knit with us. And yes, she did ask me for the recipe.

So I'm going to share it with all of you, right here. Don't blame me if these cupcakes make you famous, too.

XOXO Still Your Hometown Sweetheart

Suzanne

Suzanne's Starstruck Chocolate Cupcakes

Recipe makes about 1 dozen

4 oz. semisweet chocolate

¾ cup unsalted butter

1½ cups sugar

3 eggs

¼ cup milk

1 teaspoon vanilla

1½ cups flour (or gluten-free flour with 1:1 substitu-
tion ratio)

Heat oven to 350 degrees.

Lightly spray cupcake pan with cooking spray.
Prepare with paper cupcake liners.

Microwave chocolate and butter in a large bowl
on high, 2 minutes or until butter is melted. Stir until
chocolate is completely blended.

Add sugar and blend in.

In a separate bowl, beat eggs with milk and vanilla.
Pour into chocolate mixture and stir until blended. Add
flour and mix well.

Pour spoonfuls into cupcake liners about ½ to ²/₃ full
and place on middle rack of oven.

Bake 20 minutes and test doneness with a toothpick
or sharp knife in the middle of a cupcake.

If not done, cook another 3 to 5 minutes. Cupcakes should be moist, dense, and chewy.

These cupcakes do not puff up a huge amount. They're more like brownie bites.